THE GREATEST SHORT STORIES OF
ANTON CHEKHOV

Anton Chekhov was a celebrated Russian playwright and one of the greatest masters of the modern short story. Born in Taganrog, Russia, Chekhov was known for his ability to delve beneath the surface of everyday life, revealing the hidden motives of his characters with remarkable precision and economy of words. His best works, whether plays or short stories, are marked by their simplicity, often avoiding complex plots or tidy resolutions. Instead, he focused on seemingly mundane details to create an atmosphere that is often described as haunting or lyrical. Chekhov introduced the influential principle known as 'Chekhov's gun', which emphasizes that every element in a story must be essential to the plot. He portrayed Russian life with a straightforward technique, free of showy literary devices, making him a leading figure of the late nineteenth-century Russian realist movement.

THE GREATEST SHORT STORIES OF
ANTON CHEKHOV

Published by
Rupa Publications India Pvt. Ltd 2024
7/16, Ansari Road, Daryaganj
New Delhi 110002

Sales centres:
Bengaluru Chennai
Hyderabad Jaipur Kathmandu
Kolkata Mumbai Prayagraj

Edition copyright © Rupa Publications India Pvt. Ltd 2024

All rights reserved.
No part of this publication may be reproduced, transmitted, or stored in a retrieval system, in any form or by any means, electronic, mechanical, photocopying, recording or otherwise, without the prior permission of the publisher.

P-ISBN: 978-93-6156-729-2
E-ISBN: 978-93-6156-222-8

First impression 2024

10 9 8 7 6 5 4 3 2 1

Printed in India

This book is sold subject to the condition that it shall not, by way of trade or otherwise, be lent, resold, hired out, or otherwise circulated, without the publisher's prior consent, in any form of binding or cover other than that in which it is published.

CONTENTS

1. The Lady with the Toy Dog — 1
2. The Darling — 23
3. The Bet — 40
4. The Student — 50
5. Ward No. 6 — 56
6. The Kiss — 128
7. The Black Monk — 153
8. A Joke — 193
9. Kashtanka — 199
10. Sleepy — 226
11. Boys — 234
12. The Lottery Ticket — 243

1

THE LADY WITH THE TOY DOG

I

It was reported that a new face had been seen on the quay; a lady with a little dog. Dimitri Dimitrich Gomov, who had been a fortnight at Yalta and had got used to it, had begun to show an interest in new faces. As he sat in the pavilion at Verne's he saw a young lady, blond and fairly tall, and wearing a broad-brimmed hat, pass along the quay. After her ran a white Pomeranian.

Later he saw her in the park and in the square several times a day. She walked by herself, always in the same broad-brimmed hat, and with this white dog. Nobody knew who she was, and she was spoken of as the lady with the toy dog.

'If,' thought Gomov, 'if she is here without a husband or a friend, it would be as well to make her acquaintance.'

He was not yet forty, but he had a daughter of twelve and two boys at school. He had married young, in his second year at the University, and now his wife seemed half as old again as himself. She was a tall woman, with dark eyebrows, erect, grave, stolid, and she thought herself an intellectual woman. She read a great deal, called her husband not Dimitri, but Demitri, and in his private mind he thought her short-witted, narrow-minded and ungracious. He was afraid of her and disliked being at home. He had begun to betray her with other women long ago, betrayed her frequently, and, probably for that reason nearly always spoke ill of women, and when they were discussed in his presence he would maintain that they were an inferior race.

It seemed to him that his experience was bitter enough to give him the right to call them any name he liked, but he could not live a couple of days without the 'inferior race'. With men he was bored and ill at ease, cold and unable to talk, but when he was with women, he felt easy and knew what to talk about, and how to behave, and even when he was silent with them he felt quite comfortable. In his appearance as in his character, indeed in his whole nature, there was something attractive, indefinable, which drew women to him and charmed them; he knew it, and he, too, was drawn by some mysterious power to them.

His frequent, and, indeed, bitter experiences had taught him long ago that every affair of that kind, at first a divine diversion, a delicious smooth adventure, is in the end a source of worry for a decent man, especially for men like those at Moscow who are slow to move, irresolute, domesticated, for it becomes at last an acute and extraordinary complicated problem and a nuisance. But whenever he met and was interested in a new woman, then his experience would slip away from his memory, and he would long to live, and everything would seem so simple and amusing.

And it so happened that one evening he dined in the gardens, and the lady in the broad-brimmed hat came up at a leisurely pace and sat at the next table. Her expression, her gait, her dress, her coiffure told him that she belonged to society, that she was married, that she was paying her first visit to Yalta, that she was alone, and that she was bored.... There is a great deal of untruth in the gossip about the immorality of the place. He scorned such tales, knowing that they were for the most part concocted by people who would be only too ready to sin if they had the chance, but when the lady sat down at the next table, only a yard or two away from him, his thoughts were filled with tales of easy conquests, of trips to the mountains; and he was suddenly possessed by the alluring idea of a quick transitory liaison, a moment's affair with an unknown woman whom he knew not even by name.

He beckoned to the little dog, and when it came up to him, wagged his finger at it. The dog began to growl. Gomov again wagged his finger.

The lady glanced at him and at once cast her eyes down.

'He won't bite,' she said and blushed.

'May I give him a bone?'—and when she nodded emphatically, he asked affably: 'Have you been in Yalta long?'

'About five days.'

'And I am just dragging through my second week.'

They were silent for a while.

'Time goes quickly,' she said, 'and it is amazingly boring here.'

'It is the usual thing to say that it is boring here. People live quite happily in dull holes like Bieliev or Zhidra, but as soon as they come here they say: "How boring it is! The very dregs of dullness!" One would think they came from Spain.'

She smiled. Then both went on eating in silence as though they did not know each other; but after dinner they went off together—and then began an easy, playful conversation as though they were perfectly happy, and it was all one to them where they went or what they talked of. They walked and talked of how the sea was strangely luminous; the water lilac, so soft and warm, and athwart it the moon cast a golden streak. They said how stifling it was after the hot day. Gomov told her how he came from Moscow and was a philologist by education, but in a bank by profession; and how he had once wanted to sing in opera, but gave it up; and how he had two houses in Moscow.... And from her he learned that she came from Petersburg, was born there, but married at S. where she had been living for the last two years; that she would stay another month at Yalta, and perhaps her husband would come for her, because, he too, needed a rest. She could not tell him what her husband was—Provincial Administration or Zemstvo Council—and she seemed to think it funny. And Gomov found out that her name was Anna Sergueyevna.

In his room at night, he thought of her and how they would meet next day. They must do so. As he was going to sleep, it struck him that she could only lately have left school, and had been at her lessons even as his daughter was then; he remembered how bashful and gauche she was when she laughed and talked with a stranger—it must be, he thought, the first time she had been alone, and in such a place with men walking after her and looking at her and talking to her, all with the same secret purpose which she could not but guess. He thought of her slender white neck and her pretty, grey eyes.

'There is something touching about her,' he thought as he began to fall asleep.

II

A week passed. It was a blazing day. Indoors it was stifling, and in the streets the dust whirled along. All day long he was plagued with thirst and he came into the pavilion every few minutes and offered Anna Sergueyevna an iced drink or an ice. It was impossibly hot.

In the evening, when the air was fresher, they walked to the jetty to see the steamer come in. There was quite a crowd all gathered to meet somebody, for they carried bouquets. And among them were clearly marked the peculiarities of Yalta: the elderly ladies were youngly dressed and there were many generals.

The sea was rough and the steamer was late, and before it turned into the jetty it had to do a great deal of manoeuvring. Anna Sergueyevna looked through her lorgnette at the steamer and the passengers as though she were looking for friends, and when she turned to Gomov, her eyes shone. She talked much and her questions were abrupt, and she forgot what she had said; and then she lost her lorgnette in the crowd.

The well-dressed people went away, the wind dropped, and Gomov and Anna Sergueyevna stood as though they were waiting for somebody to come from the steamer. Anna Sergueyevna was silent. She smelled her flowers and did not look at Gomov.

'The weather has got pleasanter toward evening,' he said. 'Where shall we go now? Shall we take a carriage?'

She did not answer.

He fixed his eyes on her and suddenly embraced her and kissed her lips, and he was kindled with the perfume and the moisture of the flowers; at once he started and looked round; had not some one seen?

'Let us go to your—' he murmured.

And they walked quickly away.

Her room was stifling, and smelled of scents which she had bought at the Japanese shop. Gomov looked at her and thought: 'What strange chances there are in life!' From the past there came the memory of earlier good-natured women, gay in their love, grateful to him for their happiness, short though it might be; and of others—like his wife—who loved without sincerity, and talked overmuch and affectedly, hysterically, as though they were protesting that it was not love, nor passion, but something more important; and of the few beautiful cold women, into whose eyes there would flash suddenly a fierce expression, a stubborn desire to take, to snatch from life more than it can give; they were no longer in their first youth, they were capricious, unstable, domineering, imprudent, and when Gomov became cold toward them then their beauty roused him to hatred, and the lace on their lingerie reminded him of the scales of fish.

But here there was the shyness and awkwardness of inexperienced youth, a feeling of constraint; an impression of perplexity and wonder, as though some one had suddenly knocked at the door. Anna Sergueyevna, 'the lady with the toy dog', took what had happened somehow seriously, with a particular gravity, as though thinking that this was her downfall and very strange and improper. Her features seemed to sink and wither, and on either side of her face her long hair hung mournfully down; she sat crestfallen and musing, exactly like a woman taken in sin in some old picture.

'It is not right,' she said. 'You are the first to lose respect for me.'

There was a melon on the table. Gomov cut a slice and began to eat it slowly. At least half an hour passed in silence.

Anna Sergueyevna was very touching; she irradiated the purity of a simple, devout, inexperienced woman; the solitary candle on the table hardly lighted her face, but it showed her very wretched.

'Why should I cease to respect you?' asked Gomov. 'You don't know what you are saying.'

'God forgive me!' she said, and her eyes filled with tears. 'It is horrible.'

'You seem to want to justify yourself.'

'How can I justify myself? I am a wicked, low woman and I despise myself. I have no thought of justifying myself. It is not my husband that I have deceived, but myself. And not only now but for a long time past. My husband may be a good honest man, but he is a lackey. I do not know what work he does, but I do know that he is a lackey in his soul. I was twenty when I married him. I was overcome by curiosity. I longed for something. 'Surely,' I said to myself, 'there is another kind of life.' I longed to live! To live, and to live.... Curiosity burned me up.... You do not understand it, but I swear by God, I could no longer control myself. Something strange was going on in me. I could not hold myself in. I told my husband that I was ill and came here.... And here I have been walking about dizzily, like a lunatic.... And now I have become a low, filthy woman whom everybody may despise.'

Gomov was already bored; her simple words irritated him with their unexpected and inappropriate repentance; but for the tears in her eyes he might have thought her to be joking or playing a part.

'I do not understand,' he said quietly. 'What do you want?'
She hid her face in his bosom and pressed close to him.

'Believe, believe me, I implore you,' she said. 'I love a pure, honest life, and sin is revolting to me. I don't know myself what I am doing. Simple people say: "The devil entrapped me," and I can say of myself: "The Evil One tempted me."'

'Don't, don't,' he murmured.

He looked into her staring, frightened eyes, kissed her, spoke quietly and tenderly, and gradually quieted her and she was happy again, and they both began to laugh.

Later, when they went out, there was not a soul on the quay; the town with its cypresses looked like a city of the dead, but the sea still roared and broke against the shore; a boat swung on the waves; and in it sleepily twinkled the light of a lantern.

They found a cab and drove out to the Oreanda.

'Just now in the hall,' said Gomov, 'I discovered your name written on the board—von Didenitz. Is your husband a German?'

'No. His grandfather, I believe, was a German, but he himself is an Orthodox Russian.'

At Oreanda they sat on a bench, not far from the church, looked down at the sea and were silent. Yalta was hardly visible through the morning mist. The tops of the hills were shrouded in motionless white clouds. The leaves of the trees never stirred, the cicadas trilled, and the monotonous dull sound of the sea, coming up from below, spoke of the rest, the eternal sleep awaiting us. So the sea roared when there was neither Yalta nor Oreanda, and so it roars and will roar, dully, indifferently when we shall be no more. And in this continual indifference to the life and death of each of us, lives pent up, the pledge of our eternal salvation, of the uninterrupted movement of life on earth and its unceasing perfection. Sitting side by side with a young woman, who in the dawn seemed so beautiful, Gomov, appeased and enchanted by the sight of the fairy scene, the sea, the mountains, the clouds, the wide sky, thought how at bottom, if it were thoroughly explored, everything on earth was beautiful, everything, except what we ourselves think and do when we forget the higher purposes of life and our own human dignity.

A man came up—a coast-guard—gave a look at them, then went away. He, too, seemed mysterious and enchanted. A steamer came over from Feodossia, by the light of the morning star, its own lights already put out.

'There is dew on the grass,' said Anna Sergueyevna after a silence.

'Yes. It is time to go home.'

They returned to the town.

Then every afternoon they met on the quay, and lunched together, dined, walked, enjoyed the sea. She complained that she slept badly, that her heart beat alarmingly. She would ask the same question over and over again, and was troubled now by jealousy, now by fear that he did not sufficiently respect her. And often in the square or the gardens, when there was no one near, he would draw her close and kiss her passionately. Their complete idleness, these kisses in the full daylight, given timidly and fearfully lest any one should see, the heat, the smell of the sea and the continual brilliant parade of leisured, well-dressed, well-fed people almost regenerated him. He would tell Anna Sergueyevna how delightful she was, how tempting. He was impatiently passionate, never left her side, and she would often brood, and even asked him to confess that he did not respect her, did not love her at all, and only saw in her a loose woman. Almost every evening, rather late, they would drive out of the town, to Oreanda, or to the waterfall; and these drives were always delightful, and the impressions won during them were always beautiful and sublime.

They expected her husband to come. But he sent a letter in which he said that his eyes were bad and implored his wife to come home. Anna Sergueyevna began to worry.

'It is a good thing I am going away,' she would say to Gomov. 'It is fate.'

She went in a carriage and he accompanied her. They drove for a whole day. When she took her seat in the car of an express-train and when the second bell sounded, she said:

'Let me have another look at you.... Just one more look. Just as you are.'

She did not cry, but was sad and low-spirited, and her lips trembled.

'I will think of you—often,' she said. 'Good-bye. Good-bye. Don't think ill of me. We part for ever. We must, because we ought not to have met at all. Now, good-bye.'

The train moved off rapidly. Its lights disappeared, and in a minute or two the sound of it was lost, as though everything were agreed to put an end to this sweet, oblivious madness. Left alone on the platform, looking into the darkness, Gomov heard the trilling of the grasshoppers and the humming of the telegraph-wires, and felt as though he had just woke up. And he thought that it had been one more adventure, one more affair, and it also was finished and had left only a memory. He was moved, sad, and filled with a faint remorse; surely the young woman, whom he would never see again, had not been happy with him; he had been kind to her, friendly, and sincere, but still in his attitude toward her, in his tone and caresses, there had always been a thin shadow of raillery, the rather rough arrogance of the successful male aggravated by the fact that he was twice as old as she. And all the time she had called him kind, remarkable, noble, so that he was never really himself to her, and had involuntarily deceived her....

Here at the station, the smell of autumn was in the air, and the evening was cool.

'It is time for me to go North,' thought Gomov, as he left the platform. 'It is time.'

III

At home in Moscow, it was already like winter; the stoves were heated, and in the mornings, when the children were getting ready to go to school, and had their tea, it was dark and their nurse lighted the lamp for a short while. The frost had already begun. When the first snow falls, the first day of driving in sledges, it is good to see the white earth, the white roofs; one breathes easily, eagerly, and then one remembers the days of youth. The old lime-trees and birches, white with hoarfrost, have a kindly expression; they are nearer to the heart than cypresses and palm-trees, and with the dear familiar trees there is no need to think of mountains and the sea.

Gomov was a native of Moscow. He returned to Moscow on a fine frosty day, and when he donned his fur coat and warm gloves, and took a stroll through Petrovka, and when on Saturday evening he heard the church-bells ringing, then his recent travels and the places he had visited lost all their charm.

Little by little he sank back into Moscow life, read eagerly three newspapers a day, and said that he did not read Moscow papers as a matter of principle. He was drawn into a round of restaurants, clubs, dinner-parties, parties, and he was flattered to have his house frequented by famous lawyers and actors, and to play cards with a professor at the University club. He could eat a whole plateful of hot *sielianka*.

So a month would pass, and Anna Sergueyevna, he thought, would be lost in the mists of memory and only rarely would she visit his dreams with her touching smile, just as other women had done. But more than a month passed, full winter came, and in his memory everything was clear, as though he had parted from Anna Sergueyevna only yesterday. And his memory was lit by a light that grew ever stronger. No matter how, through the voices of his children saying their lessons, penetrating to the evening stillness of his study, through hearing a song, or the music in a restaurant, or the snow-storm howling in the chimney, suddenly the whole thing would come to life again in his memory: the meeting on the jetty, the early morning with the mists on the mountains, the steamer from Feodossia and their kisses. He would pace up and down his room and remember it all and smile, and then his memories would drift into dreams, and the past was confused in his imagination with the future. He did not dream at night of Anna Sergueyevna, but she followed him everywhere, like a shadow, watching him. As he shut his eyes, he could see her, vividly, and she seemed handsomer, tenderer, younger than in reality; and he seemed to himself better than he had been at Yalta. In the evenings she would look at him from the bookcase, from the fireplace, from the corner; he could hear her breathing and the soft rustle of her dress. In the street he would gaze at women's faces to see if there were not one like her....

He was filled with a great longing to share his memories with some one. But at home it was impossible to speak of his love, and away from home there was no one. Impossible to talk of her to the other people in the house and the men at the bank. And talk of what? Had he loved then? Was there anything fine, romantic, or elevating or even interesting in his relations with Anna Sergueyevna? And he would speak vaguely of love, of women, and nobody guessed what was the matter, and only his wife would raise her dark eyebrows and say:

'Demitri, the role of coxcomb does not suit you at all.'

One night, as he was coming out of the club with his partner, an official, he could not help saying:

'If only I could tell what a fascinating woman I met at Yalta.'

The official seated himself in his sledge and drove off, but suddenly called:

'Dimitri Dimitrich!'

'Yes.'

'You were right. The sturgeon was tainted.'

These banal words suddenly roused Gomov's indignation. They seemed to him degrading and impure. What barbarous customs and people!

What preposterous nights, what dull, empty days! Furious card-playing, gourmandizing, drinking, endless conversations about the same things, futile activities and conversations taking up the best part of the day and all the best of a man's forces, leaving only a stunted, wingless life, just rubbish; and to go away and escape was impossible—one might as well be in a lunatic asylum or in prison with hard labour.

Gomov did not sleep that night, but lay burning with indignation, and then all next day he had a headache. And the following night he slept badly, sitting up in bed and thinking, or pacing from corner to corner of his room. His children bored him, the bank bored him, and he had no desire to go out or to speak to any one.

In December when the holidays came he prepared to go on a journey and told his wife he was going to Petersburg to present a petition for a young friend of his—and went to S. Why? He did not know. He wanted to see Anna Sergueyevna, to talk to her, and if possible to arrange an assignation.

He arrived at S. in the morning and occupied the best room in the hotel, where the whole floor was covered with a grey canvas, and on the table there stood an inkstand grey with dust, adorned with a horseman on a headless horse holding a net in his raised hand. The porter gave him the necessary information: von Didenitz; Old Goucharno Street, his own house—not far from the hotel; lives well, has his own horses, every one knows him.

Gomov walked slowly to Old Goucharno Street and found the house. In front of it was a long, grey fence spiked with nails.

'No getting over a fence like that,' thought Gomov, glancing from the windows to the fence.

He thought: 'To-day is a holiday and her husband is probably at home. Besides it would be tactless to call and upset her. If he sent a note then it might fall into her husband's hands and spoil everything. It would be better to wait for an opportunity.' And he kept on walking up and down the street, and round the fence, waiting for his opportunity. He saw a beggar go in at the gate and the dogs attack him. He heard a piano and the sounds came faintly to his ears. It must be Anna Sergueyevna playing. The door suddenly opened and out of it came an old woman, and after her ran the familiar white Pomeranian. Gomov wanted to call the dog, but his heart suddenly began to thump and in his agitation he could not remember the dog's name.

He walked on, and more and more he hated the grey fence and thought with a gust of irritation that Anna Sergueyevna had already forgotten him, and was perhaps already amusing herself with some one else, as would be only natural in a young woman forced from morning to night to behold the accursed fence. He returned to his room and sat for a long time on the sofa, not knowing what to do. Then he dined and afterward slept for a long while.

'How idiotic and tiresome it all is,' he thought as he awoke and saw the dark windows; for it was evening. 'I've had sleep enough, and what shall I do to-night?'

He sat on his bed which was covered with a cheap, grey blanket, exactly like those used in a hospital, and tormented himself.

'So much for the lady with the toy dog…. So much for the great adventure…. Here you sit.'

However, in the morning, at the station, his eye had been caught by a poster with large letters: 'First Performance of "The Geisha".' He remembered that and went to the theatre.

'It is quite possible she will go to the first performance,' he thought.

The theatre was full and, as usual in all provincial theatres, there was a thick mist above the lights, the gallery was noisily restless; in the first row before the opening of the performance stood the local dandies with their hands behind their backs, and there in the governor's box, in front, sat the governor's daughter, and the governor himself sat modestly behind the curtain and only his hands were visible. The curtain quivered; the orchestra tuned up for a long time, and while the audience were coming in and taking their seats, Gomov gazed eagerly round.

At last Anna Sergueyevna came in. She took her seat in the third row, and when Gomov glanced at her his heart ached and he knew that for him there was no one in the whole world nearer, dearer, and more important than she; she was lost in this provincial rabble, the little undistinguished woman, with a common lorgnette in her hands, yet she filled his whole life; she was his grief, his joy, his only happiness, and he longed for her; and through the noise of the bad orchestra with its tenth-rate fiddles, he thought how dear she was to him. He thought and dreamed.

With Anna Sergueyevna there came in a young man with short side-whiskers, very tall, stooping; with every movement he shook and bowed continually. Probably he was the husband whom in a bitter mood at Yalta she had called a lackey. And, indeed, in his long figure, his side-whiskers, the little bald patch on the top of his head, there was something of the lackey; he had a modest sugary smile and in his buttonhole he wore a University badge exactly like a lackey's number.

In the first entr'acte the husband went out to smoke, and she was left alone. Gomov, who was also in the pit, came up to her and said in a trembling voice with a forced smile:

'How do you do?'

She looked up at him and went pale. Then she glanced at him again in terror, not believing her eyes, clasped her fan and lorgnette tightly together, apparently struggling to keep herself from fainting. Both were silent. She sat, he stood; frightened by her emotion, not daring to sit down beside her. The fiddles and flutes began to play and suddenly it seemed to them as though all the people in the boxes were looking at them. She got up and walked quickly to the exit; he followed, and both walked absently along the corridors, down the stairs, up the stairs, with the crowd shifting and shimmering before their eyes; all kinds of uniforms, judges, teachers, crown-estates, and all with badges; ladies shone and shimmered before them, like fur coats on moving rows of clothes-pegs, and there was a draught howling through the place laden with the smell of tobacco and cigar-ends. And Gomov, whose heart was thudding wildly, thought:

'Oh, Lord! Why all these men and that beastly orchestra?'

At that very moment he remembered how when he had seen Anna Sergueyevna off that evening at the station he had said to himself that everything was over between them, and they would never meet again. And now how far off they were from the end!

On a narrow, dark staircase over which was written: 'This Way to the Amphitheatre,' she stopped:

'How you frightened me!' she said, breathing heavily, still pale and apparently stupefied. 'Oh! How you frightened me! I am nearly dead. Why did you come? Why?'

'Understand me, Anna,' he whispered quickly. 'I implore you to understand....'

She looked at him fearfully, in entreaty, with love in her eyes, gazing fixedly to gather up in her memory every one of his features.

'I suffer so!' she went on, not listening to him. 'All the time, I thought only of you. I lived with thoughts of you.... And I wanted to forget, to forget, but why, why did you come?'

A little above them, on the landing, two schoolboys stood and smoked and looked down at them, but Gomov did not care. He drew her to him and began to kiss her cheeks, her hands.

'What are you doing? What are you doing?' she said in terror, thrusting him away.... 'We were both mad. Go away to-night. You must go away at once.... I implore you, by everything you hold sacred, I implore you.... The people are coming—'

Some one passed them on the stairs.

'You must go away,' Anna Sergueyevna went on in a whisper. 'Do you hear, Dimitri Dimitrich? I'll come to you in Moscow. I never was happy. Now I am unhappy and I shall never, never be happy, never! Don't make me suffer even more! I swear, I'll come to Moscow. And now let us part. My dear, dearest darling, let us part!'

She pressed his hand and began to go quickly down-stairs, all the while looking back at him, and in her eyes plainly showed that she was most unhappy. Gomov stood for a while, listened, then, when all was quiet he found his coat and left the theatre.

IV

And Anna Sergueyevna began to come to him in Moscow. Once every two or three months she would leave S., telling her husband that she was going to consult a specialist in women's diseases. Her husband half believed and half disbelieved her. At Moscow she would stay at the 'Slaviansky Bazaar' and send a message at once to Gomov. He would come to her, and nobody in Moscow knew.

Once as he was going to her as usual one winter morning— he had not received her message the night before—he had his daughter with him, for he was taking her to school which was on the way. Great wet flakes of snow were falling.

'Three degrees above freezing,' he said, 'and still the snow is falling. But the warmth is only on the surface of the earth. In the upper strata of the atmosphere there is quite a different temperature.'

'Yes, papa. Why is there no thunder in winter?'

He explained this too, and as he spoke he thought of his assignation, and that not a living soul knew of it, or ever would know. He had two lives; one obvious, which every one could see and know, if they were sufficiently interested, a life full of conventional truth and conventional fraud, exactly like the lives of his friends and acquaintances; and another, which moved underground. And by a strange conspiracy of circumstances, everything that was to him important, interesting, vital, everything that enabled him to be sincere and denied self-deception and was the very core of his being, must dwell hidden away from others, and everything that made him false, a mere shape in which he hid himself in order to conceal the truth, as for instance his work in the bank, arguments at the club, his favourite gibe about women, going to parties with his wife—all this was open. And, judging others by himself, he did not believe the things he saw, and assumed that everybody else also had his real vital life passing under a veil of mystery as under the cover of the night. Every man's intimate existence is kept mysterious, and perhaps, in part, because of that civilised people are so nervously anxious that a personal secret should be respected.

When he had left his daughter at school, Gomov went to the 'Slaviansky Bazaar'. He took off his fur coat down-stairs, went up and knocked quietly at the door. Anna Sergueyevna, wearing his favourite grey dress, tired by the journey, had been expecting him to come all night. She was pale, and looked at him without a smile, and flung herself on his breast as soon as he entered. Their kiss was long and lingering as though they had not seen each other for a couple of years.

'Well, how are you getting on down there?' he asked. 'What is your news?'

'Wait. I'll tell you presently.... I cannot.'

She could not speak, for she was weeping. She turned her face from him and dried her eyes.

'Well, let her cry a bit.... I'll wait,' he thought, and sat down.

Then he rang and ordered tea, and then, as he drank it, she stood and gazed out of the window.... She was weeping in distress, in the bitter knowledge that their life had fallen out so sadly; only seeing each other in secret, hiding themselves away like thieves! Was not their life crushed?

'Don't cry.... Don't cry,' he said.

It was clear to him that their love was yet far from its end, which there was no seeing. Anna Sergueyevna was more and more passionately attached to him; she adored him and it was inconceivable that he should tell her that their love must some day end; she would not believe it.

He came up to her and patted her shoulder fondly and at that moment he saw himself in the mirror.

His hair was already going grey. And it seemed strange to him that in the last few years he should have got so old and ugly. Her shoulders were warm and trembled to his touch. He was suddenly filled with pity for her life, still so warm and beautiful, but probably beginning to fade and wither, like his own. Why should she love him so much? He always seemed to women not what he really was, and they loved in him, not himself, but the creature of their imagination, the thing they hankered for in life, and when they had discovered their mistake, still they loved him. And not one of them was happy with him. Time passed; he met women and was friends with them, went further and parted, but never once did he love; there was everything but love.

And now at last when his hair was grey he had fallen in love, real love—for the first time in his life.

Anna Sergueyevna and he loved one another, like dear kindred, like husband and wife, like devoted friends; it seemed to them that Fate had destined them for one another, and it was inconceivable that he should have a wife, she a husband; they were like two birds of passage, a male and a female, which had been caught and forced to live in separate cages. They had forgiven each other all the past of which they were ashamed; they forgave everything in the present, and they felt that their love had changed both of them.

Formerly, when he felt a melancholy compunction, he used to comfort himself with all kinds of arguments, just as they happened to cross his mind, but now he was far removed from any such ideas; he was filled with a profound pity, and he desired to be tender and sincere....

'Don't cry, my darling,' he said. 'You have cried enough.... Now let us talk and see if we can't find some way out.'

Then they talked it all over, and tried to discover some means of avoiding the necessity for concealment and deception, and the torment of living in different towns, and of not seeing each other for a long time. How could they shake off these intolerable fetters?

'How? How?' he asked, holding his head in his hands. 'How?'

And it seemed that but a little while and the solution would be found and there would begin a lovely new life; and to both of them it was clear that the end was still very far off, and that their hardest and most difficult period was only just beginning.

2

THE DARLING

Olenka, the daughter of the retired collegiate assessor, Plemyanniakov, was sitting in her back porch, lost in thought. It was hot, the flies were persistent and teasing, and it was pleasant to reflect that it would soon be evening. Dark rainclouds were gathering from the east, and bringing from time to time a breath of moisture in the air.

Kukin, who was the manager of an open-air theatre called the Tivoli, and who lived in the lodge, was standing in the middle of the garden looking at the sky.

'Again!' he observed despairingly. 'It's going to rain again! Rain every day, as though to spite me. I might as well hang myself! It's ruin! Fearful losses every day.'

He flung up his hands, and went on, addressing Olenka:

'There! that's the life we lead, Olga Semyonovna. It's enough to make one cry. One works and does one's utmost, one wears oneself out, getting no sleep at night, and racks one's brain what to do for the best. And then what happens? To begin with, one's public is ignorant, boorish. I give them the very best operetta, a dainty masque, first rate music-hall artists. But do you suppose that's what they want! They don't understand anything of that sort. They want a clown; what they ask for is vulgarity. And then look at the weather! Almost every evening it rains. It started on the tenth of May, and it's kept it up all May and June. It's simply awful! The public doesn't come, but I've to pay the rent just the same, and pay the artists.'

The next evening the clouds would gather again, and Kukin would say with an hysterical laugh:

'Well, rain away, then! Flood the garden, drown me! Damn my luck in this world and the next! Let the artists have me up! Send me to prison!—to Siberia!—the scaffold! Ha, ha, ha!'

And next day the same thing.

Olenka listened to Kukin with silent gravity, and sometimes tears came into her eyes. In the end his misfortunes touched her; she grew to love him. He was a small thin man, with a yellow face, and curls combed forward on his forehead. He spoke in a thin tenor; as he talked his mouth worked on one side, and there was always an expression of despair on his face; yet he aroused a deep and genuine affection in her. She was always fond of some one, and could not exist without loving. In earlier days she had loved her papa, who now sat in a darkened room, breathing with difficulty; she had loved her aunt who used to come every other year from Bryansk; and before that, when she was at school, she had loved her French master. She was a gentle, soft-hearted, compassionate girl, with mild, tender eyes and very good health. At the sight of her full rosy cheeks, her soft white neck with a little dark mole on it, and the kind, naïve smile, which came into her face when she listened to anything pleasant, men thought, 'Yes, not half bad,' and smiled too, while lady visitors could not refrain from seizing her hand in the middle of a conversation, exclaiming in a gush of delight, 'You darling!'

The house in which she had lived from her birth upwards,

and which was left her in her father's will, was at the extreme end of the town, not far from the Tivoli. In the evenings and at night she could head the band playing, and the crackling and banging of fireworks, and it seemed to her that it was Kukin struggling with his destiny, storming the entrenchments of his chief foe, the indifferent public; there was a sweet thrill at her heart, she had no desire to sleep, and when he returned home at day-break, she tapped softly at her bedroom window, and showing him only her face and one shoulder through the curtain, she gave him a friendly smile....

He proposed to her, and they were married. And when he had a closer view of her neck and her plump, fine shoulders, he threw up his hands, and said:

'You darling!'

He was happy, but as it rained on the day and night of his wedding, his face still retained an expression of despair.

They got on very well together. She used to sit in his office, to look after things in the Tivoli, to put down the accounts and pay the wages. And her rosy cheeks, her sweet, naïve, radiant smile, were to be seen now at the office window, now in the refreshment bar or behind the scenes of the theatre. And already she used to say to her acquaintances that the theatre was the chief and most important thing in life and that it was only through the drama that one could derive true enjoyment and become cultivated and humane.

'But do you suppose the public understands that?' she used to say. 'What they want is a clown. Yesterday we gave "Faust Inside Out", and almost all the boxes were empty; but if Vanitchka and I had been producing some vulgar thing, I assure you the theatre would have been packed. Tomorrow Vanitchka and I are doing "Orpheus in Hell". Do come.'

And what Kukin said about the theatre and the actors she repeated. Like him she despised the public for their ignorance and their indifference to art; she took part in the rehearsals, she corrected the actors, she kept an eye on the behaviour of the musicians, and when there was an unfavourable notice in the local paper, she shed tears, and then went to the editor's office to set things right.

The actors were fond of her and used to call her 'Vanitchka and I", and 'the darling'; she was sorry for them and used to lend them small sums of money, and if they deceived her, she used to shed a few tears in private, but did not complain to her husband.

They got on well in the winter too. They took the theatre in the town for the whole winter, and let it for short terms to a Little Russian company, or to a conjurer, or to a local dramatic society. Olenka grew stouter, and was always beaming with satisfaction, while Kukin grew thinner and yellower, and continually complained of their terrible losses, although he had not done badly all the winter. He used to cough at night, and she used to give him hot raspberry tea or lime-flower water, to rub him with eau-de-Cologne and to wrap him in her warm shawls.

'You're such a sweet pet!' she used to say with perfect sincerity, stroking his hair. 'You're such a pretty dear!'

Towards Lent he went to Moscow to collect a new troupe, and without him she could not sleep, but sat all night at her window, looking at the stars, and she compared herself with the hens, who are awake all night and uneasy when the cock is not in the hen-house. Kukin was detained in Moscow, and wrote that he would be back at Easter, adding some instructions about the Tivoli. But on the Sunday before Easter, late in the evening, came a sudden ominous knock at the gate; some one was hammering on the gate as though on a barrel—boom, boom, boom! The drowsy cook went flopping with her bare feet through the puddles, as she ran to open the gate.

'Please open,' said some one outside in a thick bass. 'There is a telegram for you.'

Olenka had received telegrams from her husband before, but this time for some reason she felt numb with terror. With shaking hands she opened the telegram and read as follows:

'IVAN PETROVITCH DIED SUDDENLY TO-DAY. AWAITING IMMATE INSTRUCTIONS FUFUNERAL TUESDAY.'

That was how it was written in the telegram—'fufuneral,' and the utterly incomprehensible word 'immate'. It was signed by the stage manager of the operatic company.

'My darling!' sobbed Olenka. 'Vanka, my precious, my darling! Why did I ever meet you! Why did I know you and love you! Your poor heart-broken Olenka is alone without you!'

Kukin's funeral took place on Tuesday in Moscow, Olenka returned home on Wednesday, and as soon as she got indoors, she threw herself on her bed and sobbed so loudly that it could be heard next door, and in the street.

'Poor darling!' the neighbours said, as they crossed themselves. 'Olga Semyonovna, poor darling! How she does take on!'

Three months later Olenka was coming home from mass, melancholy and in deep mourning. It happened that one of her neighbours, Vassily Andreitch Pustovalov, returning home from church, walked back beside her. He was the manager at Babakayev's, the timber merchant's. He wore a straw hat, a white waistcoat, and a gold watch-chain, and looked more a country gentleman than a man in trade.

'Everything happens as it is ordained, Olga Semyonovna,' he said gravely, with a sympathetic note in his voice; 'and if any of our dear ones die, it must be because it is the will of God, so we ought have fortitude and bear it submissively.'

After seeing Olenka to her gate, he said good-bye and went on. All day afterwards she heard his sedately dignified voice, and whenever she shut her eyes she saw his dark beard. She liked him very much. And apparently she had made an impression on him too, for not long afterwards an elderly lady, with whom she was only slightly acquainted, came to drink coffee with her, and as soon as she was seated at table began to talk about Pustovalov, saying that he was an excellent man whom one could thoroughly depend upon, and that any girl would be glad to marry him. Three days later Pustovalov came himself. He did not stay long, only about ten minutes, and he did not say much, but when he left, Olenka loved him—loved him so much that she lay awake all night in a perfect fever, and in the morning she sent for the elderly lady. The match was quickly arranged, and then came the wedding.

Pustovalov and Olenka got on very well together when they were married.

Usually he sat in the office till dinner-time, then he went out on business, while Olenka took his place, and sat in the office till evening, making up accounts and booking orders.

'Timber gets dearer every year; the price rises twenty per cent,' she would say to her customers and friends. 'Only fancy we used to sell local timber, and now Vassitchka always has to go for wood to the Mogilev district. And the freight!' she would add, covering her cheeks with her hands in horror. 'The freight!'

It seemed to her that she had been in the timber trade for ages and ages, and that the most important and necessary thing in life was timber; and there was something intimate and touching to her in the very sound of words such as 'baulk', 'post', 'beam', 'pole', 'scantling', 'batten', 'lath', 'plank', etc.

At night when she was asleep she dreamed of perfect mountains of planks and boards, and long strings of wagons, carting timber somewhere far away. She dreamed that a whole regiment of six-inch beams forty feet high, standing on end, was marching upon the timber-yard; that logs, beams, and boards knocked together with the resounding crash of dry wood, kept falling and getting up again, piling themselves on each other. Olenka cried out in her sleep, and Pustovalov said to her tenderly: 'Olenka, what's the matter, darling? Cross yourself!'

Her husband's ideas were hers. If he thought the room was too hot, or that business was slack, she thought the same. Her husband did not care for entertainments, and on holidays he stayed at home. She did likewise.

'You are always at home or in the office,' her friends said to her. 'You should go to the theatre, darling, or to the circus.'

'Vassitchka and I have no time to go to theatres,' she would answer sedately. 'We have no time for nonsense. What's the use of these theatres?'

On Saturdays Pustovalov and she used to go to the evening service; on holidays to early mass, and they walked side by side with softened faces as they came home from church. There was a pleasant fragrance about them both, and her silk dress rustled agreeably. At home they drank tea, with fancy bread and jams of various kinds, and afterwards they ate pie. Every day at twelve o'clock there was a savoury smell of beet-root soup and of mutton or duck in their yard, and on fast-days of fish, and no one could pass the gate without feeling hungry. In the office the samovar was always boiling, and customers were regaled with tea and cracknels. Once a week the couple went to the baths and returned side by side, both red in the face.

'Yes, we have nothing to complain of, thank God,' Olenka used to say to her acquaintances. 'I wish every one were as well off as Vassitchka and I.'

When Pustovalov went away to buy wood in the Mogilev district, she missed him dreadfully, lay awake and cried. A young veterinary surgeon in the army, called Smirnin, to whom they had let their lodge, used sometimes to come in in the evening. He used to talk to her and play cards with her, and this entertained her in her husband's absence. She was particularly interested in what he told her of his home life. He was married and had a little boy, but was separated from his wife because she had been unfaithful to him, and now he hated her and used to send her forty roubles a month for the maintenance of their son. And hearing of all this, Olenka sighed and shook her head. She was sorry for him.

'Well, God keep you,' she used to say to him at parting, as she lighted him down the stairs with a candle. 'Thank you for coming to cheer me up, and may the Mother of God give you health.'

And she always expressed herself with the same sedateness and dignity, the same reasonableness, in imitation of her husband. As the veterinary surgeon was disappearing behind the door below, she would say:

'You know, Vladimir Platonitch, you'd better make it up with your wife. You should forgive her for the sake of your son. You may be sure the little fellow understands.'

And when Pustovalov came back, she told him in a low voice about the veterinary surgeon and his unhappy home life, and both sighed and shook their heads and talked about the boy, who, no doubt, missed his father, and by some strange connection of ideas, they went up to the holy ikons, bowed to the ground before them and prayed that God would give them children.

And so the Pustovalovs lived for six years quietly and peaceably in love and complete harmony.

But behold! one winter day after drinking hot tea in the office, Vassily Andreitch went out into the yard without his cap on to see about sending off some timber, caught cold and was taken ill. He had the best doctors, but he grew worse and died after four months' illness. And Olenka was a widow once more.

'I've nobody, now you've left me, my darling,' she sobbed, after her husband's funeral. 'How can I live without you, in wretchedness and misery! Pity me, good people, all alone in the world!'

She went about dressed in black with long 'weepers', and gave up wearing hat and gloves for good. She hardly ever went out, except to church, or to her husband's grave, and led the life of a nun. It was not till six months later that she took off the weepers and opened the shutters of the windows. She was sometimes seen in the mornings, going with her cook to market for provisions, but what went on in her house and how she lived now could only be surmised. People guessed, from seeing her drinking tea in her garden with the veterinary surgeon, who read the newspaper aloud to her, and from the fact that, meeting a lady she knew at the post-office, she said to her:

'There is no proper veterinary inspection in our town, and that's the cause of all sorts of epidemics. One is always hearing of people's getting infection from the milk supply, or catching diseases from horses and cows. The health of domestic animals ought to be as well cared for as the health of human beings.'

She repeated the veterinary surgeon's words, and was of the same opinion as he about everything. It was evident that she could not live a year without some attachment, and had found new happiness in the lodge. In any one else this would have been censured, but no one could think ill of Olenka; everything she did was so natural. Neither she nor the veterinary surgeon said anything to other people of the change in their relations, and tried, indeed, to conceal it, but without success, for Olenka could not keep a secret. When he had visitors, men serving in his regiment, and she poured out tea or served the supper, she would begin talking of the cattle plague, of the foot and mouth disease, and of the municipal slaughterhouses. He was dreadfully embarrassed, and when the guests had gone, he would seize her by the hand and hiss angrily:

'I've asked you before not to talk about what you don't understand. When we veterinary surgeons are talking among ourselves, please don't put your word in. It's really annoying.'

And she would look at him with astonishment and dismay, and ask him in alarm: 'But, Voloditchka, what *am* I to talk about?'

And with tears in her eyes she would embrace him, begging

him not to be angry, and they were both happy.

But this happiness did not last long. The veterinary surgeon departed, departed for ever with his regiment, when it was transferred to a distant place—to Siberia, it may be. And Olenka was left alone.

Now she was absolutely alone. Her father had long been dead, and his armchair lay in the attic, covered with dust and lame of one leg. She got thinner and plainer, and when people met her in the street they did not look at her as they used to, and did not smile to her; evidently her best years were over and left behind, and now a new sort of life had begun for her, which did not bear thinking about. In the evening Olenka sat in the porch, and heard the band playing and the fireworks popping in the Tivoli, but now the sound stirred no response. She looked into her yard without interest, thought of nothing, wished for nothing, and afterwards, when night came on she went to bed and dreamed of her empty yard. She ate and drank as it were unwillingly.

And what was worst of all, she had no opinions of any sort. She saw the objects about her and understood what she saw, but could not form any opinion about them, and did not know what to talk about. And how awful it is not to have any opinions! One sees a bottle, for instance, or the rain, or a peasant driving in his cart, but what the bottle is for, or the rain, or the peasant, and what is the meaning of it, one can't say, and could not even for a thousand roubles. When she had Kukin, or Pustovalov, or the veterinary surgeon, Olenka could explain everything, and give her opinion about anything you like, but now there was the same emptiness in her brain and in her heart as there was in her yard outside. And it was as harsh and as bitter as wormwood in the mouth.

Little by little the town grew in all directions. The road became a street, and where the Tivoli and the timber-yard had been, there were new turnings and houses. How rapidly time passes! Olenka's house grew dingy, the roof got rusty, the shed sank on one side, and the whole yard was overgrown with docks and stinging-nettles. Olenka herself had grown plain and elderly; in summer she sat in the porch, and her soul, as before, was empty and dreary and full of bitterness. In winter she sat at her window and looked at the snow. When she caught the scent of spring, or heard the chime of the church bells, a sudden rush of memories from the past came over her, there was a tender ache in her heart, and her eyes brimmed over with tears; but this was only for a minute, and then came emptiness again and the sense of the futility of life. The black kitten, Briska, rubbed against her and purred softly, but Olenka was not touched by these feline caresses. That was not what she needed. She wanted a love that would absorb her whole being, her whole soul and reason--that would give her ideas and an object in life, and would warm her old blood. And she would shake the kitten off her skirt and say with vexation:

'Get along; I don't want you!'

And so it was, day after day and year after year, and no joy, and no opinions. Whatever Mavra, the cook, said she accepted.

One hot July day, towards evening, just as the cattle were being driven away, and the whole yard was full of dust, some one suddenly knocked at the gate. Olenka went to open it herself and was dumbfounded when she looked out: she saw Smirnin, the veterinary surgeon, grey-headed, and dressed as a civilian. She suddenly remembered everything. She could not help crying and letting her head fall on his breast without uttering a word, and in the violence of her feeling she did not notice how they both walked into the house and sat down to tea.

'My dear Vladimir Platonitch! What fate has brought you?' she muttered, trembling with joy.

'I want to settle here for good, Olga Semyonovna,' he told her. 'I have resigned my post, and have come to settle down and try my luck on my own account. Besides, it's time for my boy to go to school. He's a big boy. I am reconciled with my wife, you know.'

'Where is she?' asked Olenka.

'She's at the hotel with the boy, and I'm looking for lodgings.'

'Good gracious, my dear soul! Lodgings? Why not have my house? Why shouldn't that suit you? Why, my goodness, I wouldn't take any rent!' cried Olenka in a flutter, beginning to cry again. 'You live here, and the lodge will do nicely for me. Oh dear! How glad I am!'

Next day the roof was painted and the walls were whitewashed, and Olenka, with her arms akimbo walked about the yard giving directions. Her face was beaming with her old smile, and she was brisk and alert as though she had waked from a long sleep. The veterinary's wife arrived—a thin, plain lady, with short hair and a peevish expression. With her was her little Sasha, a boy of ten, small for his age, blue-eyed, chubby, with dimples in his cheeks. And scarcely had the boy walked into the yard when he ran after the cat, and at once there was the sound of his gay, joyous laugh.

'Is that your puss, auntie?' he asked Olenka. 'When she has little ones, do give us a kitten. Mamma is awfully afraid of mice.'

Olenka talked to him, and gave him tea. Her heart warmed

and there was a sweet ache in her bosom, as though the boy had been her own child. And when he sat at the table in the evening, going over his lessons, she looked at him with deep tenderness and pity as she murmured to herself:

'You pretty pet! …My precious!…Such a fair little thing, and so clever.'

'"An island is a piece of land which is entirely surrounded by water,"' he read aloud.

'An island is a piece of land,' she repeated, and this was the first opinion to which she gave utterance with positive conviction after so many years of silence and dearth of ideas.

Now she had opinions of her own, and at supper she talked to Sasha's parents, saying how difficult the lessons were at the high schools, but that yet the high school was better than a commercial one, since with a high-school education all careers were open to one, such as being a doctor or an engineer.

Sasha began going to the high school. His mother departed to Harkov to her sister's and did not return; his father used to go off every day to inspect cattle, and would often be away from home for three days together, and it seemed to Olenka as though Sasha was entirely abandoned, that he was not wanted at home, that he was being starved, and she carried him off to her lodge and gave him a little room there.

And for six months Sasha had lived in the lodge with her. Every morning Olenka came into his bedroom and found him fast asleep, sleeping noiselessly with his hand under his cheek. She was sorry to wake him.

'Sashenka,' she would say mournfully, 'get up, darling. It's time for school.'

He would get up, dress and say his prayers, and then sit

down to breakfast, drink three glasses of tea, and eat two large cracknels and a half a buttered roll. All this time he was hardly awake and a little ill-humoured in consequence.

'You don't quite know your fable, Sashenka,' Olenka would say, looking at him as though he were about to set off on a long journey. 'What a lot of trouble I have with you! You must work and do your best, darling, and obey your teachers.'

'Oh, do leave me alone!' Sasha would say.

Then he would go down the street to school, a little figure, wearing a big cap and carrying a satchel on his shoulder. Olenka would follow him noiselessly.

'Sashenka!' she would call after him, and she would pop into his hand a date or a caramel. When he reached the street where the school was, he would feel ashamed of being followed by a tall, stout woman, he would turn round and say:

'You'd better go home, auntie. I can go the rest of the way alone.'

She would stand still and look after him fixedly till he had disappeared at the school-gate.

Ah, how she loved him! Of her former attachments not one had been so deep; never had her soul surrendered to any feeling so spontaneously, so disinterestedly, and so joyously as now that her maternal instincts were aroused. For this little boy with the dimple in his cheek and the big school cap, she would have given her whole life, she would have given it with joy and tears of tenderness. Why? Who can tell why?

When she had seen the last of Sasha, she returned home, contented and serene, brimming over with love; her face, which had grown younger during the last six months, smiled and beamed; people meeting her looked at her with pleasure.

'Good-morning, Olga Semyonovna, darling. How are you, darling?'

'The lessons at the high school are very difficult now,' she would relate at the market. 'It's too much; in the first class yesterday they gave him a fable to learn by heart, and a Latin translation and a problem. You know it's too much for a little chap.'

And she would begin talking about the teachers, the lessons, and the school books, saying just what Sasha said.

At three o'clock they had dinner together: in the evening they learned their lessons together and cried. When she put him to bed, she would stay a long time making the Cross over him and murmuring a prayer; then she would go to bed and dream of that far-away misty future when Sasha would finish his studies and become a doctor or an engineer, would have a big house of his own with horses and a carriage, would get married and have children.... She would fall asleep still thinking of the same thing, and tears would run down her cheeks from her closed eyes, while the black cat lay purring beside her: 'Mrr, mrr, mrr.'

Suddenly there would come a loud knock at the gate.

Olenka would wake up breathless with alarm, her heart throbbing. Half a minute later would come another knock.

'It must be a telegram from Harkov,' she would think, beginning to tremble from head to foot. 'Sasha's mother is sending for him from Harkov.... Oh, mercy on us!'

She was in despair. Her head, her hands, and her feet would turn chill, and she would feel that she was the most unhappy woman in the world. But another minute would pass, voices would be heard: it would turn out to be the veterinary surgeon coming home from the club.

'Well, thank God!' she would think.

And gradually the load in her heart would pass off, and she would feel at ease. She would go back to bed thinking of Sasha, who lay sound asleep in the next room, sometimes crying out in his sleep:

'I'll give it you! Get away! Shut up!'

3

THE BET

I

It was a dark autumn night. The old banker was pacing from corner to corner of his study, recalling to his mind the party he gave in the autumn fifteen years before. There were many clever people at the party and much interesting conversation. They talked among other things of capital punishment. The guests, among them not a few scholars and journalists, for the most part disapproved of capital punishment. They found it obsolete as a means of punishment, unfitted to a Christian State and immoral. Some of them thought that capital punishment should be replaced universally by life-imprisonment.

'I don't agree with you,' said the host. 'I myself have experienced neither capital punishment nor life-imprisonment, but if one may judge *a priori*, then in my opinion capital punishment is more moral and more humane than imprisonment. Execution kills instantly, life-imprisonment kills by degrees. Who is the more humane executioner, one who kills you in a few seconds or one who draws the life out of you incessantly, for years?'

'They're both equally immoral,' remarked one of the guests,

'because their purpose is the same, to take away life. The State is not God. It has no right to take away that which it cannot give back, if it should so desire.'

Among the company was a lawyer, a young man of about twenty-five. On being asked his opinion, he said:

'Capital punishment and life-imprisonment are equally immoral; but if I were offered the choice between them, I would certainly choose the second. It's better to live somehow than not to live at all.'

There ensued a lively discussion. The banker who was then younger and more nervous suddenly lost his temper, banged his fist on the table, and turning to the young lawyer, cried out:

'It's a lie. I bet you two millions you wouldn't stick in a cell even for five years.'

'If you mean it seriously,' replied the lawyer, 'then I bet I'll stay not five but fifteen.'

'Fifteen! Done!' cried the banker. 'Gentlemen, I stake two millions.'

'Agreed. You stake two millions, I my freedom,' said the lawyer.

So this wild, ridiculous bet came to pass. The banker, who at that time had too many millions to count, spoiled and capricious, was beside himself with rapture. During supper he said to the lawyer jokingly:

'Come to your senses, young roan, before it's too late. Two millions are nothing to me, but you stand to lose three or four of the best years of your life. I say three or four, because you'll never stick it out any longer. Don't forget either, you unhappy man, that voluntary is much heavier than enforced imprisonment. The idea that you have the right to free yourself at any moment will poison the whole of your life in the cell. I pity you.'

And now the banker, pacing from corner to corner, recalled all this and asked himself:

'Why did I make this bet? What's the good? The lawyer loses fifteen years of his life and I throw away two millions. Will it convince people that capital punishment is worse or better than imprisonment for life? No, no! all stuff and rubbish. On my part, it was the caprice of a well-fed man; on the lawyer's pure greed of gold.'

He recollected further what happened after the evening party. It was decided that the lawyer must undergo his imprisonment under the strictest observation, in a garden wing of the banker's house. It was agreed that during the period he would be deprived of the right to cross the threshold, to see living people, to hear human voices, and to receive letters and newspapers. He was permitted to have a musical instrument, to read books, to write letters, to drink wine and smoke tobacco. By the agreement he could communicate, but only in silence, with the outside world through a little window specially constructed for this purpose. Everything necessary, books, music, wine, he could receive in any quantity by sending a note through the window. The agreement provided for all the minutest details, which made the confinement strictly solitary, and it obliged the lawyer to remain exactly fifteen years from twelve o'clock of 14 November 1870, to twelve o'clock of 14 November 1885. The least attempt on his part to violate the conditions, to escape if only for two minutes before the time freed the banker from the obligation to pay him the two millions.

During the first year of imprisonment, the lawyer, as far as it was possible to judge from his short notes, suffered terribly from loneliness and boredom. From his wing day and night came the sound of the piano. He rejected wine and tobacco. 'Wine,' he wrote, 'excites desires, and desires are the chief foes of a prisoner; besides, nothing is more boring than to drink good wine alone,' and tobacco spoils the air in his room. During the first year the lawyer was sent books of a light character; novels with a complicated love interest, stories of crime and fantasy, comedies, and so on.

In the second year the piano was heard no longer and the lawyer asked only for classics. In the fifth year, music was heard again, and the prisoner asked for wine. Those who watched him said that during the whole of that year he was only eating, drinking, and lying on his bed. He yawned often and talked angrily to himself. Books he did not read. Sometimes at nights he would sit down to write. He would write for a long time and tear it all up in the morning. More than once he was heard to weep.

In the second half of the sixth year, the prisoner began zealously to study languages, philosophy, and history. He fell on these subjects so hungrily that the banker hardly had time to get books enough for him. In the space of four years about six hundred volumes were bought at his request. It was while that passion lasted that the banker received the following letter from the prisoner: 'My dear gaoler, I am writing these lines in six languages. Show them to experts. Let them read them. If they do not find one single mistake, I beg you to give orders to have a gun fired off in the garden. By the noise I shall know that my efforts have not been in vain. The geniuses of all ages and countries speak in different languages; but in them all burns the same flame. Oh, if you knew my heavenly happiness now that I can understand them!' The prisoner's desire was fulfilled. Two shots were fired in the garden by the banker's order.

Later on, after the tenth year, the lawyer sat immovable before his table and read only the New Testament. The banker found it strange that a man who in four years had mastered six hundred erudite volumes, should have spent nearly a year in reading one book, easy to understand and by no means thick. The New Testament was then replaced by the history of religions and theology.

During the last two years of his confinement the prisoner read an extraordinary amount, quite haphazard. Now he would apply himself to the natural sciences, then he would read Byron or Shakespeare. Notes used to come from him in which he asked to be sent at the same time a book on chemistry, a text-book of medicine, a novel, and some treatise on philosophy or theology. He read as though he were swimming in the sea among broken pieces of wreckage, and in his desire to save his life was eagerly grasping one piece after another.

II

The banker recalled all this, and thought:

'To-morrow at twelve o'clock he receives his freedom. Under the agreement, I shall have to pay him two millions. If I pay, it's all over with me. I am ruined for ever...'

Fifteen years before he had too many millions to count, but now he was afraid to ask himself which he had more of, money or debts. Gambling on the Stock-Exchange, risky speculation, and the recklessness of which he could not rid himself even in old age, had gradually brought his business to decay; and the fearless, self-confident, proud man of business had become an ordinary banker, trembling at every rise and fall in the market.

'That cursed bet,' murmured the old man clutching his head in despair... 'Why didn't the man die? He's only forty years old. He will take away my last farthing, marry, enjoy life, gamble on the Exchange, and I will look on like an envious beggar and hear the same words from him every day: "I'm obliged to you for the happiness of my life. Let me help you." No, it's too much! The only escape from bankruptcy and disgrace—is that the man should die.'

The clock had just struck three. The banker was listening. In the house every one was asleep, and one could hear only the frozen trees whining outside the windows. Trying to make no sound, he took out of his safe the key of the door which had not been opened for fifteen years, put on his overcoat, and went out of the house. The garden was dark and cold. It was raining. A damp, penetrating wind howled in the garden and gave the trees no rest. Though he strained his eyes, the banker could see neither the ground, nor the white statues, nor the garden wing, nor the trees. Approaching the garden wing, he called the watchman twice. There was no answer. Evidently the watchman had taken shelter from the bad weather and was now asleep somewhere in the kitchen or the greenhouse.

'If I have the courage to fulfil my intention,' thought the old man, 'the suspicion will fall on the watchman first of all.'

In the darkness he groped for the steps and the door and entered the hall of the garden-wing, then poked his way into a narrow passage and struck a match. Not a soul was there. Some one's bed, with no bedclothes on it, stood there, and an iron stove loomed dark in the corner. The seals on the door that led into the prisoner's room were unbroken.

When the match went out, the old man, trembling from agitation, peeped into the little window.

In the prisoner's room a candle was burning dimly. The prisoner himself sat by the table. Only his back, the hair on his head and his hands were visible. Open books were strewn about on the table, the two chairs, and on the carpet near the table.

Five minutes passed and the prisoner never once stirred. Fifteen years' confinement had taught him to sit motionless. The banker tapped on the window with his finger, but the prisoner made no movement in reply. Then the banker cautiously tore the seals from the door and put the key into the lock. The rusty lock gave a hoarse groan and the door creaked. The banker expected instantly to hear a cry of surprise and the sound of steps. Three minutes passed and it was as quiet inside as it had been before. He made up his mind to enter.

Before the table sat a man, unlike an ordinary human being. It was a skeleton, with tight-drawn skin, with long curly hair like a woman's, and a shaggy beard. The colour of his face was yellow, of an earthy shade; the cheeks were sunken, the back long and narrow, and the hand upon which he leaned his hairy head was so lean and skinny that it was painful to look upon. His hair was already silvering with grey, and no one who glanced at the senile emaciation of the face would have believed that he was only forty years old. On the table, before his bended head, lay a sheet of paper on which something was written in a tiny hand.

'Poor devil,' thought the banker, 'he's asleep and probably seeing millions in his dreams. I have only to take and throw this half-dead thing on the bed, smother him a moment with the pillow, and the most careful examination will find no trace of unnatural death. But, first, let us read what he has written here.'

The banker took the sheet from the table and read:

'To-morrow at twelve o'clock midnight, I shall obtain my freedom and the right to mix with people. But before I leave this room and see the sun I think it necessary to say a few words to you. On my own clear conscience and before God who sees me I declare to you that I despise freedom, life, health, and all that your books call the blessings of the world.

'For fifteen years I have diligently studied earthly life. True, I saw neither the earth nor the people, but in your books I drank fragrant wine, sang songs, hunted deer and wild boar in the forests, loved women... And beautiful women, like clouds ethereal, created by the magic of your poets' genius, visited me by night and whispered to me wonderful tales, which made my head drunken. In your books I climbed the summits of Elbruz and Mont Blanc and saw from there how the sun rose in the morning, and in the evening suffused the sky, the ocean and the mountain ridges with a purple gold. I saw from there how above me lightnings glimmered cleaving the clouds; I saw green forests, fields, rivers, lakes, cities; I heard syrens singing, and the playing of the pipes of Pan; I touched the wings of beautiful devils who came flying to me to speak of God... In your books I cast myself into bottomless abysses, worked miracles, burned cities to the ground, preached new religions, conquered whole countries...

'Your books gave me wisdom. All that unwearying human thought created in the centuries is compressed to a little lump in my skull. I know that I am cleverer than you all.

'And I despise your books, despise all worldly blessings and wisdom. Everything is void, frail, visionary and delusive as a mirage. Though you be proud and wise and beautiful, yet will death wipe you from the face of the earth like the mice underground; and your posterity, your history, and the immortality of your men of genius will be as frozen slag, burnt down together with the terrestrial globe.

'You are mad, and gone the wrong way. You take falsehood for truth and ugliness for beauty. You would marvel if suddenly apple and orange trees should bear frogs and lizards instead of fruit, and if roses should begin to breathe the odour of a sweating horse. So do I marvel at you, who have bartered heaven for earth. I do not want to understand you.

'That I may show you in deed my contempt for that by which you live, I waive the two millions of which I once dreamed as of paradise, and which I now despise. That I may deprive myself of my right to them, I shall come out from here five minutes before the stipulated term, and thus shall violate the agreement.'

When he had read, the banker put the sheet on the table, kissed the head of the strange man, and began to weep. He went out of the wing. Never at any other time, not even after his terrible losses on the Exchange, had he felt such contempt for himself as now. Coming home, he lay down on his bed, but agitation and tears kept him a long time from sleeping...

The next morning the poor watchman came running to him and told him that they had seen the man who lived in the wing climb through the window into the garden. He had gone to the gate and disappeared. The banker instantly went with his servants to the wing and established the escape of his prisoner. To avoid unnecessary rumours he took the paper with the renunciation from the table and, on his return, locked it in his safe.

4

THE STUDENT

At first the weather was fine and still. The thrushes were calling, and in the swamps close by something alive droned pitifully with a sound like blowing into an empty bottle. A snipe flew by, and the shot aimed at it rang out with a gay, resounding note in the spring air. But when it began to get dark in the forest a cold, penetrating wind blew inappropriately from the east, and everything sank into silence. Needles of ice stretched across the pools, and it felt cheerless, remote, and lonely in the forest. There was a whiff of winter.

Ivan Velikopolsky, the son of a sacristan, and a student of the clerical academy, returning home from shooting, walked all the time by the path in the water-side meadow. His fingers were numb and his face was burning with the wind. It seemed to him that the cold that had suddenly come on had destroyed the order and harmony of things, that nature itself felt ill at ease, and that was why the evening darkness was falling more rapidly than usual. All around it was deserted and peculiarly gloomy. The only light was one gleaming in the widows' gardens near the river; the village, over three miles away, and everything in the distance all round was plunged in the cold evening mist. The student remembered that, as he went out from the house, his mother was sitting barefoot on the floor in the entry, cleaning the samovar, while his father lay on the stove coughing; as it was Good Friday nothing had been cooked, and the student was terribly hungry. And now, shrinking from the cold, he thought that just such a wind had blown in the days of Rurik and in the time of Ivan the Terrible and Peter, and in their time there had been just the same desperate poverty and hunger, the same thatched roofs with holes in them, ignorance, misery, the same desolation around, the same darkness, the same feeling of oppression—all these had existed, did exist, and would exist, and the lapse of a thousand years would make life no better. And he did not want to go home.

The gardens were called 'the widows' because they were kept by two widows, mother and daughter. A camp fire was burning brightly with a crackling sound, throwing out light far around on the ploughed earth. The widow Vasilisa, a tall, fat old woman in a man's coat, was standing by and looking thoughtfully into the fire; her daughter Lukerya, a little pockmarked woman with a stupid-looking face, was sitting on the ground, washing a caldron and spoons. Apparently they had just had supper. There was a sound of men's voices; it was the labourers watering their horses at the river.

'Here you have winter back again,' said the student, going up to the camp fire. 'Good evening.'

Vasilisa started, but at once recognized him and smiled cordially.

'I did not know you; God bless you,' she said.

'You'll be rich.'

They talked. Vasilisa, a woman of experience, who had been in service with the gentry, first as a wet-nurse, afterwards as a children's nurse, expressed herself with refinement, and a soft, sedate smile never left her face; her daughter Lukerya, a village peasant woman, who had been beaten by her husband, simply screwed up her eyes at the student and said nothing, and she had a strange expression like that of a deaf mute.

'At just such a fire the Apostle Peter warmed himself,' said the student, stretching out his hands to the fire, 'so it must have been cold then, too. Ah, what a terrible night it must have been, granny! An utterly dismal long night!'

He looked round at the darkness, shook his head abruptly and asked:

'No doubt you have been at the reading of the Twelve Gospels?'

'Yes, I have,' answered Vasilisa.

'If you remember at the Last Supper Peter said to Jesus, "I am ready to go with Thee into darkness and unto death." And our Lord answered him thus: "I say unto thee, Peter, before the cock croweth thou wilt have denied Me thrice." After the supper Jesus went through the agony of death in the garden and prayed, and poor Peter was weary in spirit and faint, his eyelids were heavy and he could not struggle against sleep. He fell asleep. Then you heard how Judas the same night kissed Jesus and betrayed Him to His tormentors. They took Him bound to the high priest and beat Him, while Peter, exhausted, worn out with misery and alarm, hardly awake, you know, feeling that something awful was just going to happen on earth, followed behind.... He loved Jesus passionately, intensely, and now he saw from far off how He was beaten...'

Lukerya left the spoons and fixed an immovable stare upon the student.

'They came to the high priest's,' he went on; 'they began to question Jesus, and meantime the labourers made a fire in the yard as it was cold, and warmed themselves. Peter, too, stood with them near the fire and warmed himself as I am doing. A woman, seeing him, said: "He was with Jesus, too"—that is as much as to say that he, too, should be taken to be questioned. And all the labourers that were standing near the fire must have looked sourly and suspiciously at him, because he was confused and said: "I don't know Him." A little while after again someone recognized him as one of Jesus' disciples and said: "Thou, too, art one of them," but again he denied it. And for the third time someone turned to him: "Why, did I not see thee with Him in the garden to-day?" For the third time he denied it. And immediately after that time the cock crowed, and Peter, looking from afar off at Jesus, remembered the words He had said to him in the evening.... He remembered, he came to himself, went out of the yard and wept bitterly—bitterly. In the Gospel it is written: "He went out and wept bitterly." I imagine it: the still, still, dark, dark garden, and in the stillness, faintly audible, smothered sobbing...'

The student sighed and sank into thought. Still smiling, Vasilisa suddenly gave a gulp, big tears flowed freely down her cheeks, and she screened her face from the fire with her sleeve as though ashamed of her tears, and Lukerya, staring immovably at the student, flushed crimson, and her expression became strained and heavy like that of someone enduring intense pain.

The labourers came back from the river, and one of them riding a horse was quite near, and the light from the fire quivered upon him. The student said good-night to the widows and went on. And again the darkness was about him and his fingers began to be numb. A cruel wind was blowing, winter really had come back and it did not feel as though Easter would be the day after to-morrow.

Now the student was thinking about Vasilisa: since she had shed tears all that had happened to Peter the night before the Crucifixion must have some relation to her....

He looked round. The solitary light was still gleaming in the darkness and no figures could be seen near it now. The student thought again that if Vasilisa had shed tears, and her daughter had been troubled, it was evident that what he had just been telling them about, which had happened nineteen centuries ago, had a relation to the present—to both women, to the desolate village, to himself, to all people. The old woman had wept, not because he could tell the story touchingly, but because Peter was near to her, because her whole being was interested in what was passing in Peter's soul.

And joy suddenly stirred in his soul, and he even stopped for a minute to take breath. 'The past,' he thought, 'is linked with the present by an unbroken chain of events flowing one out of another.' And it seemed to him that he had just seen both ends of that chain; that when he touched one end the other quivered.

When he crossed the river by the ferry boat and afterwards, mounting the hill, looked at his village and towards the west where the cold crimson sunset lay a narrow streak of light, he thought that truth and beauty which had guided human life there in the garden and in the yard of the high priest had continued without interruption to this day, and had evidently always been the chief thing in human life and in all earthly life, indeed; and the feeling of youth, health, vigour—he was only twenty-two—and the inexpressible sweet expectation of happiness, of unknown mysterious happiness, took possession of him little by little, and life seemed to him enchanting, marvellous, and full of lofty meaning.

5

WARD NO. 6

I

In the hospital yard there stands a small lodge surrounded by a perfect forest of burdocks, nettles, and wild hemp. Its roof is rusty, the chimney is tumbling down, the steps at the front-door are rotting away and overgrown with grass, and there are only traces left of the stucco. The front of the lodge faces the hospital; at the back it looks out into the open country, from which it is separated by the grey hospital fence with nails on it. These nails, with their points upwards, and the fence, and the lodge itself, have that peculiar, desolate, God-forsaken look which is only found in our hospital and prison buildings.

If you are not afraid of being stung by the nettles, come by the narrow footpath that leads to the lodge, and let us see what is going on inside. Opening the first door, we walk into the entry. Here along the walls and by the stove every sort of hospital rubbish lies littered about. Mattresses, old tattered dressing-gowns, trousers, blue striped shirts, boots and shoes no good for anything—all these remnants are piled up in heaps, mixed up and crumpled, mouldering and giving out a sickly smell.

The porter, Nikita, an old soldier wearing rusty good-conduct stripes, is always lying on the litter with a pipe between his teeth. He has a grim, surly, battered-looking face, overhanging eyebrows which give him the expression of a sheep-dog of the steppes, and a red nose; he is short and looks thin and scraggy, but he is of imposing deportment and his fists are vigorous. He belongs to the class of simple-hearted, practical, and dull-witted people, prompt in carrying out orders, who like discipline better than anything in the world, and so are convinced that it is their duty to beat people. He showers blows on the face, on the chest, on the back, on whatever comes first, and is convinced that there would be no order in the place if he did not.

Next you come into a big, spacious room which fills up the whole lodge except for the entry. Here the walls are painted a dirty blue, the ceiling is as sooty as in a hut without a chimney—it is evident that in the winter the stove smokes and the room is full of fumes. The windows are disfigured by iron gratings on the inside. The wooden floor is grey and full of splinters. There is a stench of sour cabbage, of smouldering wicks, of bugs, and of ammonia, and for the first minute this stench gives you the impression of having walked into a menagerie.

There are bedsteads screwed to the floor. Men in blue hospital dressing-gowns, and wearing nightcaps in the old style, are sitting and lying on them. These are the lunatics.

There are five of them in all here. Only one is of the upper class, the rest are all artisans. The one nearest the door—a tall, lean workman with shining red whiskers and tear-stained eyes—sits with his head propped on his hand, staring at the same point. Day and night he grieves, shaking his head, sighing and smiling bitterly. He takes a part in conversation and usually makes no answer to questions; he eats and drinks mechanically when food is offered him. From his agonizing, throbbing cough, his thinness, and the flush on his cheeks, one may judge that he is in the first stage of consumption. Next to him is a little, alert, very lively old man, with a pointed beard and curly black hair like a negro's. By day he walks up and down the ward from window to window, or sits on his bed, cross-legged like a Turk, and, ceaselessly as a bullfinch whistles, softly sings and titters. He shows his childish gaiety and lively character at night also when he gets up to say his prayers—that is, to beat himself on the chest with his fists, and to scratch with his fingers at the door. This is the Jew Moiseika, an imbecile, who went crazy twenty years ago when his hat factory was burnt down.

And of all the inhabitants of Ward No. 6, he is the only one who is allowed to go out of the lodge, and even out of the yard into the street. He has enjoyed this privilege for years, probably because he is an old inhabitant of the hospital—a quiet, harmless imbecile, the buffoon of the town, where people are used to seeing him surrounded by boys and dogs. In his wretched gown, in his absurd night-cap, and in slippers, sometimes with bare legs and even without trousers, he walks about the streets, stopping at the gates and little shops, and begging for a copper. In one place they will give him some kvass, in another some bread, in another a copper, so that he generally goes back to the ward feeling rich and well fed. Everything that he brings back Nikita takes from him for his own benefit. The soldier does this roughly, angrily turning the Jew's pockets inside out, and calling God to witness that he will not let him go into the street again, and that breach of the regulations is worse to him than anything in the world.

Moiseika likes to make himself useful. He gives his companions water, and covers them up when they are asleep; he promises each of them to bring him back a kopeck, and to make him a new cap; he feeds with a spoon his neighbour on the left, who is paralyzed. He acts in this way, not from compassion nor from any considerations of a humane kind, but through imitation, unconsciously dominated by Gromov, his neighbour on the right hand.

Ivan Dmitritch Gromov, a man of thirty-three, who is a gentleman by birth, and has been a court usher and provincial secretary, suffers from the mania of persecution. He either lies curled up in bed, or walks from corner to corner as though for exercise; he very rarely sits down. He is always excited, agitated, and overwrought by a sort of vague, undefined expectation. The faintest rustle in the entry or shout in the yard is enough to make him raise his head and begin listening: whether they are coming for him, whether they are looking for him. And at such times his face expresses the utmost uneasiness and repulsion.

I like his broad face with its high cheek-bones, always pale and unhappy, and reflecting, as though in a mirror, a soul tormented by conflict and long-continued terror. His grimaces are strange and abnormal, but the delicate lines traced on his face by profound, genuine suffering show intelligence and sense, and there is a warm and healthy light in his eyes. I like the man himself, courteous, anxious to be of use, and extraordinarily gentle to everyone except Nikita. When anyone drops a button or a spoon, he jumps up from his bed quickly and picks it up; every day he says good-morning to his companions, and when he goes to bed he wishes them good-night.

Besides his continually overwrought condition and his

grimaces, his madness shows itself in the following way also. Sometimes in the evenings he wraps himself in his dressing-gown, and, trembling all over, with his teeth chattering, begins walking rapidly from corner to corner and between the bedsteads. It seems as though he is in a violent fever. From the way he suddenly stops and glances at his companions, it can be seen that he is longing to say something very important, but, apparently reflecting that they would not listen, or would not understand him, he shakes his head impatiently and goes on pacing up and down. But soon the desire to speak gets the upper hand of every consideration, and he will let himself go and speak fervently and passionately. His talk is disordered and feverish like delirium, disconnected, and not always intelligible, but, on the other hand, something extremely fine may be felt in it, both in the words and the voice. When he talks you recognize in him the lunatic and the man. It is difficult to reproduce on paper his insane talk. He speaks of the baseness of mankind, of violence trampling on justice, of the glorious life which will one day be upon earth, of the window-gratings, which remind him every minute of the stupidity and cruelty of oppressors. It makes a disorderly, incoherent potpourri of themes old but not yet out of date.

II

Some twelve or fifteen years ago an official called Gromov, a highly respectable and prosperous person, was living in his own house in the principal street of the town. He had two sons, Sergey and Ivan. When Sergey was a student in his fourth year he was taken ill with galloping consumption and died, and his death was, as it were, the first of a whole series of calamities which suddenly showered on the Gromov family. Within a week of Sergey's funeral the old father was put on trial for fraud and misappropriation, and he died of typhoid in the prison hospital soon afterwards. The house, with all their belongings, was sold by auction, and Ivan Dmitritch and his mother were left entirely without means.

Hitherto in his father's lifetime, Ivan Dmitritch, who was studying in the University of Petersburg, had received an allowance of sixty or seventy roubles a month, and had had no conception of poverty; now he had to make an abrupt change in his life. He had to spend his time from morning to night giving lessons for next to nothing, to work at copying, and with all that to go hungry, as all his earnings were sent to keep his mother. Ivan Dmitritch could not stand such a life; he lost heart and strength, and, giving up the university, went home.

Here, through interest, he obtained the post of teacher in the district school, but could not get on with his colleagues, was not liked by the boys, and soon gave up the post. His mother died. He was for six months without work, living on nothing but bread and water; then he became a court usher. He kept this post until he was dismissed owing to his illness.

He had never even in his young student days given the impression of being perfectly healthy. He had always been pale, thin, and given to catching cold; he ate little and slept badly. A single glass of wine went to his head and made him hysterical. He always had a craving for society, but, owing to his irritable temperament and suspiciousness, he never became very intimate with anyone, and had no friends. He always spoke with contempt of his fellow-townsmen, saying that their coarse ignorance and sleepy animal existence seemed to him loathsome and horrible. He spoke in a loud tenor, with heat, and invariably either with scorn and indignation, or with wonder and enthusiasm, and always with perfect sincerity. Whatever one talked to him about he always brought it round to the same subject: that life was dull and stifling in the town; that the townspeople had no lofty interests, but lived a dingy, meaningless life, diversified by violence, coarse profligacy, and hypocrisy; that scoundrels were well fed and clothed, while honest men lived from hand to mouth; that they needed schools, a progressive local paper, a theatre, public lectures, the co-ordination of the intellectual elements; that society must see its failings and be horrified. In his criticisms of people he laid on the colours thick, using only black and white, and no fine shades; mankind was divided for him into honest men and scoundrels: there was nothing in between. He always spoke with passion and enthusiasm of women and of love, but he had never been in love.

In spite of the severity of his judgments and his nervousness, he was liked, and behind his back was spoken of affectionately as Vanya. His innate refinement and readiness to be of service, his good breeding, his moral purity, and his shabby coat, his frail appearance and family misfortunes, aroused a kind, warm, sorrowful feeling. Moreover, he was well educated and well read; according to the townspeople's notions, he knew everything, and was in their eyes something like a walking encyclopaedia.

He had read a great deal. He would sit at the club, nervously pulling at his beard and looking through the magazines and books; and from his face one could see that he was not reading, but devouring the pages without giving himself time to digest what he read. It must be supposed that reading was one of his morbid habits, as he fell upon anything that came into his hands with equal avidity, even last year's newspapers and calendars. At home he always read lying down.

III

One autumn morning Ivan Dmitritch, turning up the collar of his greatcoat and splashing through the mud, made his way by side-streets and back lanes to see some artisan, and to collect some payment that was owing. He was in a gloomy mood, as he always was in the morning. In one of the side-streets he was met by two convicts in fetters and four soldiers with rifles in charge of them. Ivan Dmitritch had very often met convicts before, and they had always excited feelings of compassion and discomfort in him; but now this meeting made a peculiar, strange impression on him. It suddenly seemed to him for some reason that he, too, might be put into fetters and led through the mud to prison like that. After visiting the artisan, on the way home he met near the post office a police superintendent of his acquaintance, who greeted him and walked a few paces along the street with him, and for some reason this seemed to him suspicious. At home he could not get the convicts or the soldiers with their rifles out of his head all day, and an unaccountable inward agitation prevented him from reading or concentrating his mind. In the evening he did not light his lamp, and at night he could not sleep, but kept thinking that he might be arrested, put into fetters, and thrown into prison. He did not know of any harm he had done, and could be certain that he would never be guilty of murder, arson, or theft in the future either; but was it not easy to commit a crime by accident, unconsciously, and was not false witness always possible, and, indeed, miscarriage of justice? It was not without good reason that the agelong experience of the simple people teaches that beggary and prison are ills none can be safe from. A judicial mistake is very possible as legal proceedings are conducted nowadays, and there is nothing to be wondered at in it. People who have an official, professional relation to other men's sufferings—for instance, judges, police officers, doctors—in course of time, through habit, grow so callous that they cannot, even if they wish it, take any but a formal attitude to their clients; in this respect they are not different from the peasant who slaughters sheep and calves in the back-yard, and does not notice the blood. With this formal, soulless attitude to human personality the judge needs but one thing—time—in order to deprive an innocent man of all rights of property, and to condemn him to penal servitude. Only the time spent on performing certain formalities for which the judge is paid his salary, and then—it is all over. Then you may look in vain for justice and protection in this dirty, wretched little town a hundred and fifty miles from a railway station! And, indeed, is it not absurd even to think of justice when every kind of violence is accepted by society as a rational and consistent necessity, and every act of mercy—for instance, a verdict of acquittal—calls forth a perfect outburst of dissatisfied and revengeful feeling?

In the morning Ivan Dmitritch got up from his bed in a state of horror, with cold perspiration on his forehead, completely convinced that he might be arrested any minute. Since his gloomy thoughts of yesterday had haunted him so long, he thought, it must be that there was some truth in them. They could not, indeed, have come into his mind without any grounds whatever.

A policeman walking slowly passed by the windows: that was not for nothing. Here were two men standing still and silent near the house. Why were they silent? And agonizing days and nights followed for Ivan Dmitritch. Everyone who passed by the windows or came into the yard seemed to him a spy or a detective. At midday the chief of the police usually drove down the street with a pair of horses; he was going from his estate near the town to the police department; but Ivan Dmitritch fancied every time that he was driving especially quickly, and that he had a peculiar expression: it was evident that he was in haste to announce that there was a very important criminal in the town. Ivan Dmitritch started at every ring at the bell and knock at the gate, and was agitated whenever he came upon anyone new at his landlady's; when he met police officers and gendarmes he smiled and began whistling so as to seem unconcerned. He could not sleep for whole nights in succession expecting to be arrested, but he snored loudly and sighed as though in deep sleep, that his landlady might think he was asleep; for if he could not sleep it meant that he was tormented by the stings of conscience—what a piece of evidence! Facts and common sense persuaded him that all these terrors were nonsense and morbidity, that if one looked at the matter more broadly there was nothing really terrible in arrest and imprisonment—so long as the conscience is at ease; but the more sensibly and logically he reasoned, the more acute and agonizing his mental distress became. It might be compared with the story of a hermit who tried to cut a dwelling-place for himself in a virgin forest; the more zealously he worked with his axe, the thicker the forest grew. In the end Ivan Dmitritch, seeing it was useless, gave up reasoning altogether, and abandoned himself entirely to despair and terror.

He began to avoid people and to seek solitude. His official work had been distasteful to him before: now it became unbearable to him. He was afraid they would somehow get him into trouble, would put a bribe in his pocket unnoticed and then denounce him, or that he would accidentally make a mistake in official papers that would appear to be fraudulent, or would lose other people's money. It is strange that his imagination had never at other times been so agile and inventive as now, when every day he thought of thousands of different reasons for being seriously anxious over his freedom and honour; but, on the other hand, his interest in the outer world, in books in particular, grew sensibly fainter, and his memory began to fail him.

In the spring when the snow melted there were found in the ravine near the cemetery two half-decomposed corpses—the bodies of an old woman and a boy bearing the traces of death by violence. Nothing was talked of but these bodies and their unknown murderers. That people might not think he had been guilty of the crime, Ivan Dmitritch walked about the streets, smiling, and when he met acquaintances he turned pale, flushed, and began declaring that there was no greater crime than the murder of the weak and defenceless. But this duplicity soon exhausted him, and after some reflection he decided that in his position the best thing to do was to hide in his landlady's cellar. He sat in the cellar all day and then all night, then another day, was fearfully cold, and waiting till dusk, stole secretly like a thief back to his room. He stood in the middle of the room till daybreak, listening without stirring. Very early in the morning, before sunrise, some workmen came into the house. Ivan Dmitritch knew perfectly well that they had come to mend the stove in the kitchen, but terror told him that they were police officers disguised as workmen. He slipped stealthily out of the flat, and, overcome by terror, ran along the street without his cap and coat. Dogs raced after him barking, a peasant shouted somewhere behind him, the wind whistled in his ears, and it seemed to Ivan Dmitritch that the force and violence of the whole world was massed together behind his back and was chasing after him.

He was stopped and brought home, and his landlady sent for a doctor. Doctor Andrey Yefimitch, of whom we shall have more to say hereafter, prescribed cold compresses on his head and laurel drops, shook his head, and went away, telling the landlady he should not come again, as one should not interfere with people who are going out of their minds. As he had not the means to live at home and be nursed, Ivan Dmitritch was soon sent to the hospital, and was there put into the ward for venereal patients. He could not sleep at night, was full of whims and fancies, and disturbed the patients, and was soon afterwards, by Andrey Yefimitch's orders, transferred to Ward No. 6.

Within a year Ivan Dmitritch was completely forgotten in the town, and his books, heaped up by his landlady in a sledge in the shed, were pulled to pieces by boys.

IV

Ivan Dmitritch's neighbour on the left hand is, as I have said already, the Jew Moiseika; his neighbour on the right hand is a peasant so rolling in fat that he is almost spherical, with a blankly stupid face, utterly devoid of thought. This is a motionless, gluttonous, unclean animal who has long ago lost all powers of thought or feeling. An acrid, stifling stench always comes from him.

Nikita, who has to clean up after him, beats him terribly with all his might, not sparing his fists; and what is dreadful is not his being beaten—that one can get used to—but the fact that this stupefied creature does not respond to the blows with a sound or a movement, nor by a look in the eyes, but only sways a little like a heavy barrel.

The fifth and last inhabitant of Ward No. 6 is a man of the artisan class who had once been a sorter in the post office, a thinnish, fair little man with a good-natured but rather sly face. To judge from the clear, cheerful look in his calm and intelligent eyes, he has some pleasant idea in his mind, and has some very important and agreeable secret. He has under his pillow and under his mattress something that he never shows anyone, not from fear of its being taken from him and stolen, but from modesty. Sometimes he goes to the window, and turning his back to his companions, puts something on his breast, and bending his head, looks at it; if you go up to him at such a moment, he is overcome with confusion and snatches something off his breast. But it is not difficult to guess his secret.

'Congratulate me,' he often says to Ivan Dmitritch; 'I have been presented with the Stanislav order of the second degree with the star. The second degree with the star is only given to foreigners, but for some reason they want to make an exception for me,' he says with a smile, shrugging his shoulders in perplexity. 'That I must confess I did not expect.'

'I don't understand anything about that,' Ivan Dmitritch replies morosely.

'But do you know what I shall attain to sooner or later?' the former sorter persists, screwing up his eyes slyly. 'I shall certainly get the Swedish "Polar Star". That's an order it is worth working for, a white cross with a black ribbon. It's very beautiful.'

Probably in no other place is life so monotonous as in this ward. In the morning the patients, except the paralytic and the fat peasant, wash in the entry at a big tab and wipe themselves with the skirts of their dressing-gowns; after that they drink tea out of tin mugs which Nikita brings them out of the main building. Everyone is allowed one mugful. At midday they have soup made out of sour cabbage and boiled grain, in the evening their supper consists of grain left from dinner. In the intervals they lie down, sleep, look out of window, and walk from one corner to the other. And so every day. Even the former sorter always talks of the same orders.

Fresh faces are rarely seen in Ward No. 6. The doctor has not taken in any new mental cases for a long time, and the people who are fond of visiting lunatic asylums are few in this world. Once every two months Semyon Lazaritch, the barber, appears in the ward. How he cuts the patients' hair, and how Nikita helps him to do it, and what a trepidation the lunatics are always thrown into by the arrival of the drunken, smiling barber, we will not describe.

No one even looks into the ward except the barber. The patients are condemned to see day after day no one but Nikita.

A rather strange rumour has, however, been circulating in the hospital of late.

It is rumoured that the doctor has begun to visit Ward No. 6.

V

A strange rumour!

Dr Andrey Yefimitch Ragin is a strange man in his way. They say that when he was young he was very religious, and prepared himself for a clerical career, and that when he had finished his studies at the high school in 1863 he intended to enter a theological academy, but that his father, a surgeon and doctor of medicine, jeered at him and declared point-blank that he would disown him if he became a priest. How far this is true I don't know, but Andrey Yefimitch himself has more than once confessed that he has never had a natural bent for medicine or science in general.

However that may have been, when he finished his studies in the medical faculty he did not enter the priesthood. He showed no special devoutness, and was no more like a priest at the beginning of his medical career than he is now.

His exterior is heavy—coarse like a peasant's, his face, his beard, his flat hair, and his coarse, clumsy figure, suggest an overfed, intemperate, and harsh innkeeper on the highroad. His face is surly-looking and covered with blue veins, his eyes are little and his nose is red. With his height and broad shoulders he has huge hands and feet; one would think that a blow from his fist would knock the life out of anyone, but his step is soft, and his walk is cautious and insinuating; when he meets anyone in a narrow passage he is always the first to stop and make way, and to say, not in a bass, as one would expect, but in a high, soft tenor: 'I beg your pardon!' He has a little swelling on his neck which prevents him from wearing stiff starched collars, and so he always goes about in soft linen or cotton shirts.

Altogether he does not dress like a doctor. He wears the same suit for ten years, and the new clothes, which he usually buys at a Jewish shop, look as shabby and crumpled on him as his old ones; he sees patients and dines and pays visits all in the same coat; but this is not due to niggardliness, but to complete carelessness about his appearance.

When Andrey Yefimitch came to the town to take up his duties the 'institution founded to the glory of God' was in a terrible condition. One could hardly breathe for the stench in the wards, in the passages, and in the courtyards of the hospital. The hospital servants, the nurses, and their children slept in the wards together with the patients. They complained that there was no living for beetles, bugs, and mice. The surgical wards were never free from erysipelas. There were only two scalpels and not one thermometer in the whole hospital; potatoes were kept in the baths. The superintendent, the housekeeper, and the medical assistant robbed the patients, and of the old doctor, Andrey Yefimitch's predecessor, people declared that he secretly sold the hospital alcohol, and that he kept a regular harem consisting of nurses and female patients. These disorderly proceedings were perfectly well known in the town, and were even exaggerated, but people took them calmly; some justified them on the ground that there were only peasants and working men in the hospital, who could not be dissatisfied, since they were much worse off at home than in the hospital—they couldn't be fed on woodcocks! Others said in excuse that the town alone, without help from the Zemstvo, was not equal to maintaining a good hospital; thank God for having one at all, even a poor one. And the newly formed Zemstvo did not open infirmaries either in the town or the neighbourhood, relying on the fact that the town already had its hospital.

After looking over the hospital Andrey Yefimitch came to the conclusion that it was an immoral institution and extremely prejudicial to the health of the townspeople. In his opinion the most sensible thing that could be done was to let out the patients and close the hospital. But he reflected that his will alone was not enough to do this, and that it would be useless; if physical and moral impurity were driven out of one place, they would only move to another; one must wait for it to wither away of itself. Besides, if people open a hospital and put up with having it, it must be because they need it; superstition and all the nastiness and abominations of daily life were necessary, since in process of time they worked out to something sensible, just as manure turns into black earth. There was nothing on earth so good that it had not something nasty about its first origin.

When Andrey Yefimitch undertook his duties he was apparently not greatly concerned about the irregularities at the hospital. He only asked the attendants and nurses not to sleep in the wards, and had two cupboards of instruments put up; the superintendent, the housekeeper, the medical assistant, and the erysipelas remained unchanged.

Andrey Yefimitch loved intelligence and honesty intensely, but he had no strength of will nor belief in his right to organize an intelligent and honest life about him. He was absolutely unable to give orders, to forbid things, and to insist. It seemed as though he had taken a vow never to raise his voice and never to make use of the imperative. It was difficult for him to say 'Fetch' or 'Bring'; when he wanted his meals he would cough hesitatingly and say to the cook, 'How about tea?...' or 'How about dinner?...' To dismiss the superintendent or to tell him to leave off stealing, or to abolish the unnecessary parasitic post altogether, was absolutely beyond his powers. When Andrey Yefimitch was deceived or flattered, or accounts he knew to be cooked were brought him to sign, he would turn as red as a crab and feel guilty, but yet he would sign the accounts. When the patients complained to him of being hungry or of the roughness of the nurses, he would be confused and mutter guiltily: 'Very well, very well, I will go into it later.... Most likely there is some misunderstanding...'

At first Andrey Yefimitch worked very zealously. He saw patients every day from morning till dinner-time, performed operations, and even attended confinements. The ladies said of him that he was attentive and clever at diagnosing diseases, especially those of women and children. But in process of time the work unmistakably wearied him by its monotony and obvious uselessness. To-day one sees thirty patients, and to-morrow they have increased to thirty-five, the next day forty, and so on from day to day, from year to year, while the mortality in the town did not decrease and the patients did not leave off coming. To be any real help to forty patients between morning and dinner was not physically possible, so it could but lead to deception. If twelve thousand patients were seen in a year it meant, if one looked at it simply, that twelve thousand men were deceived. To put those who were seriously ill into wards, and to treat them according to the principles of science, was impossible, too, because though there were principles there was no science; if he were to put aside philosophy and pedantically follow the rules as other doctors did, the things above all necessary were cleanliness and ventilation instead of dirt, wholesome nourishment instead of broth made of stinking, sour cabbage, and good assistants instead of thieves; and, indeed, why hinder people dying if death is the normal and legitimate end of everyone? What is gained if some shop-keeper or clerk lives an extra five or ten years? If the aim of medicine is by drugs to alleviate suffering, the question forces itself on one: why alleviate it? In the first place, they say that suffering leads man to perfection; and in the second, if mankind really learns to alleviate its sufferings with pills and drops, it will completely abandon religion and philosophy, in which it has hitherto found not merely protection from all sorts of trouble, but even happiness. Pushkin suffered terrible agonies before his death, poor Heine lay paralyzed for several years; why, then, should not some Andrey Yefimitch or Matryona Savishna be ill, since their lives had nothing of importance in them, and would have been entirely empty and like the life of an amoeba except for suffering?

Oppressed by such reflections, Andrey Yefimitch relaxed his efforts and gave up visiting the hospital every day.

VI

His life was passed like this. As a rule he got up at eight o'clock in the morning, dressed, and drank his tea. Then he sat down in his study to read, or went to the hospital. At the hospital the out-patients were sitting in the dark, narrow little corridor waiting to be seen by the doctor. The nurses and the attendants, tramping with their boots over the brick floors, ran by them; gaunt-looking patients in dressing-gowns passed; dead bodies and vessels full of filth were carried by; the children were crying, and there was a cold draught. Andrey

Yefimitch knew that such surroundings were torture to feverish, consumptive, and impressionable patients; but what could be done? In the consulting-room he was met by his assistant, Sergey Sergeyitch—a fat little man with a plump, well-washed shaven face, with soft, smooth manners, wearing a new loosely cut suit, and looking more like a senator than a medical assistant. He had an immense practice in the town, wore a white tie, and considered himself more proficient than the doctor, who had no practice. In the corner of the consulting-room there stood a large ikon in a shrine with a heavy lamp in front of it, and near it a candle-stand with a white cover on it. On the walls hung portraits of bishops, a view of the Svyatogorsky Monastery, and wreaths of dried cornflowers. Sergey Sergeyitch was religious, and liked solemnity and decorum. The ikon had been put up at his expense; at his instructions some one of the patients read the hymns of praise in the consulting-room on Sundays, and after the reading Sergey Sergeyitch himself went through the wards with a censer and burned incense.

There were a great many patients, but the time was short, and so the work was confined to the asking of a few brief questions and the administration of some drugs, such as castor-oil or volatile ointment. Andrey Yefimitch would sit with his cheek resting in his hand, lost in thought and asking questions mechanically. Sergey Sergeyitch sat down too, rubbing his hands, and from time to time putting in his word.

'We suffer pain and poverty,' he would say, 'because we do not pray to the merciful God as we should. Yes!'

Andrey Yefimitch never performed any operation when he was seeing patients; he had long ago given up doing so, and the sight of blood upset him. When he had to open a child's mouth in order to look at its throat, and the child cried and tried to defend itself with its little hands, the noise in his ears made his head go round and brought tears to his eyes. He would make haste to prescribe a drug, and motion to the woman to take the child away.

He was soon wearied by the timidity of the patients and their incoherence, by the proximity of the pious Sergey Sergeyitch, by the portraits on the walls, and by his own questions which he had asked over and over again for twenty years. And he would go away after seeing five or six patients. The rest would be seen by his assistant in his absence.

With the agreeable thought that, thank God, he had no private practice now, and that no one would interrupt him, Andrey Yefimitch sat down to the table immediately on reaching home and took up a book. He read a great deal and always with enjoyment. Half his salary went on buying books, and of the six rooms that made up his abode three were heaped up with books and old magazines. He liked best of all works on history and philosophy; the only medical publication to which he subscribed was The Doctor, of which he always read the last pages first. He would always go on reading for several hours without a break and without being weary. He did not read as rapidly and impulsively as Ivan Dmitritch had done in the past, but slowly and with concentration, often pausing over a passage which he liked or did not find intelligible. Near the books there always stood a decanter of vodka, and a salted cucumber or a pickled apple lay beside it, not on a plate, but on the baize table-cloth. Every half-hour he would pour himself out a glass of vodka and drink it without taking his eyes off the book. Then without looking at it he would feel for the cucumber and bite off a bit.

At three o'clock he would go cautiously to the kitchen door; cough, and say, 'Daryushka, what about dinner?...'

After his dinner—a rather poor and untidily served one—Andrey Yefimitch would walk up and down his rooms with his arms folded, thinking. The clock would strike four, then five, and still he would be walking up and down thinking. Occasionally the kitchen door would creak, and the red and sleepy face of Daryushka would appear.

'Andrey Yefimitch, isn't it time for you to have your beer?' she would ask anxiously.

'No, it's not time yet...' he would answer. 'I'll wait a little.... I'll wait a little...'

Towards the evening the postmaster, Mihail Averyanitch, the only man in town whose society did not bore Andrey Yefimitch, would come in. Mihail Averyanitch had once been a very rich landowner, and had served in the calvary, but had come to ruin, and was forced by poverty to take a job in the post office late in life. He had a hale and hearty appearance, luxuriant grey whiskers, the manners of a well-bred man, and a loud, pleasant voice. He was good-natured and emotional, but hot-tempered. When anyone in the post office made a protest, expressed disagreement, or even began to argue, Mihail Averyanitch would turn crimson, shake all over, and shout in a voice of thunder, 'Hold your tongue!' so that the post office had long enjoyed the reputation of an institution which it was terrible to visit. Mihail Averyanitch liked and respected Andrey Yefimitch for his culture and the loftiness of his soul; he treated the other inhabitants of the town superciliously, as though they were his subordinates.

'Here I am,' he would say, going in to Andrey Yefimitch.

'Good evening, my dear fellow! I'll be bound, you are getting sick of me, aren't you?'

'On the contrary, I am delighted,' said the doctor. 'I am always glad to see you.'

The friends would sit on the sofa in the study and for some time would smoke in silence.

'Daryushka, what about the beer?' Andrey Yefimitch would say.

They would drink their first bottle still in silence, the doctor brooding and Mihail Averyanitch with a gay and animated face, like a man who has something very interesting to tell. The doctor was always the one to begin the conversation.

'What a pity,' he would say quietly and slowly, not looking his friend in the face (he never looked anyone in the face)—'what a great pity it is that there are no people in our town who are capable of carrying on intelligent and interesting conversation, or care to do so. It is an immense privation for us. Even the educated class do not rise above vulgarity; the level of their development, I assure you, is not a bit higher than that of the lower orders.'

'Perfectly true. I agree.'

'You know, of course,' the doctor went on quietly and deliberately, 'that everything in this world is insignificant and uninteresting except the higher spiritual manifestations of the human mind. Intellect draws a sharp line between the animals and man, suggests the divinity of the latter, and to some extent even takes the place of the immortality which does not exist. Consequently the intellect is the only possible source of enjoyment. We see and hear of no trace of intellect about us, so we are deprived of enjoyment. We have books, it is true, but that is not at all the same as living talk and converse. If you will allow me to make a not quite apt comparison: books are the printed score, while talk is the singing.'

'Perfectly true.'

A silence would follow. Daryushka would come out of the kitchen and with an expression of blank dejection would stand in the doorway to listen, with her face propped on her fist.

'Eh!' Mihail Averyanitch would sigh. 'To expect intelligence of this generation!'

And he would describe how wholesome, entertaining, and interesting life had been in the past. How intelligent the educated class in Russia used to be, and what lofty ideas it had of honour and friendship; how they used to lend money without an IOU, and it was thought a disgrace not to give a helping hand to a comrade in need; and what campaigns, what adventures, what skirmishes, what comrades, what women! And the Caucasus, what a marvellous country! The wife of a battalion commander, a queer woman, used to put on an officer's uniform and drive off into the mountains in the evening, alone, without a guide. It was said that she had a love affair with some princeling in the native village.

'Queen of Heaven, Holy Mother...' Daryushka would sigh.

'And how we drank! And how we ate! And what desperate liberals we were!'

Andrey Yefimitch would listen without hearing; he was musing as he sipped his beer.

'I often dream of intellectual people and conversation with them,' he said suddenly, interrupting Mihail Averyanitch. 'My father gave me an excellent education, but under the influence of the ideas of the sixties made me become a doctor. I believe if

I had not obeyed him then, by now I should have been in the very centre of the intellectual movement. Most likely I should have become a member of some university. Of course, intellect, too, is transient and not eternal, but you know why I cherish a partiality for it. Life is a vexatious trap; when a thinking man reaches maturity and attains to full consciousness he cannot help feeling that he is in a trap from which there is no escape. Indeed, he is summoned without his choice by fortuitous circumstances from non-existence into life... what for? He tries to find out the meaning and object of his existence; he is told nothing, or he is told absurdities; he knocks and it is not opened to him; death comes to him—also without his choice. And so, just as in prison men held together by common misfortune feel more at ease when they are together, so one does not notice the trap in life when people with a bent for analysis and generalization meet together and pass their time in the interchange of proud and free ideas. In that sense the intellect is the source of an enjoyment nothing can replace.'

'Perfectly true.'

Not looking his friend in the face, Andrey Yefimitch would go on, quietly and with pauses, talking about intellectual people and conversation with them, and Mihail Averyanitch would listen attentively and agree: 'Perfectly true.'

'And you do not believe in the immortality of the soul?' he would ask suddenly.

'No, honoured Mihail Averyanitch; I do not believe it, and have no grounds for believing it.'

'I must own I doubt it too. And yet I have a feeling as though I should never die. Oh, I think to myself: "Old fogey, it is time you were dead!" But there is a little voice in my soul says: "Don't believe it; you won't die."'

Soon after nine o'clock Mihail Averyanitch would go away. As he put on his fur coat in the entry he would say with a sigh:

'What a wilderness fate has carried us to, though, really! What's most vexatious of all is to have to die here. Ech!...'

VII

After seeing his friend out Andrey Yefimitch would sit down at the table and begin reading again. The stillness of the evening, and afterwards of the night, was not broken by a single sound, and it seemed as though time were standing still and brooding with the doctor over the book, and as though there were nothing in existence but the books and the lamp with the green shade. The doctor's coarse peasant-like face was gradually lighted up by a smile of delight and enthusiasm over the progress of the human intellect. Oh, why is not man immortal? he thought. What is the good of the brain centres and convolutions, what is the good of sight, speech, self-consciousness, genius, if it is all destined to depart into the soil, and in the end to grow cold together with the earth's crust, and then for millions of years to fly with the earth round the sun with no meaning and no object? To do that there was no need at all to draw man with his lofty, almost godlike intellect out of non-existence, and then, as though in mockery, to turn him into clay. The transmutation of substances! But what cowardice to comfort oneself with that cheap substitute for immortality! The unconscious processes that take place in nature are lower even than the stupidity of man, since in stupidity there is, anyway, consciousness and will, while in those processes there is absolutely nothing. Only the coward who has more fear of death than dignity can comfort himself with the fact that his body will in time live again in the grass, in the stones, in the toad. To find one's immortality in the transmutation of substances is as strange as to prophesy a brilliant future for the case after a precious violin has been broken and become useless.

When the clock struck, Andrey Yefimitch would sink back into his chair and close his eyes to think a little. And under the influence of the fine ideas of which he had been reading he would, unawares, recall his past and his present. The past was hateful—better not to think of it. And it was the same in the present as in the past. He knew that at the very time when his thoughts were floating together with the cooling earth round the sun, in the main building beside his abode people were suffering in sickness and physical impurity: someone perhaps could not sleep and was making war upon the insects, someone was being infected by erysipelas, or moaning over too tight a bandage; perhaps the patients were playing cards with the nurses and drinking vodka. According to the yearly return, twelve thousand people had been deceived; the whole hospital rested as it had done twenty years ago on thieving, filth, scandals, gossip, on gross quackery, and, as before, it was an immoral institution extremely injurious to the health of the inhabitants. He knew that Nikita knocked the patients about behind the barred windows of Ward No. 6, and that Moiseika went about the town every day begging alms.

On the other hand, he knew very well that a magical change had taken place in medicine during the last twenty-five years. When he was studying at the university he had fancied that medicine would soon be overtaken by the fate of alchemy and metaphysics; but now when he was reading at night the science of medicine touched him and excited his wonder, and even enthusiasm. What unexpected brilliance, what a revolution! Thanks to the antiseptic system operations were performed such as the great Pirogov had considered impossible even in spe. Ordinary Zemstvo doctors were venturing to perform the resection of the kneecap; of abdominal operations only one per cent. was fatal; while stone was considered such a trifle that they did not even write about it. A radical cure for syphilis had been discovered. And the theory of heredity, hypnotism, the discoveries of Pasteur and of Koch, hygiene based on statistics, and the work of Zemstvo doctors!

Psychiatry with its modern classification of mental diseases, methods of diagnosis, and treatment, was a perfect Elborus in comparison with what had been in the past. They no longer poured cold water on the heads of lunatics nor put strait-waistcoats upon them; they treated them with humanity, and even, so it was stated in the papers, got up balls and entertainments for them. Andrey Yefimitch knew that with modern tastes and views such an abomination as Ward No. 6 was possible only a hundred and fifty miles from a railway in a little town where the mayor and all the town council were half-illiterate tradesmen who looked upon the doctor as an oracle who must be believed without any criticism even if he had poured molten lead into their mouths; in any other place the public and the newspapers would long ago have torn this little Bastille to pieces.

'But, after all, what of it?' Andrey Yefimitch would ask himself, opening his eyes. 'There is the antiseptic system, there is Koch, there is Pasteur, but the essential reality is not altered a bit; ill-health and mortality are still the same. They get up balls and entertainments for the mad, but still they don't let them go free; so it's all nonsense and vanity, and there is no difference in reality between the best Vienna clinic and my hospital.' But depression and a feeling akin to envy prevented him from feeling indifferent; it must have been owing to exhaustion. His heavy head sank on to the book, he put his hands under his face to make it softer, and thought: 'I serve in a pernicious institution and receive a salary from people whom I am deceiving. I am not honest, but then, I of myself am nothing, I am only part of an inevitable social evil: all local officials are pernicious and receive their salary for doing nothing.... And so for my dishonesty it is not I who am to blame, but the times.... If I had been born two hundred years later I should have been different...'

When it struck three he would put out his lamp and go into his bedroom; he was not sleepy.

VIII

Two years before, the Zemstvo in a liberal mood had decided to allow three hundred roubles a year to pay for additional medical service in the town till the Zemstvo hospital should be opened, and the district doctor, Yevgeny Fyodoritch Hobotov, was invited to the town to assist Andrey Yefimitch. He was a very young man—not yet thirty—tall and dark, with broad cheek-bones and little eyes; his forefathers had probably come from one of the many alien races of Russia. He arrived in the town without a farthing, with a small portmanteau, and a plain young woman whom he called his cook. This woman had a baby at the breast. Yevgeny Fyodoritch used to go about in a cap with a peak, and in high boots, and in the winter wore a sheepskin. He made great friends with Sergey Sergeyitch, the medical assistant, and with the treasurer, but held aloof from the other officials, and for some reason called them aristocrats. He had only one book in his lodgings, 'The Latest Prescriptions of the Vienna Clinic for 1881.' When he went to a patient he always took this book with him. He played billiards in the evening at the club: he did not like cards. He was very fond of using in conversation such expressions as 'endless bobbery', 'canting soft soap', 'shut up with your finicking…'.

He visited the hospital twice a week, made the round of the wards, and saw out-patients. The complete absence of antiseptic treatment and the cupping roused his indignation, but he did not introduce any new system, being afraid of offending Andrey Yefimitch. He regarded his colleague as a sly old rascal, suspected him of being a man of large means, and secretly envied him. He would have been very glad to have his post.

IX

On a spring evening towards the end of March, when there was no snow left on the ground and the starlings were singing in the hospital garden, the doctor went out to see his friend the postmaster as far as the gate. At that very moment the Jew Moiseika, returning with his booty, came into the yard. He had no cap on, and his bare feet were thrust into goloshes; in his hand he had a little bag of coppers.

'Give me a kopeck!' he said to the doctor, smiling, and shivering with cold. Andrey Yefimitch, who could never refuse anyone anything, gave him a ten-kopeck piece.

'How bad that is!' he thought, looking at the Jew's bare feet with their thin red ankles. 'Why, it's wet.'

And stirred by a feeling akin both to pity and disgust, he went into the lodge behind the Jew, looking now at his bald head, now at his ankles. As the doctor went in, Nikita jumped up from his heap of litter and stood at attention.

'Good-day, Nikita,' Andrey Yefimitch said mildly. 'That Jew should be provided with boots or something, he will catch cold.'

'Certainly, your honour. I'll inform the superintendent.'

'Please do; ask him in my name. Tell him that I asked.'

The door into the ward was open. Ivan Dmitritch, lying propped on his elbow on the bed, listened in alarm to the unfamiliar voice, and suddenly recognized the doctor. He trembled all over with anger, jumped up, and with a red and wrathful face, with his eyes starting out of his head, ran out into the middle of the road.

'The doctor has come!' he shouted, and broke into a laugh. 'At last! Gentlemen, I congratulate you. The doctor is honouring us with a visit! Cursed reptile!' he shrieked, and stamped in a frenzy such as had never been seen in the ward before. 'Kill the reptile! No, killing's too good. Drown him in the midden-pit!'

Andrey Yefimitch, hearing this, looked into the ward from the entry and asked gently: 'What for?'

'What for?' shouted Ivan Dmitritch, going up to him with a menacing air and convulsively wrapping himself in his dressing-gown. 'What for? Thief!' he said with a look of repulsion, moving his lips as though he would spit at him. 'Quack! Hangman!'

'Calm yourself,' said Andrey Yefimitch, smiling guiltily. 'I assure you I have never stolen anything; and as to the rest, most likely you greatly exaggerate. I see you are angry with me. Calm yourself, I beg, if you can, and tell me coolly what are you angry for?'

'What are you keeping me here for?'

'Because you are ill.'

'Yes, I am ill. But you know dozens, hundreds of madmen are walking about in freedom because your ignorance is incapable of distinguishing them from the sane. Why am I and these poor wretches to be shut up here like scapegoats for all the rest? You, your assistant, the superintendent, and all your hospital rabble, are immeasurably inferior to every one of us morally; why then are we shut up and you not? Where's the logic of it?'

'Morality and logic don't come in, it all depends on chance. If anyone is shut up he has to stay, and if anyone is not shut up he can walk about, that's all. There is neither morality nor logic in my being a doctor and your being a mental patient, there is nothing but idle chance.'

'That twaddle I don't understand...' Ivan Dmitritch brought out in a hollow voice, and he sat down on his bed.

Moiseika, whom Nikita did not venture to search in the presence of the doctor, laid out on his bed pieces of bread, bits of paper, and little bones, and, still shivering with cold, began rapidly in a singsong voice saying something in Yiddish. He most likely imagined that he had opened a shop.

'Let me out,' said Ivan Dmitritch, and his voice quivered.

'I cannot.'

'But why, why?'

'Because it is not in my power. Think, what use will it be to you if I do let you out? Go. The townspeople or the police will detain you or bring you back.'

'Yes, yes, that's true,' said Ivan Dmitritch, and he rubbed

his forehead. 'It's awful! But what am I to do, what?'

Andrey Yefimitch liked Ivan Dmitritch's voice and his intelligent young face with its grimaces. He longed to be kind to the young man and soothe him; he sat down on the bed beside him, thought, and said:

'You ask me what to do. The very best thing in your position would be to run away. But, unhappily, that is useless. You would be taken up. When society protects itself from the criminal, mentally deranged, or otherwise inconvenient people, it is invincible. There is only one thing left for you: to resign yourself to the thought that your presence here is inevitable.'

'It is no use to anyone.'

'So long as prisons and madhouses exist someone must be shut up in them. If not you, I. If not I, some third person. Wait till in the distant future prisons and madhouses no longer exist, and there will be neither bars on the windows nor hospital gowns. Of course, that time will come sooner or later.'

Ivan Dmitritch smiled ironically.

'You are jesting,' he said, screwing up his eyes. 'Such gentlemen as you and your assistant Nikita have nothing to do with the future, but you may be sure, sir, better days will come! I may express myself cheaply, you may laugh, but the dawn of a new life is at hand; truth and justice will triumph, and—our turn will come! I shall not live to see it, I shall perish, but some people's great-grandsons will see it. I greet them with all my heart and rejoice, rejoice with them! Onward! God be your help, friends!'

With shining eyes Ivan Dmitritch got up, and stretching his hands towards the window, went on with emotion in his voice:

'From behind these bars I bless you! Hurrah for truth and justice! I rejoice!'

'I see no particular reason to rejoice,' said Andrey Yefimitch, who thought Ivan Dmitritch's movement theatrical, though he was delighted by it. 'Prisons and madhouses there will not be, and truth, as you have just expressed it, will triumph; but the reality of things, you know, will not change, the laws of nature will still remain the same. People will suffer pain, grow old, and die just as they do now. However magnificent a dawn lighted up your life, you would yet in the end be nailed up in a coffin and thrown into a hole.'

'And immortality?'

'Oh, come, now!'

'You don't believe in it, but I do. Somebody in Dostoevsky or Voltaire said that if there had not been a God men would have invented him. And I firmly believe that if there is no immortality the great intellect of man will sooner or later invent it.'

'Well said,' observed Andrey Yefimitch, smiling with pleasure; 'its a good thing you have faith. With such a belief one may live happily even shut up within walls. You have studied somewhere, I presume?'

'Yes, I have been at the university, but did not complete my studies.'

'You are a reflecting and a thoughtful man. In any surroundings you can find tranquillity in yourself. Free and deep thinking which strives for the comprehension of life, and complete contempt for the foolish bustle of the world—those are two blessings beyond any that man has ever known. And you can possess them even though you lived behind threefold bars. Diogenes lived in a tub, yet he was happier than all the kings of the earth.'

'Your Diogenes was a blockhead,' said Ivan Dmitritch

morosely. 'Why do you talk to me about Diogenes and some foolish comprehension of life?' he cried, growing suddenly angry and leaping up. 'I love life; I love it passionately. I have the mania of persecution, a continual agonizing terror; but I have moments when I am overwhelmed by the thirst for life, and then I am afraid of going mad. I want dreadfully to live, dreadfully!'

He walked up and down the ward in agitation, and said, dropping his voice:

'When I dream I am haunted by phantoms. People come to me, I hear voices and music, and I fancy I am walking through woods or by the seashore, and I long so passionately for movement, for interests.... Come, tell me, what news is there?' asked Ivan Dmitritch; 'what's happening?'

'Do you wish to know about the town or in general?'

'Well, tell me first about the town, and then in general.'

'Well, in the town it is appallingly dull.... There's no one to say a word to, no one to listen to. There are no new people. A young doctor called Hobotov has come here recently.'

'He had come in my time. Well, he is a low cad, isn't he?'

'Yes, he is a man of no culture. It's strange, you know.... Judging by every sign, there is no intellectual stagnation in our capital cities; there is a movement—so there must be real people there too; but for some reason they always send us such men as I would rather not see. It's an unlucky town!'

'Yes, it is an unlucky town,' sighed Ivan Dmitritch, and he laughed. 'And how are things in general? What are they writing in the papers and reviews?'

It was by now dark in the ward. The doctor got up, and, standing, began to describe what was being written abroad and in Russia, and the tendency of thought that could be noticed now. Ivan Dmitritch listened attentively and put questions, but suddenly, as though recalling something terrible, clutched at his head and lay down on the bed with his back to the doctor.

'What's the matter?' asked Andrey Yefimitch.

'You will not hear another word from me,' said Ivan Dmitritch rudely. 'Leave me alone.'

'Why so?'

'I tell you, leave me alone. Why the devil do you persist?'

Andrey Yefimitch shrugged his shoulders, heaved a sigh, and went out. As he crossed the entry he said: 'You might clear up here, Nikita...there's an awfully stuffy smell.'

'Certainly, your honour.'

'What an agreeable young man!' thought Andrey Yefimitch, going back to his flat. 'In all the years I have been living here I do believe he is the first I have met with whom one can talk. He is capable of reasoning and is interested in just the right things.'

While he was reading, and afterwards, while he was going to bed, he kept thinking about Ivan Dmitritch, and when he woke next morning he remembered that he had the day before made the acquaintance of an intelligent and interesting man, and determined to visit him again as soon as possible.

X

Ivan Dmitritch was lying in the same position as on the previous day, with his head clutched in both hands and his legs drawn up. His face was not visible.

'Good-day, my friend,' said Andrey Yefimitch. 'You are not asleep, are you?'

'In the first place, I am not your friend,' Ivan Dmitritch

articulated into the pillow; 'and in the second, your efforts are useless; you will not get one word out of me.'

'Strange,' muttered Andrey Yefimitch in confusion. 'Yesterday we talked peacefully, but suddenly for some reason you took offence and broke off all at once.... Probably I expressed myself awkwardly, or perhaps gave utterance to some idea which did not fit in with your convictions....'

'Yes, a likely idea!' said Ivan Dmitritch, sitting up and looking at the doctor with irony and uneasiness. His eyes were red. 'You can go and spy and probe somewhere else, it's no use your doing it here. I knew yesterday what you had come for.'

'A strange fancy,' laughed the doctor. 'So you suppose me to be a spy?'

'Yes, I do.... A spy or a doctor who has been charged to test me—it's all the same—'

'Oh excuse me, what a queer fellow you are really!'

The doctor sat down on the stool near the bed and shook his head reproachfully.

'But let us suppose you are right,' he said, 'let us suppose that I am treacherously trying to trap you into saying something so as to betray you to the police. You would be arrested and then tried. But would you be any worse off being tried and in prison than you are here? If you are banished to a settlement, or even sent to penal servitude, would it be worse than being shut up in this ward? I imagine it would be no worse.... What, then, are you afraid of?'

These words evidently had an effect on Ivan Dmitritch. He sat down quietly.

It was between four and five in the afternoon—the time when Andrey Yefimitch usually walked up and down his rooms, and Daryushka asked whether it was not time for his beer. It was a still, bright day.

'I came out for a walk after dinner, and here I have come, as you see,' said the doctor. 'It is quite spring.'

'What month is it? March?' asked Ivan Dmitritch.

'Yes, the end of March.'

'Is it very muddy?'

'No, not very. There are already paths in the garden.'

'It would be nice now to drive in an open carriage somewhere into the country,' said Ivan Dmitritch, rubbing his red eyes as though he were just awake, 'then to come home to a warm, snug study, and... and to have a decent doctor to cure one's headache.... It's so long since I have lived like a human being. It's disgusting here! Insufferably disgusting!'

After his excitement of the previous day he was exhausted and listless, and spoke unwillingly. His fingers twitched, and from his face it could be seen that he had a splitting headache.

'There is no real difference between a warm, snug study and this ward,' said Andrey Yefimitch. 'A man's peace and contentment do not lie outside a man, but in himself.'

'What do you mean?'

'The ordinary man looks for good and evil in external things—that is, in carriages, in studies—but a thinking man looks for it in himself.'

'You should go and preach that philosophy in Greece, where it's warm and fragrant with the scent of pomegranates, but here it is not suited to the climate. With whom was it I was talking of Diogenes? Was it with you?'

'Yes, with me yesterday.'

'Diogenes did not need a study or a warm habitation; it's

hot there without. You can lie in your tub and eat oranges and olives. But bring him to Russia to live: he'd be begging to be let indoors in May, let alone December. He'd be doubled up with the cold.'

'No. One can be insensible to cold as to every other pain. Marcus Aurelius says: "A pain is a vivid idea of pain; make an effort of will to change that idea, dismiss it, cease to complain, and the pain will disappear." That is true. The wise man, or simply the reflecting, thoughtful man, is distinguished precisely by his contempt for suffering; he is always contented and surprised at nothing.'

'Then I am an idiot, since I suffer and am discontented and surprised at the baseness of mankind.'

'You are wrong in that; if you will reflect more on the subject you will understand how insignificant is all that external world that agitates us. One must strive for the comprehension of life, and in that is true happiness.'

'Comprehension...' repeated Ivan Dmitritch frowning. 'External, internal.... Excuse me, but I don't understand it. I only know,' he said, getting up and looking angrily at the doctor—'I only know that God has created me of warm blood and nerves, yes, indeed! If organic tissue is capable of life it must react to every stimulus. And I do! To pain I respond with tears and outcries, to baseness with indignation, to filth with loathing. To my mind, that is just what is called life. The lower the organism, the less sensitive it is, and the more feebly it reacts to stimulus; and the higher it is, the more responsively and vigorously it reacts to reality. How is it you don't know that? A doctor, and not know such trifles! To despise suffering, to be always contented, and to be surprised at nothing, one must reach this condition'—and Ivan Dmitritch pointed to the peasant who was a mass of fat—'or to harden oneself by suffering to such a point that one loses all sensibility to it—that is, in other words, to cease to live. You must excuse me, I am not a sage or a philosopher,' Ivan Dmitritch continued with irritation, 'and I don't understand anything about it. I am not capable of reasoning.'

'On the contrary, your reasoning is excellent.'

'The Stoics, whom you are parodying, were remarkable people, but their doctrine crystallized two thousand years ago and has not advanced, and will not advance, an inch forward, since it is not practical or living. It had a success only with the minority which spends its life in savouring all sorts of theories and ruminating over them; the majority did not understand it. A doctrine which advocates indifference to wealth and to the comforts of life, and a contempt for suffering and death, is quite unintelligible to the vast majority of men, since that majority has never known wealth or the comforts of life; and to despise suffering would mean to it despising life itself, since the whole existence of man is made up of the sensations of hunger, cold, injury, and a Hamlet-like dread of death. The whole of life lies in these sensations; one may be oppressed by it, one may hate it, but one cannot despise it. Yes, so, I repeat, the doctrine of the Stoics can never have a future; from the beginning of time up to to-day you see continually increasing the struggle, the sensibility to pain, the capacity of responding to stimulus.'

Ivan Dmitritch suddenly lost the thread of his thoughts, stopped, and rubbed his forehead with vexation.

'I meant to say something important, but I have lost it,' he said. 'What was I saying? Oh, yes! This is what I mean: one of the Stoics sold himself into slavery to redeem his neighbour, so, you see, even a Stoic did react to stimulus, since, for such a generous act as the destruction of oneself for the sake of one's neighbour, he must have had a soul capable of pity and indignation. Here in prison I have forgotten everything I have learned, or else I could have recalled something else. Take Christ, for instance: Christ responded to reality by weeping, smiling, being sorrowful and moved to wrath, even overcome by misery. He did not go to meet His sufferings with a smile, He did not despise death, but prayed in the Garden of Gethsemane that this cup might pass Him by.'

Ivan Dmitritch laughed and sat down.

'Granted that a man's peace and contentment lie not outside but in himself,' he said, 'granted that one must despise suffering and not be surprised at anything, yet on what ground do you preach the theory? Are you a sage? A philosopher?'

'No, I am not a philosopher, but everyone ought to preach it because it is reasonable.'

'No, I want to know how it is that you consider yourself competent to judge of "comprehension", contempt for suffering, and so on. Have you ever suffered? Have you any idea of suffering? Allow me to ask you, were you ever thrashed in your childhood?'

'No, my parents had an aversion for corporal punishment.'

'My father used to flog me cruelly; my father was a harsh, sickly Government clerk with a long nose and a yellow neck. But let us talk of you. No one has laid a finger on you all your life, no one has scared you nor beaten you; you are as strong as a bull. You grew up under your father's wing and studied at his expense, and then you dropped at once into a sinecure. For more than twenty years you have lived rent free with heating, lighting, and service all provided, and had the right to work how you pleased and as much as you pleased, even to do nothing. You were naturally a flabby, lazy man, and so you have tried to arrange your life so that nothing should disturb you or make you move. You have handed over your work to the assistant and the rest of the rabble while you sit in peace and warmth, save money, read, amuse yourself with reflections, with all sorts of lofty nonsense, and' (Ivan Dmitritch looked at the doctor's red nose) 'with boozing; in fact, you have seen nothing of life, you know absolutely nothing of it, and are only theoretically acquainted with reality; you despise suffering and are surprised at nothing for a very simple reason: vanity of vanities, the external and the internal, contempt for life, for suffering and for death, comprehension, true happiness—that's the philosophy that suits the Russian sluggard best. You see a peasant beating his wife, for instance. Why interfere? Let him beat her, they will both die sooner or later, anyway; and, besides, he who beats injures by his blows, not the person he is beating, but himself. To get drunk is stupid and unseemly, but if you drink you die, and if you don't drink you die. A peasant woman comes with toothache...well, what of it? Pain is the idea of pain, and besides "there is no living in this world without illness; we shall all die, and so, go away, woman, don't hinder me from thinking and drinking vodka." A young man asks advice, what he is to do, how he is to live; anyone else would think before answering, but you have got the answer ready: strive for "comprehension" or for true happiness. And what is that fantastic "true happiness"? There's no answer, of course. We are kept here behind barred windows, tortured, left to rot; but that is very good and reasonable, because there is no difference at all between this ward and a warm, snug study. A convenient philosophy. You can do nothing, and your conscience is clear, and you feel you are wise.... No, sir, it is not philosophy, it's not thinking, it's not breadth of vision, but laziness, fakirism, drowsy stupefaction. Yes,' cried Ivan Dmitritch, getting angry again, 'you despise suffering, but I'll be bound if you pinch your finger in the door you will howl at the top of your voice.'

'And perhaps I shouldn't howl,' said Andrey Yefimitch, with a gentle smile.

'Oh, I dare say! Well, if you had a stroke of paralysis, or supposing some fool or bully took advantage of his position and rank to insult you in public, and if you knew he could do it with impunity, then you would understand what it means to put people off with comprehension and true happiness.'

'That's original,' said Andrey Yefimitch, laughing with pleasure and rubbing his hands. 'I am agreeably struck by your inclination for drawing generalizations, and the sketch of my character you have just drawn is simply brilliant. I must confess that talking to you gives me great pleasure. Well, I've listened to you, and now you must graciously listen to me.'

XI

The conversation went on for about an hour longer, and apparently made a deep impression on Andrey Yefimitch. He began going to the ward every day. He went there in the mornings and after dinner, and often the dusk of evening found him in conversation with Ivan Dmitritch. At first Ivan Dmitritch held aloof from him, suspected him of evil designs, and openly expressed his hostility. But afterwards he got used to him, and his abrupt manner changed to one of condescending irony.

Soon it was all over the hospital that the doctor, Andrey Yefimitch, had taken to visiting Ward No. 6. No one—neither Sergey Sergevitch, nor Nikita, nor the nurses—could conceive why he went there, why he stayed there for hours together, what he was talking about, and why he did not write prescriptions. His actions seemed strange. Often Mihail Averyanitch did not find him at home, which had never happened in the past, and Daryushka was greatly perturbed, for the doctor drank his beer now at no definite time, and sometimes was even late for dinner.

One day—it was at the end of June—Dr Hobotov went to see Andrey Yefimitch about something. Not finding him at home, he proceeded to look for him in the yard; there he was told that the old doctor had gone to see the mental patients. Going into the lodge and stopping in the entry, Hobotov heard the following conversation:

'We shall never agree, and you will not succeed in converting me to your faith,' Ivan Dmitritch was saying irritably; 'you are utterly ignorant of reality, and you have never known suffering, but have only like a leech fed beside the sufferings of others, while I have been in continual suffering from the day of my birth till to-day. For that reason, I tell you frankly, I consider myself superior to you and more competent in every respect. It's not for you to teach me.'

'I have absolutely no ambition to convert you to my faith,' said Andrey Yefimitch gently, and with regret that the other refused to understand him. 'And that is not what matters, my friend; what matters is not that you have suffered and I have not. Joy and suffering are passing; let us leave them, never mind them. What matters is that you and I think; we see in each other people who are capable of thinking and reasoning, and that is a common bond between us however different our views. If you knew, my friend, how sick I am of the universal senselessness, ineptitude, stupidity, and with what delight I always talk with you! You are an intelligent man, and I enjoyed your company.'

Hobotov opened the door an inch and glanced into the ward; Ivan Dmitritch in his night-cap and the doctor Andrey Yefimitch were sitting side by side on the bed. The madman was grimacing, twitching, and convulsively wrapping himself in his gown, while the doctor sat motionless with bowed head, and his face was red and look helpless and sorrowful. Hobotov shrugged his shoulders, grinned, and glanced at Nikita. Nikita shrugged his shoulders too.

Next day Hobotov went to the lodge, accompanied by the assistant. Both stood in the entry and listened.

'I fancy our old man has gone clean off his chump!' said Hobotov as he came out of the lodge.

'Lord have mercy upon us sinners!' sighed the decorous Sergey Sergeyitch, scrupulously avoiding the puddles that he might not muddy his polished boots. 'I must own, honoured Yevgeny Fyodoritch, I have been expecting it for a long time.'

XII

After this Andrey Yefimitch began to notice a mysterious air in all around him. The attendants, the nurses, and the patients looked at him inquisitively when they met him, and then whispered together. The superintendent's little daughter Masha, whom he liked to meet in the hospital garden, for some reason ran away from him now when he went up with a smile to stroke her on the head. The postmaster no longer said, 'Perfectly true,' as he listened to him, but in unaccountable confusion muttered, 'Yes, yes, yes...' and looked at him with a grieved and thoughtful expression; for some reason he took to advising his friend to give up vodka and beer, but as a man of delicate feeling he did not say this directly, but hinted it, telling him first about the commanding officer of his battalion, an excellent man, and then about the priest of the regiment, a capital fellow, both of whom drank and fell ill, but on giving up drinking completely regained their health. On two or three occasions Andrey Yefimitch was visited by his colleague Hobotov, who also advised him to give up spirituous liquors, and for no apparent reason recommended him to take bromide.

In August Andrey Yefimitch got a letter from the mayor of the town asking him to come on very important business. On arriving at the town hall at the time fixed, Andrey Yefimitch found there the military commander, the superintendent of the district school, a member of the town council, Hobotov, and a plump, fair gentleman who was introduced to him as a doctor. This doctor, with a Polish surname difficult to pronounce, lived at a pedigree stud-farm twenty miles away, and was now on a visit to the town.

'There's something that concerns you,' said the member of the town council, addressing Andrey Yefimitch after they had all greeted one another and sat down to the table. 'Here Yevgeny Fyodoritch says that there is not room for the dispensary in the main building, and that it ought to be transferred to one of the lodges. That's of no consequence—of course it can be transferred, but the point is that the lodge wants doing up.'

'Yes, it would have to be done up,' said Andrey Yefimitch after a moment's thought. 'If the corner lodge, for instance, were fitted up as a dispensary, I imagine it would cost at least five hundred roubles. An unproductive expenditure!'

Everyone was silent for a space.

'I had the honour of submitting to you ten years ago,' Andrey Yefimitch went on in a low voice, 'that the hospital in its present form is a luxury for the town beyond its means. It was built in the forties, but things were different then. The town spends too much on unnecessary buildings and superfluous staff. I believe with a different system two model hospitals might be maintained for the same money.'

'Well, let us have a different system, then!' the member of the town council said briskly.

'I have already had the honour of submitting to you that the medical department should be transferred to the supervision of the Zemstvo.'

'Yes, transfer the money to the Zemstvo and they will steal it,' laughed the fair-haired doctor.

'That's what it always comes to,' the member of the council assented, and he also laughed.

Andrey Yefimitch looked with apathetic, lustreless eyes at the fair-haired doctor and said: 'One should be just.'

Again there was silence. Tea was brought in. The military commander, for some reason much embarrassed, touched Andrey Yefimitch's hand across the table and said: 'You have quite forgotten us, doctor. But of course you are a hermit: you don't play cards and don't like women. You would be dull with fellows like us.'

They all began saying how boring it was for a decent person

to live in such a town. No theatre, no music, and at the last dance at the club there had been about twenty ladies and only two gentlemen. The young men did not dance, but spent all the time crowding round the refreshment bar or playing cards.

Not looking at anyone and speaking slowly in a low voice, Andrey Yefimitch began saying what a pity, what a terrible pity it was that the townspeople should waste their vital energy, their hearts, and their minds on cards and gossip, and should have neither the power nor the inclination to spend their time in interesting conversation and reading, and should refuse to take advantage of the enjoyments of the mind. The mind alone was interesting and worthy of attention, all the rest was low and petty. Hobotov listened to his colleague attentively and suddenly asked:

'Andrey Yefimitch, what day of the month is it?'

Having received an answer, the fair-haired doctor and he, in the tone of examiners conscious of their lack of skill, began asking Andrey Yefimitch what was the day of the week, how many days there were in the year, and whether it was true that there was a remarkable prophet living in Ward No. 6.

In response to the last question Andrey Yefimitch turned rather red and said: 'Yes, he is mentally deranged, but he is an interesting young man.'

They asked him no other questions.

When he was putting on his overcoat in the entry, the military commander laid a hand on his shoulder and said with a sigh:

'It's time for us old fellows to rest!'

As he came out of the hall, Andrey Yefimitch understood that it had been a committee appointed to enquire into his mental condition. He recalled the questions that had been asked him, flushed crimson, and for some reason, for the first time in his life, felt bitterly grieved for medical science.

'My God...' he thought, remembering how these doctors had just examined him; 'why, they have only lately been hearing lectures on mental pathology; they had passed an examination—what's the explanation of this crass ignorance? They have not a conception of mental pathology!'

And for the first time in his life he felt insulted and moved to anger.

In the evening of the same day Mihail Averyanitch came to see him. The postmaster went up to him without waiting to greet him, took him by both hands, and said in an agitated voice:

'My dear fellow, my dear friend, show me that you believe in my genuine affection and look on me as your friend!' And preventing Andrey Yefimitch from speaking, he went on, growing excited: 'I love you for your culture and nobility of soul. Listen to me, my dear fellow. The rules of their profession compel the doctors to conceal the truth from you, but I blurt out the plain truth like a soldier. You are not well! Excuse me, my dear fellow, but it is the truth; everyone about you has been noticing it for a long time. Dr Yevgeny Fyodoritch has just told me that it is essential for you to rest and distract your mind for the sake of your health. Perfectly true! Excellent! In a day or two I am taking a holiday and am going away for a sniff of a different atmosphere. Show that you are a friend to me, let us go together! Let us go for a jaunt as in the good old days.'

'I feel perfectly well,' said Andrey Yefimitch after a moment's thought. 'I can't go away. Allow me to show you my friendship in some other way.'

To go off with no object, without his books, without his Daryushka, without his beer, to break abruptly through the routine of life, established for twenty years—the idea for the first minute struck him as wild and fantastic, but he remembered the conversation at the Zemstvo committee and the depressing feelings with which he had returned home, and the thought of a brief absence from the town in which stupid people looked on him as a madman was pleasant to him.

'And where precisely do you intend to go?' he asked.

'To Moscow, to Petersburg, to Warsaw.... I spent the five happiest years of my life in Warsaw. What a marvellous town! Let us go, my dear fellow!'

XIII

A week later it was suggested to Andrey Yefimitch that he should have a rest—that is, send in his resignation—a suggestion he received with indifference, and a week later still, Mihail Averyanitch and he were sitting in a posting carriage driving to the nearest railway station. The days were cool and bright, with a blue sky and a transparent distance. They were two days driving the hundred and fifty miles to the railway station, and stayed two nights on the way. When at the posting station the glasses given them for their tea had not been properly washed, or the drivers were slow in harnessing the horses, Mihail Averyanitch would turn crimson, and quivering all over would shout:

'Hold your tongue! Don't argue!'

And in the carriage he talked without ceasing for a moment, describing his campaigns in the Caucasus and in Poland. What adventures he had had, what meetings! He talked loudly and opened his eyes so wide with wonder that he might well be thought to be lying. Moreover, as he talked he breathed in Andrey Yefimitch's face and laughed into his ear. This bothered the doctor and prevented him from thinking or concentrating his mind.

In the train they travelled, from motives of economy, third-class in a non-smoking compartment. Half the passengers were decent people. Mihail Averyanitch soon made friends with everyone, and moving from one seat to another, kept saying loudly that they ought not to travel by these appalling lines. It was a regular swindle! A very different thing riding on a good horse: one could do over seventy miles a day and feel fresh and well after it. And our bad harvests were due to the draining of the Pinsk marshes; altogether, the way things were done was dreadful. He got excited, talked loudly, and would not let others speak. This endless chatter to the accompaniment of loud laughter and expressive gestures wearied Andrey Yefimitch.

'Which of us is the madman?' he thought with vexation. 'I, who try not to disturb my fellow-passengers in any way, or this egoist who thinks that he is cleverer and more interesting than anyone here, and so will leave no one in peace?'

In Moscow Mihail Averyanitch put on a military coat without epaulettes and trousers with red braid on them. He wore a military cap and overcoat in the street, and soldiers saluted him. It seemed to Andrey Yefimitch, now, that his companion was a man who had flung away all that was good and kept only what was bad of all the characteristics of a country gentleman that he had once possessed. He liked to be waited on even when it was quite unnecessary. The matches would be lying before him on the table, and he would see them and shout to the waiter to give him the matches; he did not hesitate to appear before a maidservant in nothing but his underclothes; he used the familiar mode of address to all footmen indiscriminately, even old men, and when he was angry called them fools and blockheads. This, Andrey Yefimitch thought, was like a gentleman, but disgusting.

First of all Mihail Averyanitch led his friend to the Iversky Madonna. He prayed fervently, shedding tears and bowing down to the earth, and when he had finished, heaved a deep sigh and said:

'Even though one does not believe it makes one somehow easier when one prays a little. Kiss the ikon, my dear fellow.'

Andrey Yefimitch was embarrassed and he kissed the image, while Mihail Averyanitch pursed up his lips and prayed in a whisper, and again tears came into his eyes. Then they went to the Kremlin and looked there at the Tsar-cannon and the Tsar-bell, and even touched them with their fingers, admired the view over the river, visited St. Saviour's and the Rumyantsev museum.

They dined at Tyestov's. Mihail Averyanitch looked a long time at the menu, stroking his whiskers, and said in the tone of a gourmand accustomed to dine in restaurants:

'We shall see what you give us to eat to-day, angel!'

XIV

The doctor walked about, looked at things, ate and drank, but he had all the while one feeling: annoyance with Mihail Averyanitch. He longed to have a rest from his friend, to get away from him, to hide himself, while the friend thought it was his duty not to let the doctor move a step away from him, and to provide him with as many distractions as possible. When there was nothing to look at he entertained him with conversation. For two days Andrey Yefimitch endured it, but on the third he announced to his friend that he was ill and wanted to stay at home for the whole day; his friend replied that in that case he would stay too—that really he needed rest, for he was run off his legs already. Andrey Yefimitch lay on the sofa, with his face to the back, and clenching his teeth, listened to his friend, who assured him with heat that sooner or later France would certainly thrash Germany, that there were a great many scoundrels in Moscow, and that it was impossible to judge of a horse's quality by its outward appearance. The doctor began to have a buzzing in his ears and palpitations of the heart, but out of delicacy could not bring himself to beg his friend to go away or hold his tongue. Fortunately Mihail Averyanitch grew weary of sitting in the hotel room, and after dinner he went out for a walk.

As soon as he was alone Andrey Yefimitch abandoned himself to a feeling of relief. How pleasant to lie motionless on the sofa and to know that one is alone in the room! Real happiness is impossible without solitude. The fallen angel betrayed God probably because he longed for solitude, of which the angels know nothing. Andrey Yefimitch wanted to think about what he had seen and heard during the last few days, but he could not get Mihail Averyanitch out of his head.

'Why, he has taken a holiday and come with me out of friendship, out of generosity,' thought the doctor with vexation; 'nothing could be worse than this friendly supervision. I suppose he is good-natured and generous and a lively fellow, but he is a bore. An insufferable bore. In the same way there are people who never say anything but what is clever and good, yet one feels that they are dull-witted people.'

For the following days Andrey Yefimitch declared himself ill and would not leave the hotel room; he lay with his face to the back of the sofa, and suffered agonies of weariness when his friend entertained him with conversation, or rested when his friend was absent. He was vexed with himself for having come, and with his friend, who grew every day more talkative and more free-and-easy; he could not succeed in attuning his thoughts to a serious and lofty level.

'This is what I get from the real life Ivan Dmitritch talked about,' he thought, angry at his own pettiness. 'It's of no consequence, though.... I shall go home, and everything will go on as before....'

It was the same thing in Petersburg too; for whole days together he did not leave the hotel room, but lay on the sofa and only got up to drink beer.

Mihail Averyanitch was all haste to get to Warsaw.

'My dear man, what should I go there for?' said Andrey Yefimitch in an imploring voice. 'You go alone and let me get home! I entreat you!'

'On no account,' protested Mihail Averyanitch. 'It's a marvellous town.'

Andrey Yefimitch had not the strength of will to insist on his own way, and much against his inclination went to Warsaw. There he did not leave the hotel room, but lay on the sofa, furious with himself, with his friend, and with the waiters, who obstinately refused to understand Russian; while Mihail Averyanitch, healthy, hearty, and full of spirits as usual, went about the town from morning to night, looking for his old acquaintances. Several times he did not return home at night.

After one night spent in some unknown haunt he returned home early in the morning, in a violently excited condition, with a red face and tousled hair. For a long time he walked up and down the rooms muttering something to himself, then stopped and said:

'Honour before everything.'

After walking up and down a little longer he clutched his head in both hands and pronounced in a tragic voice: 'Yes, honour before everything! Accursed be the moment when the idea first entered my head to visit this Babylon! My dear friend,' he added, addressing the doctor, 'you may despise me, I have played and lost; lend me five hundred roubles!'

Andrey Yefimitch counted out five hundred roubles and gave them to his friend without a word. The latter, still crimson with shame and anger, incoherently articulated some useless vow, put on his cap, and went out. Returning two hours later he flopped into an easy-chair, heaved a loud sigh, and said:

'My honour is saved. Let us go, my friend; I do not care to remain another hour in this accursed town. Scoundrels! Austrian spies!'

By the time the friends were back in their own town it was November, and deep snow was lying in the streets. Dr Hobotov had Andrey Yefimitch's post; he was still living in his old lodgings, waiting for Andrey Yefimitch to arrive and clear out of the hospital apartments. The plain woman whom he called his cook was already established in one of the lodges.

Fresh scandals about the hospital were going the round of the town. It was said that the plain woman had quarrelled with the superintendent, and that the latter had crawled on his knees before her begging forgiveness. On the very first day he arrived

Andrey Yefimitch had to look out for lodgings.

'My friend,' the postmaster said to him timidly, 'excuse an indiscreet question: what means have you at your disposal?'

Andrey Yefimitch, without a word, counted out his money and said: 'Eighty-six roubles.'

'I don't mean that,' Mihail Averyanitch brought out in confusion, misunderstanding him; 'I mean, what have you to live on?'

'I tell you, eighty-six roubles... I have nothing else.'

Mihail Averyanitch looked upon the doctor as an honourable man, yet he suspected that he had accumulated a fortune of at least twenty thousand. Now learning that Andrey Yefimitch was a beggar, that he had nothing to live on he was for some reason suddenly moved to tears and embraced his friend.

XV

Andrey Yefimitch now lodged in a little house with three windows. There were only three rooms besides the kitchen in the little house. The doctor lived in two of them which looked into the street, while Daryushka and the landlady with her three children lived in the third room and the kitchen. Sometimes the landlady's lover, a drunken peasant who was rowdy and reduced the children and Daryushka to terror, would come for the night. When he arrived and established himself in the kitchen and demanded vodka, they all felt very uncomfortable, and the doctor would be moved by pity to take the crying children into his room and let them lie on his floor, and this gave him great satisfaction.

He got up as before at eight o'clock, and after his morning

tea sat down to read his old books and magazines: he had no money for new ones. Either because the books were old, or perhaps because of the change in his surroundings, reading exhausted him, and did not grip his attention as before. That he might not spend his time in idleness he made a detailed catalogue of his books and gummed little labels on their backs, and this mechanical, tedious work seemed to him more interesting than reading. The monotonous, tedious work lulled his thoughts to sleep in some unaccountable way, and the time passed quickly while he thought of nothing. Even sitting in the kitchen, peeling potatoes with Daryushka or picking over the buckwheat grain, seemed to him interesting. On Saturdays and Sundays he went to church. Standing near the wall and half closing his eyes, he listened to the singing and thought of his father, of his mother, of the university, of the religions of the world; he felt calm and melancholy, and as he went out of the church afterwards he regretted that the service was so soon over. He went twice to the hospital to talk to Ivan Dmitritch. But on both occasions Ivan Dmitritch was unusually excited and ill-humoured; he bade the doctor leave him in peace, as he had long been sick of empty chatter, and declared, to make up for all his sufferings, he asked from the damned scoundrels only one favour—solitary confinement. Surely they would not refuse him even that? On both occasions when Andrey Yefimitch was taking leave of him and wishing him good-night, he answered rudely and said:

'Go to hell!'

And Andrey Yefimitch did not know now whether to go to him for the third time or not. He longed to go.

In old days Andrey Yefimitch used to walk about his rooms and think in the interval after dinner, but now from dinner-time till evening tea he lay on the sofa with his face to the back and gave himself up to trivial thoughts which he could not struggle against. He was mortified that after more than twenty years of service he had been given neither a pension nor any assistance. It is true that he had not done his work honestly, but, then, all who are in the Service get a pension without distinction whether they are honest or not. Contemporary justice lies precisely in the bestowal of grades, orders, and pensions, not for moral qualities or capacities, but for service whatever it may have been like. Why was he alone to be an exception? He had no money at all. He was ashamed to pass by the shop and look at the woman who owned it. He owed thirty-two roubles for beer already. There was money owing to the landlady also. Daryushka sold old clothes and books on the sly, and told lies to the landlady, saying that the doctor was just going to receive a large sum of money.

He was angry with himself for having wasted on travelling the thousand roubles he had saved up. How useful that thousand roubles would have been now! He was vexed that people would not leave him in peace. Hobotov thought it his duty to look in on his sick colleague from time to time. Everything about him was revolting to Andrey Yefimitch—his well-fed face and vulgar, condescending tone, and his use of the word 'colleague', and his high top-boots; the most revolting thing was that he thought it was his duty to treat Andrey Yefimitch, and thought that he really was treating him. On every visit he brought a bottle of bromide and rhubarb pills.

Mihail Averyanitch, too, thought it his duty to visit his friend and entertain him. Every time he went in to Andrey Yefimitch with an affectation of ease, laughed constrainedly, and began assuring him that he was looking very well to-day, and that, thank God, he was on the highroad to recovery, and from this it might be concluded that he looked on his friend's condition as hopeless. He had not yet repaid his Warsaw debt, and was overwhelmed by shame; he was constrained, and so tried to laugh louder and talk more amusingly. His anecdotes and descriptions seemed endless now, and were an agony both to Andrey Yefimitch and himself.

In his presence Andrey Yefimitch usually lay on the sofa with his face to the wall, and listened with his teeth clenched; his soul was oppressed with rankling disgust, and after every visit from his friend he felt as though this disgust had risen higher, and was mounting into his throat.

To stifle petty thoughts he made haste to reflect that he himself, and Hobotov, and Mihail Averyanitch, would all sooner or later perish without leaving any trace on the world. If one imagined some spirit flying by the earthly globe in space in a million years he would see nothing but clay and bare rocks. Everything—culture and the moral law—would pass away and not even a burdock would grow out of them. Of what consequence was shame in the presence of a shopkeeper, of what consequence was the insignificant Hobotov or the wearisome friendship of Mihail Averyanitch? It was all trivial and nonsensical.

But such reflections did not help him now. Scarcely had he imagined the earthly globe in a million years, when Hobotov in his high top-boots or Mihail Averyanitch with his forced laugh would appear from behind a bare rock, and he even heard the shamefaced whisper: 'The Warsaw debt.... I will repay it in a day or two, my dear fellow, without fail....'

XVI

One day Mihail Averyanitch came after dinner when Andrey Yefimitch was lying on the sofa. It so happened that Hobotov arrived at the same time with his bromide. Andrey Yefimitch got up heavily and sat down, leaning both arms on the sofa.

'You have a much better colour to-day than you had yesterday, my dear man,' began Mihail Averyanitch. 'Yes, you look jolly. Upon my soul, you do!'

'It's high time you were well, dear colleague,' said Hobotov, yawning. 'I'll be bound, you are sick of this bobbery.'

'And we shall recover,' said Mihail Averyanitch cheerfully. 'We shall live another hundred years! To be sure!'

'Not a hundred years, but another twenty,' Hobotov said reassuringly. 'It's all right, all right, colleague; don't lose heart.... Don't go piling it on!'

'We'll show what we can do,' laughed Mihail Averyanitch, and he slapped his friend on the knee. 'We'll show them yet! Next summer, please God, we shall be off to the Caucasus, and we will ride all over it on horseback—trot, trot, trot! And when we are back from the Caucasus I shouldn't wonder if we will all dance at the wedding.' Mihail Averyanitch gave a sly wink. 'We'll marry you, my dear boy, we'll marry you....'

Andrey Yefimitch felt suddenly that the rising disgust had mounted to his throat, his heart began beating violently.

'That's vulgar,' he said, getting up quickly and walking away to the window. 'Don't you understand that you are talking vulgar nonsense?'

He meant to go on softly and politely, but against his will he suddenly clenched his fists and raised them above his head.

'Leave me alone,' he shouted in a voice unlike his own, blushing crimson and shaking all over. 'Go away, both of you!'

Mihail Averyanitch and Hobotov got up and stared at him first with amazement and then with alarm.

'Go away, both!' Andrey Yefimitch went on shouting. 'Stupid people! Foolish people! I don't want either your friendship or your medicines, stupid man! Vulgar! Nasty!'

Hobotov and Mihail Averyanitch, looking at each other in bewilderment, staggered to the door and went out. Andrey Yefimitch snatched up the bottle of bromide and flung it after them; the bottle broke with a crash on the door-frame.

'Go to the devil!' he shouted in a tearful voice, running out into the passage. 'To the devil!'

When his guests were gone Andrey Yefimitch lay down on the sofa, trembling as though in a fever, and went on for a long while repeating: 'Stupid people! Foolish people!'

When he was calmer, what occurred to him first of all was the thought that poor Mihail Averyanitch must be feeling fearfully ashamed and depressed now, and that it was all dreadful. Nothing like this had ever happened to him before. Where was his intelligence and his tact? Where was his comprehension of things and his philosophical indifference?

The doctor could not sleep all night for shame and vexation with himself, and at ten o'clock next morning he went to the post office and apologized to the postmaster.

'We won't think again of what has happened,' Mihail Averyanitch, greatly touched, said with a sigh, warmly pressing his hand. 'Let bygones be bygones. Lyubavkin,' he suddenly shouted so loud that all the postmen and other persons present started, 'hand a chair; and you wait,' he shouted to a peasant woman who was stretching out a registered letter to him through the grating. 'Don't you see that I am busy? We will not remember the past,' he went on, affectionately addressing Andrey Yefimitch; 'sit down, I beg you, my dear fellow.'

For a minute he stroked his knees in silence, and then said:

'I have never had a thought of taking offence. Illness is no joke, I understand. Your attack frightened the doctor and me yesterday, and we had a long talk about you afterwards. My dear friend, why won't you treat your illness seriously? You can't go on like this.... Excuse me speaking openly as a friend,' whispered Mihail Averyanitch. 'You live in the most unfavourable surroundings, in a crowd, in uncleanliness, no one to look after you, no money for proper treatment.... My dear friend, the doctor and I implore you with all our hearts, listen to our advice: go into the hospital! There you will have wholesome food and attendance and treatment. Though, between ourselves, Yevgeny Fyodoritch is mauvais ton, yet he does understand his work, you can fully rely upon him. He has promised me he will look after you.'

Andrey Yefimitch was touched by the postmaster's genuine sympathy and the tears which suddenly glittered on his cheeks.

'My honoured friend, don't believe it!' he whispered, laying his hand on his heart; 'don't believe them. It's all a sham. My illness is only that in twenty years I have only found one intelligent man in the whole town, and he is mad. I am not ill at all, it's simply that I have got into an enchanted circle which there is no getting out of. I don't care; I am ready for anything.'

'Go into the hospital, my dear fellow.'

'I don't care if it were into the pit.'

'Give me your word, my dear man, that you will obey Yevgeny Fyodoritch in everything.'

'Certainly I will give you my word. But I repeat, my honoured friend, I have got into an enchanted circle. Now everything, even the genuine sympathy of my friends, leads to the same thing—to my ruin. I am going to my ruin, and I have the manliness to recognize it.'

'My dear fellow, you will recover.'

'What's the use of saying that?' said Andrey Yefimitch, with irritation. 'There are few men who at the end of their lives do not experience what I am experiencing now. When you are told that you have something such as diseased kidneys or enlarged heart, and you begin being treated for it, or are told you are mad or a criminal—that is, in fact, when people suddenly turn their attention to you—you may be sure you have got into an enchanted circle from which you will not escape. You will try to escape and make things worse. You had better give in, for no human efforts can save you. So it seems to me.'

Meanwhile the public was crowding at the grating. That he might not be in their way, Andrey Yefimitch got up and began to take leave. Mihail Averyanitch made him promise on his honour once more, and escorted him to the outer door.

Towards evening on the same day Hobotov, in his sheepskin and his high top-boots, suddenly made his appearance, and said to Andrey Yefimitch in a tone as though nothing had happened the day before:

'I have come on business, colleague. I have come to ask you whether you would not join me in a consultation. Eh?'

Thinking that Hobotov wanted to distract his mind with

an outing, or perhaps really to enable him to earn something, Andrey Yefimitch put on his coat and hat, and went out with him into the street. He was glad of the opportunity to smooth over his fault of the previous day and to be reconciled, and in his heart thanked Hobotov, who did not even allude to yesterday's scene and was evidently sparing him. One would never have expected such delicacy from this uncultured man.

'Where is your invalid?' asked Andrey Yefimitch.

'In the hospital…. I have long wanted to show him to you. A very interesting case.'

They went into the hospital yard, and going round the main building, turned towards the lodge where the mental cases were kept, and all this, for some reason, in silence. When they went into the lodge Nikita as usual jumped up and stood at attention.

'One of the patients here has a lung complication.' Hobotov said in an undertone, going into the yard with Andrey Yefimitch. 'You wait here, I'll be back directly. I am going for a stethoscope.'

And he went away.

XVII

It was getting dusk. Ivan Dmitritch was lying on his bed with his face thrust unto his pillow; the paralytic was sitting motionless, crying quietly and moving his lips. The fat peasant and the former sorter were asleep. It was quiet.

Andrey Yefimitch sat down on Ivan Dmitritch's bed and waited. But half an hour passed, and instead of Hobotov, Nikita came into the ward with a dressing-gown, some underlinen, and a pair of slippers in a heap on his arm.

'Please change your things, your honour,' he said softly. 'Here is your bed; come this way,' he added, pointing to an empty bedstead which had obviously recently been brought into the ward. 'It's all right; please God, you will recover.'

Andrey Yefimitch understood it all. Without saying a word he crossed to the bed to which Nikita pointed and sat down; seeing that Nikita was standing waiting, he undressed entirely and he felt ashamed. Then he put on the hospital clothes; the drawers were very short, the shirt was long, and the dressing-gown smelt of smoked fish.

'Please God, you will recover,' repeated Nikita, and he gathered up Andrey Yefimitch's clothes into his arms, went out, and shut the door after him.

'No matter...' thought Andrey Yefimitch, wrapping himself in his dressing-gown in a shamefaced way and feeling that he looked like a convict in his new costume. 'It's no matter.... It does not matter whether it's a dress-coat or a uniform or this dressing-gown.'

But how about his watch? And the notebook that was in the side-pocket? And his cigarettes? Where had Nikita taken his clothes? Now perhaps to the day of his death he would not put on trousers, a waistcoat, and high boots. It was all somehow strange and even incomprehensible at first. Andrey Yefimitch was even now convinced that there was no difference between his landlady's house and Ward No. 6, that everything in this world was nonsense and vanity of vanities. And yet his hands were trembling, his feet were cold, and he was filled with dread at the thought that soon Ivan Dmitritch would get up and see that he was in a dressing-gown. He got up and walked across the room and sat down again.

Here he had been sitting already half an hour, an hour,

and he was miserably sick of it: was it really possible to live here a day, a week, and even years like these people? Why, he had been sitting here, had walked about and sat down again; he could get up and look out of window and walk from corner to corner again, and then what? Sit so all the time, like a post, and think? No, that was scarcely possible.

Andrey Yefimitch lay down, but at once got up, wiped the cold sweat from his brow with his sleeve and felt that his whole face smelt of smoked fish. He walked about again.

'It's some misunderstanding...' he said, turning out the palms of his hands in perplexity. 'It must be cleared up. There is a misunderstanding.'

Meanwhile Ivan Dmitritch woke up; he sat up and propped his cheeks on his fists. He spat. Then he glanced lazily at the doctor, and apparently for the first minute did not understand; but soon his sleepy face grew malicious and mocking.

'Aha! so they have put you in here, too, old fellow?' he said in a voice husky from sleepiness, screwing up one eye. 'Very glad to see you. You sucked the blood of others, and now they will suck yours. Excellent!'

'It's a misunderstanding...' Andrey Yefimitch brought out, frightened by Ivan Dmitritch's words; he shrugged his shoulders and repeated: 'It's some misunderstanding.'

Ivan Dmitritch spat again and lay down.

'Cursed life,' he grumbled, 'and what's bitter and insulting, this life will not end in compensation for our sufferings, it will not end with apotheosis as it would in an opera, but with death; peasants will come and drag one's dead body by the arms and the legs to the cellar. Ugh! Well, it does not matter.... We shall have our good time in the other world.... I shall come here as a ghost from the other world and frighten these reptiles. I'll turn their hair grey.'

Moiseika returned, and, seeing the doctor, held out his hand.

'Give me one little kopeck,' he said.

XVIII

Andrey Yefimitch walked away to the window and looked out into the open country. It was getting dark, and on the horizon to the right a cold crimson moon was mounting upwards. Not far from the hospital fence, not much more than two hundred yards away, stood a tall white house shut in by a stone wall. This was the prison.

'So this is real life,' thought Andrey Yefimitch, and he felt frightened.

The moon and the prison, and the nails on the fence, and the far-away flames at the bone-charring factory were all terrible. Behind him there was the sound of a sigh. Andrey Yefimitch looked round and saw a man with glittering stars and orders on his breast, who was smiling and slyly winking. And this, too, seemed terrible.

Andrey Yefimitch assured himself that there was nothing special about the moon or the prison, that even sane persons wear orders, and that everything in time will decay and turn to earth, but he was suddenly overcome with desire; he clutched at the grating with both hands and shook it with all his might. The strong grating did not yield.

Then that it might not be so dreadful he went to Ivan Dmitritch's bed and sat down.

'I have lost heart, my dear fellow,' he muttered, trembling

and wiping away the cold sweat, 'I have lost heart.'

'You should be philosophical,' said Ivan Dmitritch ironically.

'My God, my God.... Yes, yes.... You were pleased to say once that there was no philosophy in Russia, but that all people, even the paltriest, talk philosophy. But you know the philosophizing of the paltriest does not harm anyone,' said Andrey Yefimitch in a tone as if he wanted to cry and complain. 'Why, then, that malignant laugh, my friend, and how can these paltry creatures help philosophizing if they are not satisfied? For an intelligent, educated man, made in God's image, proud and loving freedom, to have no alternative but to be a doctor in a filthy, stupid, wretched little town, and to spend his whole life among bottles, leeches, mustard plasters! Quackery, narrowness, vulgarity! Oh, my God!'

'You are talking nonsense. If you don't like being a doctor you should have gone in for being a statesman.'

'I could not, I could not do anything. We are weak, my dear friend.... I used to be indifferent. I reasoned boldly and soundly, but at the first coarse touch of life upon me I have lost heart.... Prostration.... We are weak, we are poor creatures... and you, too, my dear friend, you are intelligent, generous, you drew in good impulses with your mother's milk, but you had hardly entered upon life when you were exhausted and fell ill.... Weak, weak!'

Andrey Yefimitch was all the while at the approach of evening tormented by another persistent sensation besides terror and the feeling of resentment. At last he realized that he was longing for a smoke and for beer.

'I am going out, my friend,' he said. 'I will tell them to bring a light; I can't put up with this.... I am not equal to it....'

Andrey Yefimitch went to the door and opened it, but at once Nikita jumped up and barred his way.

'Where are you going? You can't, you can't!' he said. 'It's bedtime.'

'But I'm only going out for a minute to walk about the yard,' said Andrey Yefimitch.

'You can't, you can't; it's forbidden. You know that yourself.'

'But what difference will it make to anyone if I do go out?' asked Andrey Yefimitch, shrugging his shoulders. 'I don't understand. Nikita, I must go out!' he said in a trembling voice. 'I must.'

'Don't be disorderly, it's not right,' Nikita said peremptorily.

'This is beyond everything,' Ivan Dmitritch cried suddenly, and he jumped up. 'What right has he not to let you out? How dare they keep us here? I believe it is clearly laid down in the law that no one can be deprived of freedom without trial! It's an outrage! It's tyranny!'

'Of course it's tyranny,' said Andrey Yefimitch, encouraged by Ivan Dmitritch's outburst. 'I must go out, I want to. He has no right! Open, I tell you.'

'Do you hear, you dull-witted brute?' cried Ivan Dmitritch, and he banged on the door with his fist. 'Open the door, or I will break it open! Torturer!'

'Open the door,' cried Andrey Yefimitch, trembling all over; 'I insist!'

'Talk away!' Nikita answered through the door, 'talk away....'

'Anyhow, go and call Yevgeny Fyodoritch! Say that I beg him to come for a minute!'

'His honour will come of himself to-morrow.'

'They will never let us out,' Ivan Dmitritch was going on

meanwhile. 'They will leave us to rot here! Oh, Lord, can there really be no hell in the next world, and will these wretches be forgiven? Where is justice? Open the door, you wretch! I am choking!' he cried in a hoarse voice, and flung himself upon the door. 'I'll dash out my brains, murderers!'

Nikita opened the door quickly, and roughly with both his hands and his knee shoved Andrey Yefimitch back, then swung his arm and punched him in the face with his fist. It seemed to Andrey Yefimitch as though a huge salt wave enveloped him from his head downwards and dragged him to the bed; there really was a salt taste in his mouth: most likely the blood was running from his teeth. He waved his arms as though he were trying to swim out and clutched at a bedstead, and at the same moment felt Nikita hit him twice on the back.

Ivan Dmitritch gave a loud scream. He must have been beaten too.

Then all was still, the faint moonlight came through the grating, and a shadow like a net lay on the floor. It was terrible. Andrey Yefimitch lay and held his breath: he was expecting with horror to be struck again. He felt as though someone had taken a sickle, thrust it into him, and turned it round several times in his breast and bowels. He bit the pillow from pain and clenched his teeth, and all at once through the chaos in his brain there flashed the terrible unbearable thought that these people, who seemed now like black shadows in the moonlight, had to endure such pain day by day for years. How could it have happened that for more than twenty years he had not known it and had refused to know it? He knew nothing of pain, had no conception of it, so he was not to blame, but his conscience, as inexorable and as rough as Nikita, made him turn cold from the crown of his head to his heels. He leaped up, tried to cry out with all his might, and to run in haste to kill Nikita, and then Hobotov, the superintendent and the assistant, and then himself; but no sound came from his chest, and his legs would not obey him. Gasping for breath, he tore at the dressing-gown and the shirt on his breast, rent them, and fell senseless on the bed.

XIX

Next morning his head ached, there was a droning in his ears and a feeling of utter weakness all over. He was not ashamed at recalling his weakness the day before. He had been cowardly, had even been afraid of the moon, had openly expressed thoughts and feelings such as he had not expected in himself before; for instance, the thought that the paltry people who philosophized were really dissatisfied. But now nothing mattered to him.

He ate nothing; he drank nothing. He lay motionless and silent.

'It is all the same to me,' he thought when they asked him questions. 'I am not going to answer.... It's all the same to me.'

After dinner Mihail Averyanitch brought him a quarter pound of tea and a pound of fruit pastilles. Daryushka came too and stood for a whole hour by the bed with an expression of dull grief on her face. Dr Hobotov visited him. He brought a bottle of bromide and told Nikita to fumigate the ward with something.

Towards evening Andrey Yefimitch died of an apoplectic stroke. At first he had a violent shivering fit and a feeling of sickness; something revolting as it seemed, penetrating through his whole body, even to his finger-tips, strained from his stomach to his head and flooded his eyes and ears. There was a greenness before his eyes. Andrey Yefimitch understood that his end had come, and remembered that Ivan Dmitritch, Mihail Averyanitch, and millions of people believed in immortality. And what if it really existed? But he did not want immortality—and he thought of it only for one instant. A herd of deer, extraordinarily beautiful and graceful, of which he had been reading the day before, ran by him; then a peasant woman stretched out her hand to him with a registered letter.... Mihail Averyanitch said something, then it all vanished, and Andrey Yefimitch sank into oblivion for ever.

The hospital porters came, took him by his arms and legs, and carried him away to the chapel.

There he lay on the table, with open eyes, and the moon shed its light upon him at night. In the morning Sergey Sergeyitch came, prayed piously before the crucifix, and closed his former chief's eyes.

Next day Andrey Yefimitch was buried. Mihail Averyanitch and Daryushka were the only people at the funeral.

6

THE KISS

At eight o'clock on the evening of the twentieth of May all the six batteries of the N——Reserve Artillery Brigade halted for the night in the village of Myestetchki on their way to camp. When the general commotion was at its height, while some officers were busily occupied around the guns, while others, gathered together in the square near the church enclosure, were listening to the quartermasters, a man in civilian dress, riding a strange horse, came into sight round the church. The little dun-coloured horse with a good neck and a short tail came, moving not straight forward, but as it were sideways, with a sort of dance step, as though it were being lashed about the legs. When he reached the officers the man on the horse took off his hat and said:

'His Excellency Lieutenant-General von Rabbek invites the gentlemen to drink tea with him this minute....'

The horse turned, danced, and retired sideways; the messenger raised his hat once more, and in an instant disappeared with his strange horse behind the church.

'What the devil does it mean?' grumbled some of the officers, dispersing to their quarters. 'One is sleepy, and here this Von Rabbek with his tea! We know what tea means.'

The officers of all the six batteries remembered vividly an

incident of the previous year, when during manoeuvres they, together with the officers of a Cossack regiment, were in the same way invited to tea by a count who had an estate in the neighbourhood and was a retired army officer: the hospitable and genial count made much of them, fed them, and gave them drink, refused to let them go to their quarters in the village and made them stay the night. All that, of course, was very nice—nothing better could be desired, but the worst of it was, the old army officer was so carried away by the pleasure of the young men's company that till sunrise he was telling the officers anecdotes of his glorious past, taking them over the house, showing them expensive pictures, old engravings, rare guns, reading them autograph letters from great people, while the weary and exhausted officers looked and listened, longing for their beds and yawning in their sleeves; when at last their host let them go, it was too late for sleep.

Might not this Von Rabbek be just such another? Whether he were or not, there was no help for it. The officers changed their uniforms, brushed themselves, and went all together in search of the gentleman's house. In the square by the church they were told they could get to His Excellency's by the lower path—going down behind the church to the river, going along the bank to the garden, and there an avenue would taken them to the house; or by the upper way—straight from the church by the road which, half a mile from the village, led right up to His Excellency's granaries. The officers decided to go by the upper way.

'What Von Rabbek is it?' they wondered on the way. 'Surely not the one who was in command of the N——cavalry division at Plevna?'

'No, that was not Von Rabbek, but simply Rabbe and no "von".'

'What lovely weather!'

At the first of the granaries the road divided in two: one branch went straight on and vanished in the evening darkness, the other led to the owner's house on the right. The officers turned to the right and began to speak more softly.... On both sides of the road stretched stone granaries with red roofs, heavy and sullen-looking, very much like barracks of a district town. Ahead of them gleamed the windows of the manor-house.

'A good omen, gentlemen,' said one of the officers. 'Our setter is the foremost of all; no doubt he scents game ahead of us!...'

Lieutenant Lobytko, who was walking in front, a tall and stalwart fellow, though entirely without moustache (he was over five-and-twenty, yet for some reason there was no sign of hair on his round, well-fed face), renowned in the brigade for his peculiar faculty for divining the presence of women at a distance, turned round and said:

'Yes, there must be women here; I feel that by instinct.'

On the threshold the officers were met by Von Rabbek himself, a comely-looking man of sixty in civilian dress. Shaking hands with his guests, he said that he was very glad and happy to see them, but begged them earnestly for God's sake to excuse him for not asking them to stay the night; two sisters with their children, some brothers, and some neighbours, had come on a visit to him, so that he had not one spare room left.

The General shook hands with every one, made his apologies, and smiled, but it was evident by his face that he was by no means so delighted as their last year's count, and that he had invited the officers simply because, in his opinion, it was a social obligation to do so. And the officers themselves, as they walked up the softly carpeted stairs, as they listened to him, felt that they had been invited to this house simply because it would have been awkward not to invite them; and at the sight of the footmen, who hastened to light the lamps in the entrance below and in the anteroom above, they began to feel as though they had brought uneasiness and discomfort into the house with them. In a house in which two sisters and their children, brothers, and neighbours were gathered together, probably on account of some family festivity, or event, how could the presence of nineteen unknown officers possibly be welcome?

At the entrance to the drawing-room the officers were met by a tall, graceful old lady with black eyebrows and a long face, very much like the Empress Eugénie. Smiling graciously and majestically, she said she was glad and happy to see her guests, and apologized that her husband and she were on this occasion unable to invite *messieurs les officiers* to stay the night. From her beautiful majestic smile, which instantly vanished from her face every time she turned away from her guests, it was evident that she had seen numbers of officers in her day, that she was in no humour for them now, and if she invited them to her house and apologized for not doing more, it was only because her breeding and position in society required it of her.

When the officers went into the big dining-room, there were about a dozen people, men and ladies, young and old, sitting at tea at the end of a long table. A group of men was dimly visible behind their chairs, wrapped in a haze of cigar smoke; and in the midst of them stood a lanky young man with red whiskers, talking loudly, with a lisp, in English. Through a door beyond the group could be seen a light room with pale blue furniture.

'Gentlemen, there are so many of you that it is impossible to introduce you all!' said the General in a loud voice, trying to sound very cheerful. 'Make each other's acquaintance, gentlemen, without any ceremony!'

The officers—some with very serious and even stern faces, others with forced smiles, and all feeling extremely awkward—somehow made their bows and sat down to tea.

The most ill at ease of them all was Ryabovitch—a little officer in spectacles, with sloping shoulders, and whiskers like a lynx's. While some of his comrades assumed a serious expression, while others wore forced smiles, his face, his lynx-like whiskers, and spectacles seemed to say: 'I am the shyest, most modest, and most undistinguished officer in the whole brigade!' At first, on going into the room and sitting down to the table, he could not fix his attention on any one face or object. The faces, the dresses, the cut-glass decanters of brandy, the steam from the glasses, the moulded cornices—all blended in one general impression that inspired in Ryabovitch alarm and a desire to hide his head. Like a lecturer making his first appearance before the public, he saw everything that was before his eyes, but apparently only had a dim understanding of it (among physiologists this condition, when the subject sees but does not understand, is called psychical blindness). After a little while, growing accustomed to his surroundings, Ryabovitch saw clearly and began to observe. As a shy man, unused to society, what struck him first was that in which he had always been deficient—namely, the extraordinary boldness of his new acquaintances. Von Rabbek, his wife, two elderly ladies, a young lady in a lilac dress, and the young man with the red whiskers, who was, it appeared, a younger son of Von Rabbek, very cleverly, as though they had rehearsed it beforehand, took seats between the officers, and at once got up a heated discussion in which the visitors could not help taking part. The lilac young lady hotly asserted that the artillery had a much better time than the cavalry and the infantry, while Von Rabbek and the elderly ladies maintained the opposite. A brisk interchange of talk followed. Ryabovitch watched the lilac young lady who argued so hotly about what was unfamiliar and utterly uninteresting to her, and watched artificial smiles come and go on her face.

Von Rabbek and his family skilfully drew the officers into the discussion, and meanwhile kept a sharp lookout over their glasses and mouths, to see whether all of them were drinking, whether all had enough sugar, why some one was not eating cakes or not drinking brandy. And the longer Ryabovitch watched and listened, the more he was attracted by this insincere but splendidly disciplined family.

After tea the officers went into the drawing-room. Lieutenant Lobytko's instinct had not deceived him. There were a great number of girls and young married ladies. The 'setter' lieutenant was soon standing by a very young, fair girl in a black dress, and, bending down to her jauntily, as though leaning on an unseen sword, smiled and shrugged his shoulders coquettishly. He probably talked very interesting nonsense, for the fair girl looked at his well-fed face condescendingly and asked indifferently, 'Really?' And from that uninterested 'Really?' the setter, had he been intelligent, might have concluded that she would never call him to heel.

The piano struck up; the melancholy strains of a valse floated out of the wide open windows, and every one, for some reason, remembered that it was spring, a May evening. Every one was conscious of the fragrance of roses, of lilac, and of the young leaves of the poplar. Ryabovitch, in whom the brandy he had drunk made itself felt, under the influence of the music stole a glance towards the window, smiled, and began watching the movements of the women, and it seemed to him that the smell of roses, of poplars, and lilac came not from the garden, but from the ladies' faces and dresses.

Von Rabbek's son invited a scraggy-looking young lady to dance, and waltzed round the room twice with her. Lobytko, gliding over the parquet floor, flew up to the lilac young lady and whirled her away. Dancing began.... Ryabovitch stood near the door among those who were not dancing and looked on. He had never once danced in his whole life, and he had never once in his life put his arm round the waist of a respectable woman. He was highly delighted that a man should in the sight of all take a girl he did not know round the waist and offer her his shoulder to put her hand on, but he could not imagine himself in the position of such a man. There were times when he envied the boldness and swagger of his companions and was inwardly wretched; the consciousness that he was timid, that he was round-shouldered and uninteresting, that he had a long waist and lynx-like whiskers, had deeply mortified him, but with years he had grown used to this feeling, and now, looking at his comrades dancing or loudly talking, he no longer envied them, but only felt touched and mournful.

When the quadrille began, young Von Rabbek came up to those who were not dancing and invited two officers to have a game at billiards. The officers accepted and went with him out of the drawing-room. Ryabovitch, having nothing to do and wishing to take part in the general movement, slouched after them. From the big drawing-room they went into the little drawing-room, then into a narrow corridor with a glass roof, and thence into a room in which on their entrance three sleepy-looking footmen jumped up quickly from the sofa. At last, after passing through a long succession of rooms, young Von Rabbek and the officers came into a small room where there was a billiard-table. They began to play.

Ryabovitch, who had never played any game but cards, stood near the billiard-table and looked indifferently at the players, while they in unbuttoned coats, with cues in their hands, stepped about, made puns, and kept shouting out unintelligible words.

The players took no notice of him, and only now and then one of them, shoving him with his elbow or accidentally touching him with the end of his cue, would turn round and say 'Pardon!' Before the first game was over he was weary of it, and began to feel he was not wanted and in the way.... He felt disposed to return to the drawing-room, and he went out.

On his way back he met with a little adventure. When he had gone half-way he noticed he had taken a wrong turning. He distinctly remembered that he ought to meet three sleepy footmen on his way, but he had passed five or six rooms, and those sleepy figures seemed to have vanished into the earth. Noticing his mistake, he walked back a little way and turned to the right; he found himself in a little dark room which he had not seen on his way to the billiard-room. After standing there a little while, he resolutely opened the first door that met his eyes and walked into an absolutely dark room. Straight in front could be seen the crack in the doorway through which there was a gleam of vivid light; from the other side of the door came the muffled sound of a melancholy mazurka. Here, too, as in the drawing-room, the windows were wide open and there was a smell of poplars, lilac and roses....

Ryabovitch stood still in hesitation.... At that moment, to his surprise, he heard hurried footsteps and the rustling of a dress, a breathless feminine voice whispered 'At last!' And two soft, fragrant, unmistakably feminine arms were clasped about his neck; a warm cheek was pressed to his cheek, and simultaneously there was the sound of a kiss. But at once the bestower of the kiss uttered a faint shriek and skipped back from him, as it seemed to Ryabovitch, with aversion. He, too, almost shrieked and rushed towards the gleam of light at the door....

When he went back into the drawing-room his heart was beating and his hands were trembling so noticeably that he made haste to hide them behind his back. At first he was tormented by shame and dread that the whole drawing-room knew that he had just been kissed and embraced by a woman. He shrank into himself and looked uneasily about him, but as he became convinced that people were dancing and talking as calmly as ever, he gave himself up entirely to the new sensation which he had never experienced before in his life. Something strange was happening to him... His neck, round which soft, fragrant arms had so lately been clasped, seemed to him to be anointed with oil; on his left cheek near his moustache where the unknown had kissed him there was a faint chilly tingling sensation as from peppermint drops, and the more he rubbed the place the more distinct was the chilly sensation; all over, from head to foot, he was full of a strange new feeling which grew stronger and stronger.... He wanted to dance, to talk, to run into the garden, to laugh aloud.... He quite forgot that he was round-shouldered and uninteresting, that he had lynx-like whiskers and an 'undistinguished appearance' (that was how his appearance had been described by some ladies whose conversation he had accidentally overheard). When Von Rabbek's wife happened to pass by him, he gave her such a broad and friendly smile that she stood still and looked at him inquiringly.

'I like your house immensely!' he said, setting his spectacles straight.

The General's wife smiled and said that the house had belonged to her father; then she asked whether his parents were living, whether he had long been in the army, why he was so thin, and so on.... After receiving answers to her questions, she went on, and after his conversation with her his smiles were more friendly than ever, and he thought he was surrounded by splendid people....

At supper Ryabovitch ate mechanically everything offered him, drank, and without listening to anything, tried to understand what had just happened to him.... The adventure was of a mysterious and romantic character, but it was not difficult to explain it. No doubt some girl or young married lady had arranged a tryst with some one in the dark room; had waited a long time, and being nervous and excited had taken Ryabovitch for her hero; this was the more probable as Ryabovitch had stood still hesitating in the dark room, so that he, too, had seemed like a person expecting something.... This was how Ryabovitch explained to himself the kiss he had received.

'And who is she?' he wondered, looking round at the women's faces. 'She must be young, for elderly ladies don't give rendezvous. That she was a lady, one could tell by the rustle of her dress, her perfume, her voice....'

His eyes rested on the lilac young lady, and he thought her very attractive; she had beautiful shoulders and arms, a clever face, and a delightful voice. Ryabovitch, looking at her, hoped that she and no one else was his unknown.... But she laughed somehow artificially and wrinkled up her long nose, which seemed to him to make her look old. Then he turned his eyes upon the fair girl in a black dress. She was younger, simpler and more genuine, had a charming brow, and drank very daintily out of her wineglass. Ryabovitch now hoped that it was she. But soon he began to think her face flat, and fixed his eyes upon the one next her.

'It's difficult to guess,' he thought, musing. 'If one takes the shoulders and arms of the lilac one only, adds the brow of the fair one and the eyes of the one on the left of Lobytko, then...'

He made a combination of these things in his mind and so formed the image of the girl who had kissed him, the image that he wanted her to have, but could not find at the table....

After supper, replete and exhilarated, the officers began to take leave and say thank you. Von Rabbek and his wife began again apologizing that they could not ask them to stay the night.

'Very, very glad to have met you, gentlemen,' said Von Rabbek, and this time sincerely (probably because people are far more sincere and good-humoured at speeding their parting guests than on meeting them). 'Delighted. I hope you will come on your way back! Don't stand on ceremony! Where are you going? Do you want to go by the upper way? No, go across the garden; it's nearer here by the lower way.'

The officers went out into the garden. After the bright light and the noise the garden seemed very dark and quiet. They walked in silence all the way to the gate. They were a little drunk, pleased, and in good spirits, but the darkness and silence made them thoughtful for a minute. Probably the same idea occurred to each one of them as to Ryabovitch: would there ever come a time for them when, like Von Rabbek, they would have a large house, a family, a garden—when they, too, would be able to welcome people, even though insincerely, feed them, make them drunk and contented?

Going out of the garden gate, they all began talking at once and laughing loudly about nothing. They were walking now along the little path that led down to the river, and then ran along the water's edge, winding round the bushes on the bank, the pools, and the willows that overhung the water. The bank and the path were scarcely visible, and the other bank was entirely plunged in darkness. Stars were reflected here and there on the dark water; they quivered and were broken up on the surface—and from that alone it could be seen that the river was flowing rapidly. It was still. Drowsy curlews cried plaintively on the further bank, and in one of the bushes on the nearest side a nightingale was trilling loudly, taking no notice of the crowd of officers. The officers stood round the bush, touched it, but the nightingale went on singing.

'What a fellow!' they exclaimed approvingly. 'We stand beside him and he takes not a bit of notice! What a rascal!'

At the end of the way the path went uphill, and, skirting the church enclosure, turned into the road. Here the officers, tired with walking uphill, sat down and lighted their cigarettes. On the other side of the river a murky red fire came into sight, and having nothing better to do, they spent a long time in discussing whether it was a camp fire or a light in a window, or something else.... Ryabovitch, too, looked at the light, and he fancied that the light looked and winked at him, as though it knew about the kiss.

On reaching his quarters, Ryabovitch undressed as quickly as possible and got into bed. Lobytko and Lieutenant Merzlyakov—a peaceable, silent fellow, who was considered in his own circle a highly educated officer, and was always, whenever it was possible, reading the 'Vyestnik Evropi', which he carried about with him everywhere—were quartered in the same hut with Ryabovitch. Lobytko undressed, walked up and down the room for a long while with the air of a man who has not been satisfied, and sent his orderly for beer. Merzlyakov got into bed, put a candle by his pillow and plunged into reading the 'Vyestnik Evropi'.

'Who was she?' Ryabovitch wondered, looking at the smoky ceiling.

His neck still felt as though he had been anointed with oil, and there was still the chilly sensation near his mouth as though from peppermint drops. The shoulders and arms of the young lady in lilac, the brow and the truthful eyes of the fair girl in black, waists, dresses, and brooches, floated through his imagination. He tried to fix his attention on these images, but they danced about, broke up and flickered. When these images vanished altogether from the broad dark background which every man sees when he closes his eyes, he began to hear hurried footsteps, the rustle of skirts, the sound of a kiss and—an intense groundless joy took possession of him.... Abandoning himself to this joy, he heard the orderly return and announce that there was no beer. Lobytko was terribly indignant, and began pacing up and down again.

'Well, isn't he an idiot?' he kept saying, stopping first before Ryabovitch and then before Merzlyakov. 'What a fool and a dummy a man must be not to get hold of any beer! Eh? Isn't he a scoundrel?'

'Of course you can't get beer here,' said Merzlyakov, not removing his eyes from the 'Vyestnik Evropi'.

'Oh! Is that your opinion?' Lobytko persisted. 'Lord have mercy upon us, if you dropped me on the moon I'd find you beer and women directly! I'll go and find some at once.... You may call me an impostor if I don't!'

He spent a long time in dressing and pulling on his high boots, then finished smoking his cigarette in silence and went out.

'Rabbek, Grabbek, Labbek,' he muttered, stopping in the outer room. 'I don't care to go alone, damn it all! Ryabovitch, wouldn't you like to go for a walk? Eh?'

Receiving no answer, he returned, slowly undressed and got into bed. Merzlyakov sighed, put the 'Vyestnik Evropi' away, and put out the light.

'H'm!...' muttered Lobytko, lighting a cigarette in the dark.

Ryabovitch pulled the bed-clothes over his head, curled himself up in bed, and tried to gather together the floating images in his mind and to combine them into one whole. But nothing came of it. He soon fell asleep, and his last thought was that some one had caressed him and made him happy—that something extraordinary, foolish, but joyful and delightful, had come into his life. The thought did not leave him even in his sleep.

When he woke up the sensations of oil on his neck and the chill of peppermint about his lips had gone, but joy flooded his heart just as the day before. He looked enthusiastically at the window-frames, gilded by the light of the rising sun, and listened to the movement of the passers-by in the street. People were talking loudly close to the window. Lebedetsky, the commander of Ryabovitch's battery, who had only just overtaken the brigade, was talking to his sergeant at the top of his voice, being always accustomed to shout.

'What else?' shouted the commander.

'When they were shoeing yesterday, your high nobility, they drove a nail into Pigeon's hoof. The vet. put on clay and vinegar; they are leading him apart now. And also, your honour, Artemyev got drunk yesterday, and the lieutenant ordered him to be put in the limber of a spare gun-carriage.'

The sergeant reported that Karpov had forgotten the new cords for the trumpets and the rings for the tents, and that their honours, the officers, had spent the previous evening visiting General Von Rabbek. In the middle of this conversation the red-bearded face of Lebedetsky appeared in the window. He screwed up his short-sighted eyes, looking at the sleepy faces of the officers, and said good-morning to them.

'Is everything all right?' he asked.

'One of the horses has a sore neck from the new collar,' answered Lobytko, yawning.

The commander sighed, thought a moment, and said in a loud voice:

'I am thinking of going to see Alexandra Yevgrafovna. I must call on her. Well, good-bye. I shall catch you up in the evening.'

A quarter of an hour later the brigade set off on its way. When it was moving along the road by the granaries, Ryabovitch looked at the house on the right. The blinds were down in all the windows. Evidently the household was still asleep. The one who had kissed Ryabovitch the day before was asleep, too. He tried to imagine her asleep. The wide-open windows of the bedroom, the green branches peeping in, the morning freshness, the scent of the poplars, lilac, and roses, the bed, a chair, and on it the skirts that had rustled the day before, the little slippers, the little watch on the table—all this he pictured to himself clearly and distinctly, but the features of the face, the sweet sleepy smile, just what was characteristic and important, slipped through his imagination like quicksilver through the fingers. When he had ridden on half a mile, he looked back: the yellow church, the house, and the river, were all bathed in light; the river with its bright green banks, with the blue sky reflected in it and glints of silver in the sunshine here and there, was very beautiful. Ryabovitch gazed for the last time at Myestetchki, and he felt as sad as though he were parting with something very near and dear to him.

And before him on the road lay nothing but long familiar, uninteresting pictures.... To right and to left, fields of young rye and buckwheat with rooks hopping about in them. If one looked ahead, one saw dust and the backs of men's heads; if one looked back, one saw the same dust and faces.... Foremost of all marched four men with sabres—this was the vanguard. Next, behind, the crowd of singers, and behind them the trumpeters on horseback. The vanguard and the chorus of singers, like torch-bearers in a funeral procession, often forgot to keep the regulation distance and pushed a long way ahead.... Ryabovitch was with the first cannon of the fifth battery. He could see all the four batteries moving in front of him. For any one not a military man this long tedious procession of a moving brigade seems an intricate and unintelligible muddle; one cannot understand why there are so many people round one cannon, and why it is drawn by so many horses in such a strange network of harness, as though it really were so terrible and heavy. To Ryabovitch it was all perfectly comprehensible and therefore uninteresting. He had known for ever so long why at the head of each battery there rode a stalwart bombardier, and why he was called a bombardier; immediately behind this bombardier could be seen the horsemen of the first and then of the middle units. Ryabovitch knew that the horses on which they rode, those on the left, were called one name, while those on the right were called another—it was extremely uninteresting. Behind the horsemen came two shaft-horses. On one of them sat a rider with the dust of yesterday on his back and a clumsy and funny-looking piece of wood on his leg. Ryabovitch knew the object of this piece of wood, and did not think it funny. All the riders waved their whips mechanically and shouted from time to time. The cannon itself was ugly. On the fore part lay sacks of oats covered with canvas, and the cannon itself was hung all over with kettles, soldiers' knapsacks, bags, and looked like some small harmless animal surrounded for some unknown reason by men and horses. To the leeward of it marched six men, the gunners, swinging their arms. After the cannon there came again more bombardiers, riders, shaft-horses, and behind them another cannon, as ugly and unimpressive as the first. After the second followed a third, a fourth; near the fourth an officer, and so on. There were six batteries in all in the brigade, and four cannons in each battery. The procession covered half a mile; it ended in a string of wagons near which an extremely attractive creature—the ass, Magar, brought by a battery commander from Turkey—paced pensively with his long-eared head drooping.

Ryabovitch looked indifferently before and behind, at the backs of heads and at faces; at any other time he would have been half asleep, but now he was entirely absorbed in his new agreeable thoughts. At first when the brigade was setting off on the march he tried to persuade himself that the incident of the kiss could only be interesting as a mysterious little adventure, that it was in reality trivial, and to think of it seriously, to say the least of it, was stupid; but now he bade farewell to logic and gave himself up to dreams.... At one moment he imagined himself in Von Rabbek's drawing-room beside a girl who was like the young lady in lilac and the fair girl in black; then he would close his eyes and see himself with another, entirely unknown girl, whose features were very vague. In his imagination he talked, caressed her, leaned on her shoulder, pictured war, separation, then meeting again, supper with his wife, children....

'Brakes on!' the word of command rang out every time they went downhill.

He, too, shouted 'Brakes on!' and was afraid this shout would disturb his reverie and bring him back to reality....

As they passed by some landowner's estate Ryabovitch looked over the fence into the garden. A long avenue, straight as a ruler, strewn with yellow sand and bordered with young birch-trees, met his eyes.... With the eagerness of a man given up to dreaming, he pictured to himself little feminine feet tripping along yellow sand, and quite unexpectedly had a clear vision in his imagination of the girl who had kissed him and whom he had succeeded in picturing to himself the evening before at supper. This image remained in his brain and did not desert him again.

At midday there was a shout in the rear near the string of wagons:

'Easy! Eyes to the left! Officers!'

The general of the brigade drove by in a carriage with a pair of white horses. He stopped near the second battery, and shouted something which no one understood. Several officers, among them Ryabovitch, galloped up to them.

'Well?' asked the general, blinking his red eyes. 'Are there any sick?'

Receiving an answer, the general, a little skinny man, chewed, thought for a moment and said, addressing one of the officers:

'One of your drivers of the third cannon has taken off his leg-guard and hung it on the fore part of the cannon, the rascal. Reprimand him.'

He raised his eyes to Ryabovitch and went on:

'It seems to me your front strap is too long.'

Making a few other tedious remarks, the general looked at Lobytko and grinned.

'You look very melancholy today, Lieutenant Lobytko,' he said. 'Are you pining for Madame Lopuhov? Eh? Gentlemen, he is pining for Madame Lopuhov.'

The lady in question was a very stout and tall person who had long passed her fortieth year. The general, who had a predilection for solid ladies, whatever their ages, suspected a similar taste in his officers. The officers smiled respectfully. The general, delighted at having said something very amusing and biting, laughed loudly, touched his coachman's back, and saluted. The carriage rolled on....

'All I am dreaming about now which seems to me so impossible and unearthly is really quite an ordinary thing,' thought Ryabovitch, looking at the clouds of dust racing after the general's carriage. 'It's all very ordinary, and every one goes through it.... That general, for instance, has once been in love;

now he is married and has children. Captain Vahter, too, is married and beloved, though the nape of his neck is very red and ugly and he has no waist.... Salrnanov is coarse and very Tatar, but he has had a love affair that has ended in marriage....I am the same as every one else, and I, too, shall have the same experience as every one else, sooner or later....'

And the thought that he was an ordinary person, and that his life was ordinary, delighted him and gave him courage. He pictured her and his happiness as he pleased, and put no rein on his imagination.

When the brigade reached their halting-place in the evening, and the officers were resting in their tents, Ryabovitch, Merzlyakov, and Lobytko were sitting round a box having supper. Merzlyakov ate without haste, and, as he munched deliberately, read the 'Vyestnik Evropi', which he held on his knees. Lobytko talked incessantly and kept filling up his glass with beer, and Ryabovitch, whose head was confused from dreaming all day long, drank and said nothing. After three glasses he got a little drunk, felt weak, and had an irresistible desire to impart his new sensations to his comrades.

'A strange thing happened to me at those Von Rabbeks',' he began, trying to put an indifferent and ironical tone into his voice. 'You know I went into the billiard-room....'

He began describing very minutely the incident of the kiss, and a moment later relapsed into silence.... In the course of that moment he had told everything, and it surprised him dreadfully to find how short a time it took him to tell it. He had imagined that he could have been telling the story of the kiss till next morning. Listening to him, Lobytko, who was a great liar and consequently believed no one, looked at him sceptically and laughed. Merzlyakov twitched his eyebrows and, without removing his eyes from the 'Vyestnik Evropi', said:

'That's an odd thing! How strange!... throws herself on a man's neck, without addressing him by name.... She must be some sort of hysterical neurotic.'

'Yes, she must,' Ryabovitch agreed.

'A similar thing once happened to me,' said Lobytko, assuming a scared expression. 'I was going last year to Kovno.... I took a second-class ticket. The train was crammed, and it was impossible to sleep. I gave the guard half a rouble; he took my luggage and led me to another compartment.... I lay down and covered myself with a rug.... It was dark, you understand. Suddenly I felt some one touch me on the shoulder and breathe in my face. I made a movement with my hand and felt somebody's elbow.... I opened my eyes and only imagine—a woman. Black eyes, lips red as a prime salmon, nostrils breathing passionately—a bosom like a buffer....'

'Excuse me,' Merzlyakov interrupted calmly, 'I understand about the bosom, but how could you see the lips if it was dark?'

Lobytko began trying to put himself right and laughing at Merzlyakov's unimaginativeness. It made Ryabovitch wince. He walked away from the box, got into bed, and vowed never to confide again.

Camp life began.... The days flowed by, one very much like another. All those days Ryabovitch felt, thought, and behaved as though he were in love. Every morning when his orderly handed him water to wash with, and he sluiced his head with cold water, he thought there was something warm and delightful in his life.

In the evenings when his comrades began talking of love and women, he would listen, and draw up closer; and he wore the expression of a soldier when he hears the description of a battle in which he has taken part. And on the evenings when the officers, out on the spree with the setter—Lobytko—at their head, made Don Juan excursions to the 'suburb,' and Ryabovitch took part in such excursions, he always was sad, felt profoundly guilty, and inwardly begged her forgiveness.... In hours of leisure or on sleepless nights, when he felt moved to recall his childhood, his father and mother—everything near and dear, in fact, he invariably thought of Myestetchki, the strange horse, Von Rabbek, his wife who was like the Empress Eugénie, the dark room, the crack of light at the door....

On the thirty-first of August he went back from the camp, not with the whole brigade, but with only two batteries of it. He was dreaming and excited all the way, as though he were going back to his native place. He had an intense longing to see again the strange horse, the church, the insincere family of the Von Rabbeks, the dark room. The 'inner voice,' which so often deceives lovers, whispered to him for some reason that he would be sure to see her... and he was tortured by the questions, How he should meet her? What he would talk to her about? Whether she had forgotten the kiss? If the worst came to the worst, he thought, even if he did not meet her, it would be a pleasure to him merely to go through the dark room and recall the past....

Towards evening there appeared on the horizon the familiar church and white granaries. Ryabovitch's heart beat....He did not hear the officer who was riding beside him and saying something to him, he forgot everything, and looked eagerly at the river shining in the distance, at the roof of the house, at the dovecote round which the pigeons were circling in the light of the setting sun.

When they reached the church and were listening to the billeting orders, he expected every second that a man on horseback would come round the church enclosure and invite the officers to tea, but... the billeting orders were read, the officers were in haste to go on to the village, and the man on horseback did not appear.

'Von Rabbek will hear at once from the peasants that we have come and will send for us,' thought Ryabovitch, as he went into the hut, unable to understand why a comrade was lighting a candle and why the orderlies were hurriedly setting samovars....

A painful uneasiness took possession of him. He lay down, then got up and looked out of the window to see whether the messenger were coming. But there was no sign of him.

He lay down again, but half an hour later he got up, and, unable to restrain his uneasiness, went into the street and strode towards the church. It was dark and deserted in the square near the church.... Three soldiers were standing silent in a row where the road began to go downhill. Seeing Ryabovitch, they roused themselves and saluted. He returned the salute and began to go down the familiar path.

On the further side of the river the whole sky was flooded with crimson: the moon was rising; two peasant women, talking loudly, were picking cabbage in the kitchen garden; behind the kitchen garden there were some dark huts.... And everything on the near side of the river was just as it had been in May: the path, the bushes, the willows overhanging the water... but there was no sound of the brave nightingale, and no scent of poplar and fresh grass.

Reaching the garden, Ryabovitch looked in at the gate. The

garden was dark and still.... He could see nothing but the white stems of the nearest birch-trees and a little bit of the avenue; all the rest melted together into a dark blur. Ryabovitch looked and listened eagerly, but after waiting for a quarter of an hour without hearing a sound or catching a glimpse of a light, he trudged back....

He went down to the river. The General's bath-house and the bath-sheets on the rail of the little bridge showed white before him.... He went on to the bridge, stood a little, and, quite unnecessarily, touched the sheets. They felt rough and cold. He looked down at the water.... The river ran rapidly and with a faintly audible gurgle round the piles of the bath-house. The red moon was reflected near the left bank; little ripples ran over the reflection, stretching it out, breaking it into bits, and seemed trying to carry it away.

'How stupid, how stupid!' thought Ryabovitch, looking at the running water. 'How unintelligent it all is!'

Now that he expected nothing, the incident of the kiss, his impatience, his vague hopes and disappointment, presented themselves in a clear light. It no longer seemed to him strange that he had not seen the General's messenger, and that he would never see the girl who had accidentally kissed him instead of some one else; on the contrary, it would have been strange if he had seen her....

The water was running, he knew not where or why, just as it did in May. In May it had flowed into the great river, from the great river into the sea; then it had risen in vapour, turned into rain, and perhaps the very same water was running now before Ryabovitch's eyes again.... What for? Why?

And the whole world, the whole of life, seemed to Ryabovitch an unintelligible, aimless jest.... And turning his eyes from the water and looking at the sky, he remembered again how fate in the person of an unknown woman had by chance caressed him, he remembered his summer dreams and fancies, and his life struck him as extraordinarily meagre, poverty-stricken, and colourless....

When he went back to his hut he did not find one of his comrades. The orderly informed him that they had all gone to 'General von Rabbek's, who had sent a messenger on horseback to invite them....'

For an instant there was a flash of joy in Ryabovitch's heart, but he quenched it at once, got into bed, and in his wrath with his fate, as though to spite it, did not go to the General's.

7

THE BLACK MONK

I

Andrei Vasilyevitch Kovrin, Magister, had worn himself out, and unsettled his nerves. He made no effort to undergo regular treatment; but only incidentally, over a bottle of wine, spoke to his friend the doctor; and his friend the doctor advised him to spend all the spring and summer in the country. And in the nick of time came a long letter from Tánya Pesótsky, asking him to come and stay with her father at Borisovka. He decided to go.

But first (it was in April) he travelled to his own estate, to his native Kovrinka, and spent three weeks in solitude; and only when the fine weather came drove across the country to his former guardian and second parent, Pesótsky, the celebrated Russian horti-culturist. From Kovrinka to Borisovka, the home of the Pesótskys, was a distance of some seventy versts, and in the easy, springed calêche the drive along the roads, soft in springtime, promised real enjoyment.

The house at Borisovka was, large, faced with a colonnade, and adorned with figures of lions with the plaster falling off. At the door stood a servant in livery. The old park, gloomy and severe, laid out in English fashion, stretched for nearly a verst from the house down to the river, and ended there in a steep clay bank covered with pines whose bare roots resembled shaggy paws. Below sparkled a deserted stream; overhead the snipe circled about with melancholy cries—all, in short, seemed to invite a visitor to sit down and write a ballad. But the gardens and orchards, which together with the seed-plots occupied some eighty acres, inspired very different feelings. Even in the worst of weather they were bright and joy-inspiring. Such wonderful roses, lilies, camelias, such tulips, such a host of flowering plants of every possible kind and colour, from staring white to sooty black,—such a wealth of blossoms Kovrin had never seen before. The spring was only beginning, and the greatest rareties were hidden under glass; but already enough bloomed in the alleys and beds to make up an empire of delicate shades. And most charming of all was it in the early hours of morning, when dewdrops glistened on every petal and leaf.

In childhood the decorative part of the garden, called contemptuously by Pesótsky 'the rubbish,' had produced on Kovrin a fabulous impression. What miracles of art, what studied monstrosities, what monkeries of nature! Espaliers of fruit trees, a pear tree shaped like a pyramidal poplar, globular oaks and lindens, apple-tree houses, arches, monograms, candelabra—even the date 1862 in plum trees, to commemorate the year in which Pesótsky first engaged in the art of gardening. There were stately, symmetrical trees, with trunks erect as those of palms, which after examination proved to be gooseberry or currant trees. But what most of all enlivened the garden and gave it its joyous tone was the constant movement of Pesótsky's gardeners. From early morning to late at night, by the trees, by the bushes, in the alleys, and on the beds swarmed men as busy as ants, with barrows, spades, and watering-pots.

Kovrin arrived at Borisovka at nine o'clock. He found Tánya and her father in great alarm. The clear starlight night foretold frost, and the head gardener, Ivan Karlitch, had gone to town, so that there was no one who could be relied upon. At supper they spoke only of the impending frost; and it was decided that Tánya should not go to bed at all, but should inspect the gardens at one o'clock and see if all were in order, while Yegor Semiónovitch should rise at three o'clock, or even earlier.

Kovrin sat with Tánya all the evening, and after midnight accompanied her to the garden. The air already smelt strongly of burning. In the great orchard, called 'the commercial,' which every year brought Yegor Semiónovitch thousands of roubles profit, there already crept along the ground the thick, black, sour smoke which was to clothe the young leaves and save the plants. The trees were marshalled like chessmen in straight rows—like ranks of soldiers; and this pedantic regularity, together with the uniformity of height, made the garden seem monotonous and even tiresome. Kovrin and Tánya walked up and down the alleys, and watched the fires of dung, straw, and litter; but seldom met the workmen, who wandered in the smoke like shadows. Only the cherry and plum trees and a few apple trees were in blossom, but the whole garden was shrouded in smoke, and it was only when they reached the seed-plots that Kovrin was able to breathe.

'I remember when I was a child sneezing from the smoke,' he said, shrugging his shoulders, 'but to this day I cannot understand how smoke saves plants from the frost.'

'Smoke is a good substitute when there are no clouds,'

answered Tánya.

'But what do you want the clouds for?'

'In dull and cloudy weather we have no morning frosts.'

'Is that so?' said Kovrin.

He laughed and took Tánya by the hand. Her broad, very serious, chilled face; her thick, black eyebrows; the stiff collar on her jacket which prevented her from moving her head freely; her dress tucked up out of the dew; and her whole figure, erect and slight, pleased him.

'Heavens! how she has grown!' he said to himself. 'When I was here last time, five years ago, you were quite a child. You were thin, long-legged, and untidy, and wore a short dress, and I used to tease you. What a change in five years!'

'Yes, five years!' sighed Tánya. 'A lot of things have happened since then. Tell me, Andrei, honestly,' she said, looking merrily into his face, 'do you feel that you have got out of touch with us? But why do I ask? You are a man, you live your own interesting life, you.... Some estrangement is natural. But whether that is so or not, Andrusha, I want you now to look on us as your own. We have a right to that.'

'I do, already, Tánya.'

'Your word of honour?'

'My word of honour.'

'You were surprised that we had so many of your photographs. But surely you know how my father adores you, worships you. You are a scholar, and not an ordinary man; you have built up a brilliant career, and he is firmly convinced that you turned out a success because he educated you. I do not interfere with his delusion. Let him believe it!'

Already dawn. The sky paled, and the foliage and clouds of

smoke began to show themselves more clearly. The nightingale sang, and from the fields came the cry of quails.

'It is time for bed!' said Tánya. 'It is cold too.' She took Kovrin by the hand. 'Thanks, Andrusha, for coming. We are cursed with most uninteresting acquaintances, and not many even of them. With us it is always garden, garden, garden, and nothing else. Trunks, timbers,' she laughed, 'pippins, rennets, budding, pruning, grafting…. All our life goes into the garden, we never even dream of anything but apples and pears. Of course this is all very good and useful, but sometimes I cannot help wishing for change. I remember when you used to come and pay us visits, and when you came home for the holidays, how the whole house grew fresher and brighter, as if someone had taken the covers off the furniture; I was then a very little girl, but I understood….'

Tánya spoke for a time, and spoke with feeling. Then suddenly it came into Kovrin's head that during the summer he might become attached to this little, weak, talkative being, that he might get carried away, fall in love—in their position what was more probable and natural? The thought pleased him, amused him, and as he bent down to the kind, troubled face, he hummed to himself Pushkin's couplet:

'Oniégin; I will not conceal
That I love Tatyana madly.'

By the time they reached the house Yegor Semiónovitch had risen. Kovrin felt no desire to sleep; he entered into conversation with the old man, and returned with him to the garden. Yegor Semiónovitch was tall, broad-shouldered, and fat. He suffered from shortness of breath, yet walked so quickly that it was difficult to keep up with him. His expression was always troubled and hurried, and he seemed to be thinking that if he were a single second late everything would be destroyed.

'There, brother, is a mystery for you!' he began, stopping to recover breath. 'On the surface of the ground, as you see, there is frost, but raise the thermometer a couple of yards on your stick, and it is quite warm…. Why is that?'

'I confess I don't know,' said Kovrin, laughing.

'No!… You can't know everything…. The biggest brain cannot comprehend everything. You are still engaged with your philosophy?'

'Yes,… I am studying psychology, and philosophy generally.'

'And it doesn't bore you?'

'On the contrary, I couldn't live without it.'

'Well, God grant…' began Yegor Semiónovitch, smoothing his big whiskers thoughtfully. 'Well, God grant… I am very glad for your sake, brother, very glad….'

Suddenly he began to listen, and making a terrible face, ran off the path and soon vanished among the trees in a cloud of smoke.

'Who tethered this horse to the tree?' rang out a despairing voice. 'Which of you thieves and murderers dared to tether this horse to the apple tree? My God, my God! Ruined, ruined, spoiled, destroyed! The garden is ruined, the garden is destroyed! My God!'

When he returned to Kovrin his face bore an expression of injury and impotence.

'What on earth can you do with these accursed people?' he asked in a whining voice, wringing his hands. 'Stepka brought a manure cart here last night and tethered the horse to an apple tree… tied the reins, the idiot, so tight, that the bark is rubbed off in three places. What can you do with men like this? I speak to him and he blinks his eyes and looks stupid. He ought to be hanged!'

When at last he calmed down, he embraced Kovrin and kissed him on the cheek.

'Well, God grant...God grant! ...' he stammered. 'I am very, very glad that you have come. I cannot say how glad. Thanks!'

Then, with the same anxious face, and walking with the same quick step, he went round the whole garden, showing his former ward the orangery, the hothouses, the sheds, and two beehives which he described as the miracle of the century.

As they walked about, the sun rose, lighting up the garden. It grew hot. When he thought of the long, bright day before him, Kovrin remembered that it was but the beginning of May, and that he had before him a whole summer of long, bright, and happy days; and suddenly through him pulsed the joyous, youthful feeling which he had felt when as a child he played in this same garden. And in turn, he embraced the old man and kissed him tenderly. Touched by remembrances, the pair went into the house and drank tea out of the old china cups, with cream and rich biscuits; and these trifles again reminded Kovrin of his childhood and youth. The splendid present and the awakening memories of the past mingled, and a feeling of intense happiness filled his heart.

He waited until Tánya awoke, and having drunk coffee with her, walked through the garden, and then went to his room and began to work. He read attentively, making notes; and only lifted his eyes from his books when he felt that he must look out of the window or at the fresh roses, still wet with dew, which stood in vases on his table. It seemed to hint that every little vein in his body trembled and pulsated with joy.

II

But in the country Kovrin continued to live the same nervous and untranquil life as he had lived in town. He read much, wrote much, studied Italian; and when he went for walks, thought all the time of returning to work. He slept so little that he astonished the household; if by chance he slept in the daytime for half an hour, he could not sleep all the following night. Yet after these sleepless nights he felt active and gay.

He talked much, drank wine, and smoked expensive cigars. Often, nearly every day, young girls from the neighbouring country-houses drove over to Borisovka, played the piano with Tánya, and sang. Sometimes the visitor was a young man, also a neighbour, who played the violin well. Kovrin listened eagerly to their music and singing, but was exhausted by it, so exhausted sometimes that his eyes closed involuntarily, and his head drooped on his shoulder.

One evening after tea he sat upon the balcony, reading. In the drawing-room Tánya—a soprano, one of her friends—a contralto, and the young violinist studied the well-known serenade of Braga. Kovrin listened to the words, but though they were Russian, could not understand their meaning. At last, laying down his book and listening attentively, he understood. A girl with a disordered imagination heard by night in a garden some mysterious sounds, sounds so beautiful and strange that she was forced to recognize their harmony and holiness, which to us mortals are incomprehensible, and therefore flew back to heaven. Kovrin's eyelids drooped. He rose, and in exhaustion walked up and down the drawing-room, and then up and down the hall. When the music ceased, he took Tánya by the hand and went out with her to the balcony.

'All day—since early morning,' he began, 'my head has been taken up with a strange legend. I cannot remember whether I read it, or where I heard it, but the legend is very remarkable and not very coherent. I may begin by saying that it is not very clear. A thousand years ago a monk, robed in black, wandered in the wilderness—somewhere in Syria or Arabia...Some miles away the fishermen saw another black monk moving slowly over the surface of the lake. The second monk was a mirage. Now put out of your mind all the laws of optics, which legend, of course, does not recognize, and listen. From the first mirage was produced another mirage, from the second a third, so that the image of the Black Monk is eternally reflected from one stratum of the atmosphere to another. At one time it was seen in Africa, then in Spain, then in India, then in the Far North. At last it issued from the limits of the earth's atmosphere, but never came across conditions which would cause it to disappear. Maybe it is seen to-day in Mars or in the constellation of the Southern Cross. Now the whole point, the very essence of the legend, lies in the prediction that exactly a thousand years after the monk went into the wilderness, the mirage will again be cast into the atmosphere of the earth and show itself to the world of men. This term of a thousand years, it appears, is now expiring.... According to the legend we must expect the Black Monk to-day or to-morrow.'

'It is a strange story,' said Tánya, whom the legend did not please.

'But the most astonishing thing,' laughed Kovrin, 'is that

I cannot remember how this legend came into my head. Did I read it? Did I hear it? Or can it be that I dreamed of the Black Monk? I cannot remember. But the legend interests me. All day long I thought of nothing else.'

Releasing Tánya, who returned to her visitors, he went out of the house, and walked lost in thought beside the flower-beds. Already the sun was setting. The freshly watered flowers exhaled a damp, irritating smell. In the house the music had again begun, and from the distance the violin produced the effect of a human voice. Straining his memory in an attempt to recall where he had heard the legend, Kovrin walked slowly across the park, and then, not noticing where he went, to the river-bank.

By the path which ran down among the uncovered roots to the water's edge Kovrin descended, frightening the snipe, and disturbing two ducks. On the dark pine trees glowed the rays of the setting sun, but on the surface of the river darkness had already fallen. Kovrin crossed the stream. Before him now lay a broad field covered with young rye. Neither human dwelling nor human soul was visible in the distance; and it seemed that the path must lead to the unexplored, enigmatical region in the west where the sun had already set—where still, vast and majestic, flamed the afterglow.

'How open it is—how peaceful and free!' thought Kovrin, walking along the path. 'It seems as if all the world is looking at me from a hiding-place and waiting for me to comprehend it.'

A wave passed over the rye, and the light evening breeze blew softly on his uncovered head. Yet a minute more and the breeze blew again, this time more strongly, the rye rustled, and from behind came the dull murmur of the pines. Kovrin stopped in amazement On the horizon, like a cyclone or waterspout, a great, black pillar rose up from earth to heaven. Its outlines were undefined; but from the first it might be seen that it was not standing still, but moving with inconceivable speed towards Kovrin; and the nearer it came the smaller and smaller it grew. Involuntarily Kovrin rushed aside and made a path for it. A monk in black clothing, with grey hair and black eyebrows, crossing his hands upon his chest, was borne past. His bare feet were above the ground. Having swept some twenty yards past Kovrin, he looked at him, nodded his head, and smiled kindly and at the same time slyly. His face was pale and thin. When he had passed by Kovrin he again began to grow, flew across the river, struck inaudibly against the clay bank and pine trees, and, passing through them, vanished like smoke.

'You see,' stammered Kovrin, 'after all, the legend was true!'

Making no attempt to explain this strange phenomenon; satisfied with the fact that he had so closely and so plainly seen not only the black clothing but even the face and eyes of the monk; agitated agreeably, he returned home.

In the park and in the garden visitors were walking quietly; in the house the music continued. So he alone had seen the Black Monk. He felt a strong desire to tell what he had seen to Tánya and Yegor Semiónovitch, but feared that they would regard it as a hallucination, and decided to keep his counsel. He laughed loudly, sang, danced a mazurka, and felt in the best of spirits; and the guests and Tánya noticed upon his face a peculiar expression of ecstasy and inspiration, and found him very interesting.

III

When supper was over and the visitors had gone, he went to his own room, and lay on the sofa. He wished to think of the monk. But in a few minutes Tánya entered.

'There, Andrusha, you can read father's articles ...' she said. 'They are splendid articles. He writes very well.'

'Magnificent!' said Yegor Semiónovitch, coming in after her, with a forced smile. 'Don't listen to her, please!... Or read them only if you want to go to sleep—they are a splendid soporific.'

'In my opinion they are magnificent,' said Tánya, deeply convinced. 'Read them, Andrusha, and persuade father to write more often. He could write a whole treatise on gardening.'

Yegor Semiónovitch laughed, blushed, and stammered out the conventional phrases used by abashed authors. At last he gave in.

'If you must read them, read first these papers of Gauche's, and the Russian articles,' he stammered, picking out the papers with trembling hands. 'Otherwise you won't understand them. Before you read my replies you must know what I am replying to. But it won't interest you...stupid. And it's time for bed.'

Tánya went out. Yegor Semiónovitch sat on the end of the sofa and sighed loudly.

'Akh, brother mine ...' he began after a long silence. As you see, my dear Magister, I write articles, and exhibit at shows, and get medals sometimes....Pesótsky, they say, has apples as big as your head.... Pesótsky has made a fortune out of his gardens.... In one word:

"Rich and glorious is Kotchubéi."

'But I should like to ask you what is going to be the end of all this? The gardens—there is no question of that—are splendid, they are models.... Not gardens at all, in short, but a whole institution of high political importance, and a step towards a new era in Russian agriculture and Russian industry.... But for what purpose? What ultimate object?'

'That question is easily answered.'

'I do not mean in that sense. What I want to know is what will happen with the garden when I die? As things are, it would not last without me a single month. The secret does not lie in the fact that the garden is big and the workers many, but in the fact that I love the work—you understand? I love it, perhaps, more than I love myself. Just look at me! I work from morning to night. I do everything with my own hands. All grafting, all pruning, all planting—everything is done by me. When I am helped I feel jealous, and get irritated to the point of rudeness. The whole secret is in love, in a sharp master's eye, in a master's hands, and in the feeling when I drive over to a friend and sit down for half an hour, that I have left my heart behind me and am not myself—all the time I am in dread that something has happened to the garden. Now suppose I die to-morrow, who will replace all this? Who will do the work? The head gardeners? The workmen? Why the whole burden of my present worries is that my greatest enemy is not the hare or the beetle or the frost, but the hands of the stranger.'

'But Tánya?' said Kovrin, laughing. 'Surely she is not more dangerous than a hare?...She loves and understands the work.'

'Yes, Tánya loves it and understands it. If after my death the garden should fall to her as mistress, then I could wish for nothing better. But suppose—which God forbid—she should marry!' Yegor Semiónovitch whispered and look at Kovrin with frightened eyes. 'That's the whole crux. She might marry, there would be children, and there would be no time to attend to the garden. That is bad enough. But what I fear most of all is that she may marry some spendthrift who is always in want of money, who will lease the garden to tradesmen, and the whole thing will go to the devil in the first year. In a business like this a woman, is the scourge of God.'

Yegor Semiónovitch sighed and was silent for a few minutes.

'Perhaps you may call it egoism. But I do not want Tánya to marry. I am afraid! You've seen that fop who comes along with a fiddle and makes a noise. I know Tánya would never marry him, yet I cannot bear the sight of him.... In short, brother, I am a character...and I know it.'

Yegor Semiónovitch rose and walked excitedly up and down the room. It was plain that he had something very serious to say, but could not bring himself to the point.

'I love you too sincerely not to talk to you frankly,' he said, thrusting his hands into his pockets. 'In all delicate questions I say what I think, and dislike mystification. I tell you plainly, therefore, that you are the only man whom I should not be afraid of Tánya marrying. You are a clever man, you have a heart, and you would not see my life's work ruined. And what is more, I love you as my own son...and am proud of you. So if you and Tánya were to end...in a sort of romance...I should be very glad and very happy. I tell you this straight to your face, without shame, as becomes an honest man.'

Kovrin smiled. Yegor Semiónovitch opened the door, and was leaving the room, but stopped suddenly on the threshold.

'And if you and Tánya had a son, I could make a horti-culturist out of him,' he added. 'But that is an idle fancy. Good night!'

Left alone, Kovrin settled himself comfortably, and took up his host's articles. The first was entitled 'Intermediate Culture,' the second 'A Few Words in Reply to the Remarks of Mr Z. about the Treatment of the Soil of a New Garden,' the third 'More about Grafting.' The others were similar in scope. But all breathed restlessness and sickly irritation. Even a paper with the peaceful title of 'Russian Apple Trees' exhaled irritability. Yegor Semiónovitch began with the words 'Audi alteram partem', and ended it with 'Sapienti sat'; and between these learned quotations flowed a whole torrent of acid words directed against 'the learned ignorance of our patent horticulturists who observe nature from their academic chairs', and against M. Gauche, 'whose fame is founded on the admiration of the profane and dilletanti'. And finally Kovrin came across an uncalled-for and quite insincere expression of regret that it is no longer legal to flog peasants who are caught stealing fruit and injuring trees.

'His is good work, wholesome and fascinating,' thought Kovrin, 'yet in these pamphlets we have nothing but bad temper and war to the knife. I suppose it is the same everywhere; in all careers men of ideas are nervous, and victims of this kind of exalted sensitiveness. I suppose it must be so.'

He thought of Tánya, so delighted with her father's articles, and then of Yegor Semiónovitch. Tánya, small, pale, and slight, with her collar-bone showing, with her widely-opened, her dark and clever eyes, which it seemed were always searching for something. And Yegor Semiónovitch with his little, hurried steps. He thought again of Tánya, fond of talking, fond of argument, and always accompanying even the most insignificant phrases with mimicry and gesticulation. Nervous—she must be nervous in the highest degree. Again Kovrin began to read, but he understood nothing, and threw down his books. The agreeable emotion with which he had danced the mazurka and listened to the music still held possession of him, and aroused a multitude of thoughts. It flashed upon him that if this strange, unnatural monk had been seen by him alone, he must be ill, ill to the point of suffering from hallucinations. The thought frightened him, but not for long.

He sat on the sofa, and held his head in his hands, curbing the inexplicable joy which filled his whole being; and then walked up and down the room for a minute, and returned to his work. But the thoughts which he read in books no longer satisfied him. He longed for something vast, infinite, astonishing. Towards morning he undressed and went unwillingly to bed; he felt that he had better rest. When at last he heard Yegor Semiónovitch going to his work in the garden, he rang, and ordered the servant to bring him some wine. He drank several glasses; his consciousness became dim, and he slept.

IV

Yegor Semiónovitch and Tánya often quarrelled and said disagreeable things to one another. This morning they had both been irritated, and Tánya burst out crying and went to her room, coming down neither to dinner nor to tea At first Yegor Semiónovitch marched about, solemn and dignified, as if wishing to give everyone to understand that for him justice and order were the supreme interests of life. But he was unable to keep this up for long; his spirits fell, and he wandered about the park and sighed, 'Akh, my God!' At dinner he ate nothing, and at last, tortured by his conscience, he knocked softly at the closed door, and called timidly:

'Tánya! Tánya!'

Through the door came a Weak voice, tearful but determined:

'Leave me alone!...I implore you.'

The misery of father and daughter reacted on the whole household, even on the labourers in the garden. Kovrin, as usual, was immersed in his own interesting work, but at last even he felt tired and uncomfortable. He determined to interfere, and disperse the cloud before evening. He knocked at Tánya's door, and was admitted.

'Come, come! What a shame!' he began jokingly; and then looked with surprise at her tear-stained and afflicted face covered with red spots. 'Is it so serious, then? Well, well!'

'But if you knew how he tortured me!' she said, and a flood of tears gushed out of her big eyes. 'He tormented me!' she continued, wringing her hands. 'I never said a word to him.... I only said there was no need to keep unnecessary labourers, if...if we can get day workmen.... You know the men have done nothing for the whole week. I...I only said this, and he roared at me, and said a lot of things...most offensive...deeply insulting. And all for nothing.'

'Never mind!' said Kovrin, straightening her hair. 'You have had your scoldings and your cryings, and that is surely enough. You can't keep up this for ever...it is not right...all the more since you know he loves you infinitely.'

'He has ruined my whole life,' sobbed Tánya. 'I never hear anything but insults and affronts. He regards me as superfluous in his own house. Let him! He will have cause! I shall leave here to-morrow, and study for a position as telegraphist.... Let him!'

'Come, come. Stop crying, Tánya. It does you no good.... You are both irritable and impulsive, and both in the wrong. Come, and I will make peace!'

Kovrin spoke gently and persuasively, but Tánya continued to cry, twitching her shoulders and wringing her hands as if she had been overtaken by a real misfortune. Kovrin felt all the sorrier owing to the smallness of the cause of her sorrow. What a trifle it took to make this little creature unhappy for a whole day, or, as she had expressed it, for a whole life! And as he consoled Tánya, it occurred to him that except this girl and her father there was not one in the world who loved him as a kinsman; and had it not been for them, he, left fatherless and motherless in early childhood, must have lived his whole life without feeling one sincere caress, or tasting ever that simple, unreasoning love which we feel only for those akin to us by blood. And he felt that his tired, strained nerves, like magnets, responded to the nerves of this crying, shuddering girl. He felt, too, that he could never love a healthy, rosy-cheeked woman; but pale, weak, unhappy Tánya appealed to him.

He felt pleasure in looking at her hair and her shoulders; and he pressed her hand, and wiped away her tears.... At last she ceased crying. But she still continued to complain of her father, and of her insufferable life at home, imploring Kovrin to try to realize her position. Then by degrees she began to smile, and to sigh that God had cursed her with such a wicked temper; and in the end laughed aloud, called herself a fool, and ran out of the room. A little later Kovrin went into the garden. Yegor Semiónovitch and Tánya, as if nothing had happened, We were walking side by side up the alley, eating rye-bread and salt, we both were very hungry.

V

Pleased with his success as peacemaker, Kovrin went into the park. As he sat on a bench and mused, he heal'd the rattle of a carnage and a woman's laugh—visitors evidently again. Shadows fell in the garden, the sound of a violin, the music of a woman's voice reached him almost inaudibly; and this reminded him of the Black Monk. Whither, to what country, to what planet, had that optical absurdity flown? Hardly had he called to mind the legend and painted in imagination the black apparition in the rye-field when from behind the pine trees opposite to him, walked inaudibly—without the faintest rustling—a man of middle height. His grey head was uncovered, he was dressed in black, and barefooted like a beggar. On his pallid, corpse-like face stood out sharply a number of black spots. Nodding his head politely the stranger or beggar walked noiselessly to the bench and sat down, and Kovrin recognized the Black Monk. For a minute they looked at one another, Kovrin with astonishment, but the monk kindly and, as before, with a sly expression on his face.

'But you are a mirage,' said Kovrin. 'Why are you here, and why do you sit in one place? That is not in accordance with the legend.'

'It is all the same,' replied the monk softly, turning his face towards Kovrin. 'The legend, the mirage, I—all are products of your own excited imagination. I am a phantom.'

'That is to say you don't exist?' asked Kovrin. 'Think as you like,' replied the monk, smiling faintly. 'I exist in your imagination, and as your imagination is a part of Nature, I must exist also in Nature.'

'You have a clever, a distinguished face—it seems to me as if in reality you had lived more than a thousand years,' said Kovrin. 'I did not know that my imagination was capable of creating such a phenomenon. Why do you look at me with such rapture? Are you pleased with me?'

'Yes. For you are one of the few who can justly be named the elected of God. You serve eternal truth. Your thoughts, your intentions, your astonishing science, all your life bear the stamp of divinity, a heavenly impress; they are dedicated to the rational and the beautiful, and that is, to the Eternal.'

'You say, to eternal truth. Then can eternal truth be accessible and necessary to men if there is no eternal life?'

'There is eternal life,' said the monk.

'You believe in the immortality of men.'

'Of course. For you, men, there awaits a great and a beautiful future. And the more the world has of men like you the nearer will this future be brought. Without you, ministers to the highest principles, living freely and consciously, humanity would be nothing; developing in the natural order it must wait the end of its earthly history. But you, by some thousands of years, hasten it into the kingdom of eternal truth—and in this is your high service. You embody in yourself the blessing of God which rested upon the people.'

'And what is the object of eternal life?' asked Kovrin.

'The same as all life—enjoyment. True enjoyment is in knowledge, and eternal life presents innumerable, inexhaustible fountains of knowledge; it is in this sense it was said: "In My Father's house are many mansions...."'

'You cannot conceive what a joy it is to me to listen to you,' said Kovrin, rubbing his hands with delight.

'I am glad.'

'Yet I know that when you leave me I shall be tormented by doubt as to your reality. You are a phantom, a hallucination. But that means that I am psychically diseased, that I am not in a normal state?'

'What if you are? That need not worry you. You are ill because you have overstrained your powers, because you have borne your health in sacrifice to one idea, and the time is near when you will sacrifice not merely it but your life also. What more could you desire? It is what all gifted and noble natures aspire to.'

'But if I am psychically diseased, how can I trust myself?'

'And how do you know that the men of genius whom all the world trusts have not also seen visions? Genius, they tell you now, is akin to insanity. Believe me, the healthy and the normal are but ordinary men—the herd. Fears as to a nervous age, over-exhaustion and degeneration can trouble seriously only those whose aims in life lie in the present—that is the herd.'

'The Romans had as their ideal: *mens sana in corpore sano*.'

'All that the Greeks and Romans said is not true. Exaltations, aspirations, excitements, ecstasies—all those things which distinguish poets, prophets, martyrs to ideas from ordinary men are incompatible with the animal life, that is, with physical health. I repeat, if you wish to be healthy and normal go with the herd.'

'How strange that you should repeat what I myself have so often thought!' said Kovrin. 'It seems as if you had watched me and listened to my secret thoughts. But do not talk about me. What do you imply by the words: eternal truth?'

The monk made no answer. Kovrin looked at him, but

could not make out his face. His features clouded and melted away; his head and arms disappeared; his body faded into the bench and into the twilight, and vanished utterly.

'The hallucination has gone,' said Kovrin, laughing. 'It is a pity.'

He returned to the house lively and happy. What the Black Monk had said to him flattered, not his self-love, but his soul, his whole being. To be the elected, to minister to eternal truth, to stand in the ranks of those who hasten by thousands of years the making mankind worthy of the kingdom of Christ, to deliver humanity from thousands of years of struggle, sin, and suffering, to give to one idea everything, youth, strength, health, to die for the general welfare—what an exalted, what a glorious ideal! And when through his memory flowed his past life, a life pure and chaste and full of labour, when he remembered what he had learnt and what he had taught, he concluded that in the words of the monk there was no exaggeration. Through the park, to meet him, came Tánya. She was wearing a different dress from that in which he had last seen her.

'You here?' she cried. 'We were looking for you, looking.... But what has happened?' she asked in surprise, looking into his glowing, enraptured face, and into his eyes, now full of tears. 'How strange you are, Andrusha!'

'I am satisfied, Tánya,' said Kovrin, laying his hand upon her shoulder. 'I am more than satisfied; I am happy! Tánya, dear Tánya, you are inexpressibly dear to me. Tánya, I am so glad!'

He kissed both her hands warmly, and continued: 'I have just lived through the brightest, most wonderful, most unearthly moments.... But I cannot tell you all, for you would call me mad, or refuse to believe me.... Let me speak of you! Tánya,

I love you, and have long loved you. To have you near me, to meet you ten times a day, has become a necessity for me. I do not know how I shall live without you when I go home.'

'No!' laughed Tánya. 'You will forget us all in two days. We are little people, and you are a great man.'

'Let us talk seriously,' said he. 'I will take you with me, Tánya! Yes? You will come? You will be mine?'

Tánya cried 'What?' and tried to laugh again. But the laugh did not come, and, instead, red spots stood out on her cheeks. She breathed quickly, and walked on rapidly into the park.

'I did not think...I never thought of this...never thought,' she said, pressing her hands together as if in despair.

But Kovrin hastened after her, and, with the same glowing, enraptured face, continued to speak.

'I wish for a love which will take possession of me altogether, and this love only you, Tánya, can give me. I am happy! How happy!'

She was overcome, bent, withered up, and seemed suddenly to have aged ten years. But Kovrin found her beautiful, and loudly expressed his ecstasy: 'How lovely she is!'

VI

When he learned from Kovrin that not only had a romance resulted, but that a wedding was to follow, Yegor Semiónovitch walked from corner to corner, and tried to conceal his agitation. His hands shook, his neck seemed swollen and purple; he ordered the horses to be put into his racing droschky, and drove away. Tánya, seeing how he whipped the horses and how he pushed his cap down over his ears, understood his mood, locked herself into her room, and cried all day.

In the orangery the peaches and plums were already ripe. The packing and despatch to Moscow of such a delicate load required much attention, trouble, and bustle. Owing to the heat of the summer every tree had to be watered; the process was costly in time and working-power; and many caterpillars appeared, which the workmen, and even Yegor Semiónovitch and Tánya, crushed with their fingers, to the great disgust of Kovrin. The autumn orders for fruit and trees had to be attended to, and a vast correspondence carried on. And at the very busiest time, when it seemed no one had a free moment, work began in the fields and deprived the garden of half its workers. Yegor Semiónovitch, very sunburnt, very irritated, and very worried, galloped about, now to the garden, now to the fields; and all the time shouted that they were tearing him to bits, and that he would put a bullet through his brain.

On top of all came the bustle over Tánya's trousseau, to which the Pesótskys attributed infinite significance. With the eternal snipping of scissors, rattle of sewing-machines, smell of flat-irons, and the caprices of the nervous and touchy dressmaker, the whole house seemed to spin round. And, to make matters worse, visitors arrived every day, and these visitors had to be amused, fed, and lodged for the night. Yet work and worry passed unnoticed in a mist of joy. Tánya felt as if love and happiness had suddenly burst upon her, although ever since her fourteenth year she had been certain that Kovrin would marry nobody but herself. She was eternally in a state of astonishment, doubt, and disbelief in herself. At one moment she was seized by such great joy that she felt she must fly away to the clouds and pray to God; but a moment later she remembered that when August came she would have to leave the home of her childhood and forsake her father; and she was frightened by the thought—God knows whence it came—that she was trivial, insignificant, and unworthy of a great man like Kovrin. When such thoughts came she would run up to her room, lock herself in, and cry bitterly for hours. But when visitors were present, it broke in upon her that Kovrin was a singularly handsome man, that all the women loved him and envied her; and in these moments her heart was as full of rapture and pride as if she had conquered the whole world. When he dared to smile on any other woman she trembled with jealousy, went to her room, and again—tears. These new feelings possessed her altogether; she helped her father mechanically, noticing neither pears nor caterpillars, nor workmen, nor how swiftly time was passing by.

Yegor Semiónovitch was in much the same state of mind. He still worked from morning to night, Hew about the gardens, and lost his temper; but all the while he was wrapped in a magic reverie. In his sturdy body contended two men, one the real Yegor Semiónovitch, who, when he listened to the gardener, Ivan Karlovitch's report of some mistake or disorder, went mad with excitement, and tore his hair; and the other the unreal Yegor Semiónovitch—a half-intoxicated old man, who broke off an important conversation in the middle of a word, seized the gardener by the shoulder, and stammered:

'You may say what you like, but blood is thicker than water. His mother was an astonishing, a most noble, a most brilliant woman. It was a pleasure to see her good, pure, open, angel face. She painted beautifully, wrote poetry, spoke five foreign languages, and sang.... Poor thing, Heaven rest her soul, she died of consumption!'

The unreal Yegor Semiónovitch sighed, and after a moment's silence continued:

'When he was a boy growing up to manhood in my house he had just such an angel face, open and good. His looks, his movements, his words were as gentle and graceful as his mother's. And his intellect It is not for nothing he has the degree of Magister. But you just wait, Ivan Karlovitch; you'll see what he'll be in ten years' time. Why, he'll be out of sight!' But here the real Yegor Semiónovitch remembered himself, seized his head and roared:

'Devils! Frost-bitten! Ruined, destroyed! The garden is ruined; the garden is destroyed!'

Kovrin worked with all his former ardour, and hardly noticed the bustle about him. Love only poured oil on the flames. After every meeting with Tánya, he returned to his rooms in rapture and happiness, and set to work with his books and manuscripts with the same passion with which he had kissed her and sworn his love. What the Black Monk had told him of his election by God, of eternal truth, and of the glorious future of humanity, gave to all his work a peculiar, unusual significance. Once or twice every week, either in the park or in the house, he met the monk, and talked with him for hours; but this did not frighten, but on the contrary delighted him, for he was now assured that such apparitions visit only the elect and exceptional who dedicate themselves to the ministry of ideas.

Assumption passed unobserved. Then came the wedding, celebrated by the determined wish of Yegor Semiónovitch with what was called éclat, that is, with meaningless festivities which lasted for two days. Three thousand roubles were consumed in food and drink; but what with the vile music, the noisy toasts, the fussing servants, the clamour, and the closeness of the atmosphere, no one appreciated the expensive wines or the astonishing hors d'oeuvres specially ordered from Moscow.

VII

One of the long winter nights. Kovrin lay in bed, reading a French novel. Poor Tánya, whose head every evening ached as the result of the unaccustomed life in town, had long been sleeping, muttering incoherent phrases in her dreams.

The dock struck three. Kovrin put out the candle and lay down, lay for a long time with dosed eyes unable to sleep owing to the heat of the room and Tánya's continued muttering. At half-past four he again lighted the candle. The Black Monk was sitting in a chair beside his bed.

'Good night!' said the monk, and then, after a moment's silence, asked, 'What are you thinking of now?'

'Of glory,' answered Kovrin. 'In a French novel which I have just been reading, the hero is a young man who does foolish things, and dies from a passion for glory. To me this passion is inconceivable.'

'Because you are too clever. You look indifferently on fame as a toy which cannot interest you.'

'That is true.'

'Celebrity has no attractions for you. What flattery, joy, or instruction can a man draw from the knowledge that his name will be graven on a monument, when time will efface the inscription sooner or later? Yes, happily there are too many of you for brief human memory to remember all your names.'

'Of course,' said Kovrin. 'And why remember them?... But

let us talk of something else. Of happiness, for instance. What is this happiness?'

When the clock struck five he was sitting on the bed with his feet trailing on the carpet and his head turned to the monk, and saying:

'In ancient times a man became frightened at his happiness, so great it was, and to placate the gods laid before them in sacrifice his beloved ring. You have heard? Now I, like Polycrates, am a little frightened at my own happiness. From morning to night I experience only joy—joy absorbs me and stifles all other feelings. I do not know the meaning of grief affliction, or weariness. I speak seriously, I am beginning to doubt.'

'Why?' asked the monk in an astonished tone. 'Then you think joy is a supernatural feeling? You think it is not the normal condition of things? No! The higher a man has climbed in mental and moral development the freer he is, the greater satisfaction he draws from life. Socrates, Diogenes, Marcus Aurelius knew joy and not sorrow. And the apostle said, "Rejoice exceedingly." Rejoice and be happy!'

'And suddenly the gods will be angered,' said Kovrin jokingly. 'But it would hardly be to my taste if they were to steal my happiness and force me to shiver and starve.'

Tánya awoke, and looked at her husband with amazement and terror. He spoke, he turned to the chair, he gesticulated, and laughed; his eyes glittered and his laughter sounded strange.

'Andrusha, whom are you speaking to?' she asked, seizing the hand which he had stretched out to the monk. 'Andrusha, who is it?'

'Who?' answered Kovrin. 'Why, the monk!... He is sitting there.' He pointed to the Black Monk.

'There is no one there,...no one, Andrusha; you are ill.'

Tánya embraced her husband, and, pressing against him as if to defend him against the apparition, covered his eyes with her hand.

'You are ill,' she sobbed, trembling all over. 'Forgive me, darling, but for a long time I have fancied you were unnerved in some way.... You are ill,...psychically, Andrusha.'

The shudder communicated itself to him. He looked once more at the chair, now empty, and suddenly felt weakness in his arms and legs. He began to dress. 'It is nothing, Tánya, nothing,...' he stammered, and still shuddered. 'But I am a little unwell.... It is time to recognize it.'

'I have noticed it for a long time, and father noticed it,' she said, trying to restrain her sobs. 'You have been speaking so funnily to yourself, and smiling so strangely,...and you do not sleep. O, my God, my God, save us!' she cried in terror. 'But do not be afraid, Andrusha, do not fear,...for God's sake do not be afraid....'

She also dressed.... It was only as he looked at her that Kovrin understood the danger of his position, and realized the meaning of the Black Monk and of their conversations. It became plain to him that he was mad.

Both, themselves not knowing why, dressed and went into the hall; she first, he after her. There they found Yegor Semiónovitch in his dressing-gown. He was staying with them, and had been awakened by Tánya's sobs.

'Do not be afraid, Andrusha,' said Tánya, trembling as if in fever. 'Do not be afraid...father, this will pass off...it will pass off.'

Kovrin was so agitated that he could hardly speak. But he

tried to treat the matter as a joke. He turned to his father-in-law and attempted to say: 'Congratulate me...it seems I have gone out of my mind.' But his lips only moved, and he smiled bitterly.

At nine o'clock they put on his overcoat and a fur cloak, wrapped him up in a shawl, and drove him to the doctor's. He began a course of treatment.

VIII

Again summer. By the doctor's orders Kovrin returned to the country. He had recovered his health, and no longer saw the Black Monk. It only remained for him to recruit his physical strength. He lived with his father-in-law, drank much milk, worked only two hours a day, never touched wine, and gave up smoking.

On the evening of 19 June, before Elijah's day, a vesper service was held in the house. When the priest took the censor from the sexton, and the vast hall began to smell like a church, Kovrin felt tired. He went into the garden. Taking no notice of the gorgeous blossoms around him he walked up and down, sat for a while on a bench, and then walked through the park. He descended the sloping bank to the margin of the river, and stood still, looking questioningly at the water. The great pines, with their shaggy roots, which a year before had seen him so young, so joyous, so active, no longer whispered, but stood silent and motionless, as if not recognizing him.... And, indeed, with his short-dipped hair, his feeble walk, and his changed face, so heavy and pale and changed since last year, he would hardly have been recognized anywhere.

He crossed the stream. In the field, last year covered with

rye, lay rows of reaped oats. The sun had set, and on the horizon flamed a broad, red afterglow, fore-telling stormy weather. All was quiet; and, gazing towards the point at which a year before he had first seen the Black Monk, Kovrin stood twenty minutes watching the crimson fade. When he returned to the house, tired and unsatisfied, Yegor Semiónovitch and Tánya were sitting on the steps of the terrace, drinking tea. They were talking together, and, seeing Kovrin, stopped. But Kovrin knew by their faces that they had been speaking of him.

'It is time for you to have your milk,' said Tánya to her husband.

'No, not yet,' he answered, sitting down on the lowest step. 'You drink it. I do not want it.' Tánya timidly exchanged glances with her father, and said in a guilty voice:

'You know very well that the milk does you good.'

'Yes, any amount of good,' laughed Kovrin. 'I congratulate you, I have gained a pound in weight since last Friday.' He pressed his hands to his head and said in a pained voice: 'Why…why have you cured me? Bromide mixtures, idleness, warm baths, watching in trivial terror over every mouthful, every step…all this in the end will drive me to idiocy. I had gone out of my mind…I had the mania of greatness.…But for all that I was bright, active, and even happy…. I was interesting and original. Now I have become rational and solid, just like the rest of the world. I am a mediocrity, and it is tiresome for me to live…. Oh, how cruelly… how cruelly you have treated me! I had hallucinations…but what harm did that cause to anyone? I ask you what harm?'

'God only knows what you mean!' sighed Yegor Semiónovitch. 'It is stupid even to listen to you.'

'Then you need not listen.'

The presence of others, especially of Yegor Semiónovitch, now irritated Kovrin; he answered his father-in-law drily, coldly, even rudely, and could not look on him without contempt and hatred. And Yegor Semiónovitch felt confused, and coughed guiltily, although he could not see how he was in the wrong. Unable to understand the cause of such a sudden reversal of their former hearty relations, Tánya leaned against her father, and looked with alarm into his eyes. It was becoming plain to her that their relations every day grew worse and worse, that her father had aged greatly, and that her husband had become irritable, capricious, excitable, and uninteresting. She no longer laughed and sang, she ate nothing, and whole nights never slept, but lived under the weight of some impending terror, torturing herself so much that she lay insensible from dinner-time till evening. When the service was being held, it had seemed to her that her father was crying; and now as she sat on the terrace she made an effort not to think of it.

'How happy were Buddha and Mahomet and Shakespeare that their kind-hearted kinsmen and doctors did not cure them of ecstasy and inspiration!' said Kovrin. 'If Mahomet had taken potassium bromide for his nerves, worked only two hours a day, and drunk milk, that astonishing man would have left as little behind him as his dog. Doctors and kind-hearted relatives only do their best to make humanity stupid, and the time will come when mediocrity will be considered genius, and humanity will perish. If you only had some idea,' concluded Kovrin peevishly, 'if you only had some idea how grateful I am!' He felt strong irritation, and to prevent himself saying too much, rose and went into the house. It was a windless night, and into the window was borne the smell of tobacco plants and jalap. Through the windows of the great dark hall, on the floor and on the piano, fell the moonrays. Kovrin recalled the raptures of the summer before, when the air, as now, was full of the smell of jalap and the moonrays poured through the window.... To awaken the mood of last year he went to his room, lighted a strong cigar, and ordered the servant to bring him wine. But now the cigar was bitter and distasteful, and the wine had lost its flavour of the year before. How much it means to get out of practice! From a single cigar, and two sips of wine, his head went round, and he was obliged to take bromide of potassium.

Before going to bed Tánya said to him:

'Listen. Father worships you, but you are annoyed with him about something, and that is killing him. Look at his face; he is growing old, not by days but by hours! I implore you, Andrusha, for the love of Christ, for the sake of your own dead father, for the sake of my peace of mind—be kind to him again!'

'I cannot, and I do not want to.'

'But why?' Tánya trembled all over. 'Explain to me why!'

'Because I do not like him; that is all,' answered Kovrin carelessly, shrugging his shoulders. 'But better not talk of that; he is your father.'

'I cannot, cannot understand,' said Tánya. She pressed her hands to her forehead and fixed her eyes on one point. 'Something terrible, something incomprehensible is going on in this house. You, Ahdrusha, have changed; you are no longer yourself.... You—a clever, an exceptional man—get irritated over trifles....You are annoyed by such little things that at any other time you yourself would have refused to believe it. No...do not be angry, do not be angry,' she continued, kissing his hands, and frightened by her own words. 'You are clever, good, and noble. You will be just to father. He is so good.'

'He is not good, but merely good-humoured. These vaudeville uncles—of your father's type—with well-fed, easy-going faces, are characters in their way, and once used to amuse me, whether in novels, in comedies, or in life. But they are now hateful to me. They are egoists to the marrow of their bones.... Most disgusting of all is their satiety, and this stomachic, purely bovine—or swinish—optimism.'

Tánya sat on the bed, and laid her head on a pillow. 'This is torture!' she said; and from her voice it was plain that she was utterly weary and found it hard to speak. 'Since last winter not a moment of rest....It is terrible, my God! I suffer ...'

'Yes, of course! I am Herod, and you and your papa the massacred infants. Of course!'

His face seemed to Tánya ugly and disagreeable. The expression of hatred and contempt did not suit it. She even observed that something was lacking in his face; ever since his hair had been cut off, it seemed changed. She felt an almost irresistible desire to say something insulting, but restrained herself in time, and overcome with terror, went out of the bedroom.

IX

Kovrin received an independent chair. His inaugural address was fixed for 2 December, and a notice to that effect was posted in the corridors of the University. But when the day came a telegram was received by the University authorities that he could not fulfil the engagement, owing to illness.

Blood came from his throat. He spat it up, and twice in

one month it flowed in streams. He felt terribly weak, and fell into a somnolent condition. But this illness did not frighten him, for he knew that his dead mother had lived with the same complaint more than ten years. His doctors, too, declared that there was no danger, and advised him merely not to worry, to lead a regular life, and to talk less.

In January the lecture was postponed for the same reason, and in February it was too late to begin the course. It was postponed till the following year.

He no longer lived with Tánya, but with another woman, older than himself, who looked after him as if he were a child. His temper was calm and obedient; he submitted willingly, and when Varvara Nikolaievna—that was her name—made arrangements for taking him to the Crimea, he consented to go, although he felt that from the change no good would come.

They reached Sevastopol late one evening, and stopped there to rest, intending to drive to Yalta on the following day. Both were tired by the journey. Varvara Nikolaievna drank tea, and went to bed. But Kovrin remained up. An hour before leaving home for the railway station he had received a letter from Tánya, which he had not read; and the thought of this letter caused him unpleasant agitation. In the depths of his heart he knew that his marriage with Tánya had been a mistake. He was glad that he was finally parted from her; but the remembrance of this woman, who towards the last had seemed to turn into a walking, living mummy, in which all had died except the great, clever eyes, awakened in him only pity and vexation against himself. The writing on the envelope reminded him that two years before he had been guilty of cruelty and injustice, and that he had avenged on people in no way guilty his spiritual vacuity, his solitude, his disenchantment with life…. He remembered how he had once torn into fragments his dissertation and all the articles written by him since the time of his illness, and thrown them out of the window, how the fragments flew in the wind and rested on the trees and flowers; in every page he had seen strange and baseless pretensions, frivolous irritation, and a mania for greatness. And all this had produced upon him an impression that he had written a description of his own faults. Yet when the last copybook had been torn up and thrown out of the window, he felt bitterness and vexation, and went to his wife and spoke to her cruelly. Heavens, how he had ruined her life! He remembered how once, wishing to cause her pain, he had told her that her father had played in their romance an unusual role, and had even asked him to marry her; and Yegor Semiónovitch, happening to overhear him, had rushed into the room, so dumb with consternation that he could not utter a word, but only stamped his feet on one spot and bellowed strangely as if his tongue had been cut out. And Tánya, looking at her father, cried out in a heartrending voice, and fell insensible on the floor. It was hideous.

The memory of all this returned to him at the sight of the well-known handwriting. He went out on to the balcony. It was warm and calm, and a salt smell came to him from the sea. The moonlight, and the lights around, were imaged on the surface of the wonderful bay—a surface of a hue impossible to name. It was a tender and soft combination of dark blue and green; in parts the water resembled copperas, and in parts, instead of water, liquid moonlight filled the bay. And all these combined in a harmony of hues which exhaled tranquillity and exaltation.

In the lower story of the inn, underneath the balcony, the

windows were evidently open, for women's voices and laughter could plainly be heard. There must be an entertainment.

Kovrin made an effort over himself, unsealed the letter, and, returning to his room, began to read:

'My father has just died. For this I am indebted to you, for it was you who killed him. Our garden is being ruined; it is managed by strangers; what my poor father so dreaded is taking place. For this also I am indebted to you. I hate you with all my soul, and wish that you may perish soon! Oh, how I suffer I My heart bums with an intolerable pain!... May you be accursed! I took you for an exceptional man, for a genius; I loved you, and you proved a madman....'

Kovrin could read no more; he tore up the letter and threw the pieces away.... He was overtaken by restlessness—almost by terror.... On the other side of the screen, slept Varvara Nikolaievna; he could hear her breathing. From the story beneath came the women's voices and laughter, but he felt that in the whole hotel there was not one living soul except himself. The fact that wretched, overwhelmed Tánya had cursed him in her letter, and wished him ill, caused him pain; and he looked fearfully at the door as if fearing to see again that unknown power which in two years had brought about so much ruin in his own life and in the lives of all who were dearest to him.

By experience he knew that when the nerves give way the best refuge lies in work. He used to sit at the table and concentrate his mind upon some definite thought. He took from his red portfolio a copybook containing the conspect of a small work of compilation which he intended to carry out during his stay in the Crimea, if he became tired of inactivity.... He sat at the table, and worked on this conspect, and it seemed to him that he was regaining his former peaceful, resigned, impersonal mood. His conspect led him to speculation on the vanity of the world. He thought of the great price which life demands for the most trivial and ordinary benefits which it gives to men. To reach a chair of philosophy under forty years of age; to be an ordinary professor; to expound commonplace thoughts—and those thoughts the thoughts of others—in feeble, tiresome, heavy language; in one word, to attain the position of a learned mediocrity, he had studied fifteen years, worked day and night, passed through a severe psychical disease, survived an unsuccessful marriage—been guilty of many follies and injustices which it was torture to remember. Kovrin now clearly realized that he was a mediocrity, and he was willingly reconciled to it, for he knew that every man must be satisfied with what he is.

The conspect calmed him, but the torn letter lay upon the floor and hindered the concentration of his thoughts. He rose, picked up the fragments, and threw them out of the window. But a light wind blew from the sea, and the papers fluttered back on to the window sill. Again he was overtaken by restlessness akin to terror, and it seemed to him that in the whole hotel except himself there was not one living soul.... He went on to the balcony. The bay, as if alive, stared up at him from its multitude of light-and dark-blue eyes, its eyes of turquoise and fire, and beckoned him. It was warm and stifling; how delightful, he thought, to bathe!

Suddenly beneath the balcony a violin was played, and two women's voices sang. All this was known to him. The song which they sang told of a young girl, diseased in imagination, who heard by night in a garden mysterious sounds, and found in them a harmony and a holiness incomprehensible to us mortals....

Kovrin held his breath, his heart ceased to beat, and the magical, ecstatic rapture which he had long forgotten trembled in his heart again.

A high, black pillar, like a cyclone or waterspout, appeared on the opposite coast. It swept with incredible swiftness across the bay towards the hotel; it became smaller and smaller, and Kovrin stepped aside to make room for it.... The monk, with uncovered grey head, with black eyebrows, barefooted, folding his arms upon his chest, swept past him, and stopped in the middle of the room.

'Why did you not believe me?' he asked in a tone of reproach, looking caressingly at Kovrin. 'If you had believed me when I said you were a genius, these last two years would not have been passed so sadly and so barrenly.'

Kovrin again believed that he was the elected of God and a genius; he vividly remembered all his former conversation with the Black Monk, and wished to reply. But the blood flowed from his throat on to his chest, and he, not knowing what to do, moved his hands about his chest till his cuffs were red with the blood. He wished to call Varvara Nikolaievna, who slept behind the screen, and making an effort to do so, cried: 'Tánya!'

He fell on the floor, and raising his hands, again cried: 'Tánya!'

He cried to Tánya, cried to the great garden with the miraculous flowers, cried to the park, to the pines with their shaggy roots, to the rye-field, cried to his marvellous science, to his youth, his daring, his joy, cried to the life which had been so beautiful. He saw on the floor before him a great pool of blood, and from weakness could not utter a single word. But an inexpressible, infinite joy filled his whole being. Beneath the balcony the serenade was being played, and the Black Monk whispered to him that he was a genius, and died only because his feeble, mortal body had lost its balance, and could no longer serve as the covering of genius.

When Varvara Nikolaievna awoke, and came from behind her screen, Kovrin was dead. But on his face was frozen an immovable smile of happiness.

8

A JOKE

It was a bright winter midday.... There was a sharp snapping frost and the curls on Nadenka's temples and the down on her upper lip were covered with silvery frost. She was holding my arm and we were standing on a high hill. From where we stood to the ground below there stretched a smooth sloping descent in which the sun was reflected as in a looking-glass. Beside us was a little sledge lined with bright red cloth.

'Let us go down, Nadyezhda Petrovna!' I besought her. 'Only once! I assure you we shall be all right and not hurt.'

But Nadenka was afraid. The slope from her little goloshes to the bottom of the ice hill seemed to her a terrible, immensely deep abyss. Her spirit failed her, and she held her breath as she looked down, when I merely suggested her getting into the sledge, but what would it be if she were to risk flying into the abyss! She would die, she would go out of her mind.

'I entreat you!' I said. 'You mustn't be afraid! You know it's poor-spirited, it's cowardly!'

Nadenka gave way at last, and from her face I saw that she gave way in mortal dread. I sat her in the sledge, pale and trembling, put my arm round her and with her cast myself down the precipice.

The sledge flew like a bullet. The air cleft by our flight beat in our faces, roared, whistled in our ears, tore at us, nipped us cruelly in its anger, tried to tear our heads off our shoulders. We had hardly strength to breathe from the pressure of the wind. It seemed as though the devil himself had caught us in his claws and was dragging us with a roar to hell. Surrounding objects melted into one long furiously racing streak...another moment and it seemed we should perish.

'I love you, Nadya!' I said in a low voice.

The sledge began moving more and more slowly, the roar of the wind and the whirr of the runners was no longer so terrible, it was easier to breathe, and at last we were at the bottom. Nadenka was more dead than alive. She was pale and scarcely breathing.... I helped her to get up.

'Nothing would induce me to go again,' she said, looking at me with wide eyes full of horror. 'Nothing in the world! I almost died!'

A little later she recovered herself and looked enquiringly into my eyes, wondering had I really uttered those four words or had she fancied them in the roar of the hurricane. And I stood beside her smoking and looking attentively at my glove.

She took my arm and we spent a long while walking near the ice-hill. The riddle evidently would not let her rest.... Had those words been uttered or not?...Yes or no? Yes or no? It was the question of pride, or honour, of life—a very important question, the most important question in the world. Nadenka kept impatiently, sorrowfully looking into my face with a penetrating glance; she answered at random, waiting to see whether I would not speak. Oh, the play of feeling on that sweet face! I saw that she was struggling with herself, that she wanted to say something, to ask some question, but she could not find the words; she felt awkward and frightened and troubled by her joy....

'Do you know what,' she said without looking at me.

'Well?' I asked.

'Let us...slide down again.'

We clambered up the ice-hill by the steps again. I sat Nadenka, pale and trembling, in the sledge; again we flew into the terrible abyss, again the wind roared and the runners whirred, and again when the flight of our sledge was at its swiftest and noisiest, I said in a low voice:

'I love you, Nadenka!'

When the sledge stopped, Nadenka flung a glance at the hill down which we had both slid, then bent a long look upon my face, listened to my voice which was unconcerned and passionless, and the whole of her little figure, every bit of it, even her muff and her hood expressed the utmost bewilderment, and on her face was written: 'What does it mean? Who uttered those words? Did he, or did I only fancy it?'

The uncertainty worried her and drove her out of all patience. The poor girl did not answer my questions, frowned, and was on the point of tears.

'Hadn't we better go home?' I asked.

'Well, I...I like this tobogganing,' she said, flushing. 'Shall we go down once more?'

She 'liked' the tobogganing, and yet as she got into the sledge she was, as both times before, pale, trembling, hardly able to breathe for terror.

We went down for the third time, and I saw she was looking at my face and watching my lips. But I put my handkerchief to my lips, coughed, and when we reached the middle of the hill I succeeded in bringing out:

'I love you, Nadya!'

And the mystery remained a mystery! Nadenka was silent, pondering on something.... I saw her home, she tried to walk slowly, slackened her pace and kept waiting to see whether I would not say those words to her, and I saw how her soul was suffering, what effort she was making not to say to herself:

'It cannot be that the wind said them! And I don't want it to be the wind that said them!'

Next morning I got a little note:

'If you are tobogganning to-day, come for me.—N.'

And from that time I began going every day tobogganning with Nadenka, and as we flew down in the sledge, every time I pronounced in a low voice the same words: 'I love you, Nadya!'

Soon Nadenka grew used to that phrase as to alcohol or morphia. She could not live without it. It is true that flying down the ice-hill terrified her as before, but now the terror and danger gave a peculiar fascination to words of love—words which as before were a mystery and tantalized the soul. The same two—the wind and I were still suspected.... Which of the two was making love to her she did not know, but apparently by now she did not care; from which goblet one drinks matters little if only the beverage is intoxicating.

It happened I went to the skating-ground alone at midday; mingling with the crowd I saw Nadenka go up to the ice-hill and look about for me...then she timidly mounted the steps.... She was frightened of going alone—oh, how frightened! She was white as the snow, she was trembling, she went as though to the scaffold, but she went, she went without looking back, resolutely. She had evidently determined to put it to the test at last: would those sweet amazing words be heard when I was not there? I saw her, pale, her lips parted with horror, get into the sledge, shut her eyes and saying good-bye for ever to the earth, set off.... 'Whrrr!' whirred the runners. Whether Nadenka heard those words I do not know. I only saw her getting up from the sledge looking faint and exhausted. And one could tell from her face that she could not tell herself whether she had heard anything or not. Her terror while she had been flying down had deprived of her all power of hearing, of discriminating sounds, of understanding.

But then the month of March arrived...the spring sunshine was more kindly.... Our ice-hill turned dark, lost its brilliance and finally melted. We gave up tobogganing. There was nowhere now where poor Nadenka could hear those words, and indeed no one to utter them, since there was no wind and I was going to Petersburg—for long, perhaps for ever.

It happened two days before my departure I was sitting in the dusk in the little garden which was separated from the yard of Nadenka's house by a high fence with nails in it.... It was still pretty cold, there was still snow by the manure heap, the trees looked dead but there was already the scent of spring and the rooks were cawing loudly as they settled for their night's rest. I went up to the fence and stood for a long while peeping through a chink. I saw Nadenka come out into the porch and fix a mournful yearning gaze on the sky.... The spring wind was blowing straight into her pale dejected face.... It reminded her of the wind which roared at us on the ice-hill when she heard those four words, and her face became very, very sorrowful, a tear trickled down her cheek, and the poor child held out both arms as though begging the wind to bring her those words once more. And waiting for the wind I said in a low voice:

'I love you, Nadya!'

Mercy! The change that came over Nadenka! She uttered a cry, smiled all over her face and looking joyful, happy and beautiful, held out her arms to meet the wind.

And I went off to pack up....

That was long ago. Now Nadenka is married; she married—whether of her own choice or not does not matter—a secretary of the Nobility Wardenship and now she has three children. That we once went tobogganning together, and that the wind brought her the words 'I love you, Nadenka,' is not forgotten; it is for her now the happiest, most touching, and beautiful memory in her life....

But now that I am older I cannot understand why I uttered those words, what was my motive in that joke....

9

KASHTANKA

I
Misbehaviour

A young dog, a reddish mongrel, between a dachshund and a 'yard-dog', very like a fox in face, was running up and down the pavement looking uneasily from side to side. From time to time she stopped and, whining and lifting first one chilled paw and then another, tried to make up her mind how it could have happened that she was lost.

She remembered very well how she had passed the day, and how, in the end, she had found herself on this unfamiliar pavement.

The day had begun by her master Luka Alexandritch's putting on his hat, taking something wooden under his arm wrapped up in a red handkerchief, and calling: 'Kashtanka, come along!'

Hearing her name the mongrel had come out from under the work-table, where she slept on the shavings, stretched herself voluptuously and run after her master. The people Luka Alexandritch worked for lived a very long way off, so that, before he could get to any one of them, the carpenter had several times to step into a tavern to fortify himself. Kashtanka remembered that on the way she had behaved extremely improperly. In her delight that she was being taken for a walk she jumped about, dashed barking after the trains, ran into yards, and chased other dogs. The carpenter was continually losing sight of her, stopping, and angrily shouting at her. Once he had even, with an expression of fury in his face, taken her fox-like ear in his fist, smacked her, and said emphatically: 'Pla-a-ague take you, you pest!'

After having left the work where it had been bespoken, Luka Alexandritch went into his sister's and there had something to eat and drink; from his sister's he had gone to see a bookbinder he knew; from the bookbinder's to a tavern, from the tavern to another crony's, and so on. In short, by the time Kashtanka found herself on the unfamiliar pavement, it was getting dusk, and the carpenter was as drunk as a cobbler. He was waving his arms and, breathing heavily, muttered:

'In sin my mother bore me! Ah, sins, sins! Here now we are walking along the street and looking at the street lamps, but when we die, we shall burn in a fiery Gehenna....'

Or he fell into a good-natured tone, called Kashtanka to him, and said to her: 'You, Kashtanka, are an insect of a creature, and nothing else. Beside a man, you are much the same as a joiner beside a cabinet-maker....'

While he talked to her in that way, there was suddenly a burst of music. Kashtanka looked round and saw that a regiment of soldiers was coming straight towards her. Unable to endure the music, which unhinged her nerves, she turned round and round and wailed. To her great surprise, the carpenter, instead of being frightened, whining and barking, gave a broad grin, drew himself up to attention, and saluted with all his five fingers. Seeing that her master did not protest, Kashtanka whined louder than ever, and dashed across the road to the opposite pavement.

When she recovered herself, the band was not playing and the regiment was no longer there. She ran across the road to the spot where she had left her master, but alas, the carpenter was no longer there. She dashed forward, then back again and ran across the road once more, but the carpenter seemed to have vanished into the earth. Kashtanka began sniffing the pavement, hoping to find her master by the scent of his tracks, but some wretch had been that way just before in new rubber goloshes, and now all delicate scents were mixed with an acute stench of india-rubber, so that it was impossible to make out anything.

Kashtanka ran up and down and did not find her master, and meanwhile it had got dark. The street lamps were lighted on both sides of the road, and lights appeared in the windows. Big, fluffy snowflakes were falling and painting white the pavement, the horses' backs and the cabmen's caps, and the darker the evening grew the whiter were all these objects. Unknown customers kept walking incessantly to and fro, obstructing her field of vision and shoving against her with their feet. (All mankind Kashtanka divided into two uneven parts: masters and customers; between them there was an essential difference: the first had the right to beat her, and the second she had the right to nip by the calves of their legs.) These customers were hurrying off somewhere and paid no attention to her.

When it got quite dark, Kashtanka was overcome by despair and horror. She huddled up in an entrance and began whining piteously. The long day's journeying with Luka Alexandritch had exhausted her, her ears and her paws were freezing, and, what was more, she was terribly hungry. Only twice in the whole day had she tasted a morsel: she had eaten a little paste at the bookbinder's, and in one of the taverns she had found a sausage skin on the floor, near the counter —that was all. If she had been a human being she would have certainly thought: 'No, it is impossible to live like this! I must shoot myself!'

II
A Mysterious Stranger

But she thought of nothing, she simply whined. When her head and back were entirely plastered over with the soft feathery snow, and she had sunk into a painful doze of exhaustion, all at once the door of the entrance clicked, creaked, and struck her on the side. She jumped up. A man belonging to the class of customers came out. As Kashtanka whined and got under his feet, he could not help noticing her. He bent down to her and asked:

'Doggy, where do you come from? Have I hurt you? O, poor thing, poor thing…. Come, don't be cross, don't be cross…. I am sorry.'

Kashtanka looked at the stranger through the snow-flakes that hung on her eyelashes, and saw before her a short, fat little man, with a plump, shaven face wearing a top hat and a fur coat that swung open.

'What are you whining for?' he went on, knocking the snow off her back with his fingers. 'Where is your master? I suppose you are lost? Ah, poor doggy! What are we going to do now?'

Catching in the stranger's voice a warm, cordial note, Kashtanka licked his hand, and whined still more pitifully.

'Oh, you nice funny thing!' said the stranger. 'A regular fox! Well, there's nothing for it, you must come along with me!

Perhaps you will be of use for something.... Well!'

He clicked with his lips, and made a sign to Kashtanka with his hand, which could only mean one thing: 'Come along!' Kashtanka went.

Not more than half an hour later she was sitting on the floor in a big, light room, and, leaning her head against her side, was looking with tenderness and curiosity at the stranger who was sitting at the table, dining. He ate and threw pieces to her.... At first he gave her bread and the green rind of cheese, then a piece of meat, half a pie and chicken bones, while through hunger she ate so quickly that she had not time to distinguish the taste, and the more she ate the more acute was the feeling of hunger.

'Your masters don't feed you properly,' said the stranger, seeing with what ferocious greediness she swallowed the morsels without munching them. 'And how thin you are! Nothing but skin and bones....'

Kashtanka ate a great deal and yet did not satisfy her hunger, but was simply stupefied with eating. After dinner she lay down in the middle of the room, stretched her legs and, conscious of an agreeable weariness all over her body, wagged her tail. While her new master, lounging in an easy-chair, smoked a cigar, she wagged her tail and considered the question, whether it was better at the stranger's or at the carpenter's. The stranger's surroundings were poor and ugly; besides the easy-chairs, the sofa, the lamps and the rugs, there was nothing, and the room seemed empty. At the carpenter's the whole place was stuffed full of things: he had a table, a bench, a heap of shavings, planes, chisels, saws, a cage with a goldfinch, a basin.... The stranger's room smelt of nothing, while there was always a thick fog in the carpenter's room, and a glorious smell of glue, varnish, and shavings. On the other hand, the stranger had one great superiority—he gave her a great deal to eat and, to do him full justice, when Kashtanka sat facing the table and looking wistfully at him, he did not once hit or kick her, and did not once shout: 'Go away, damned brute!'

When he had finished his cigar her new master went out, and a minute later came back holding a little mattress in his hands.

'Hey, you dog, come here!' he said, laying the mattress in the corner near the dog. 'Lie down here, go to sleep!'

Then he put out the lamp and went away. Kashtanka lay down on the mattress and shut her eyes; the sound of a bark rose from the street, and she would have liked to answer it, but all at once she was overcome with unexpected melancholy. She thought of Luka Alexandritch, of his son Fedyushka, and her snug little place under the bench.... She remembered on the long winter evenings, when the carpenter was planing or reading the paper aloud, Fedyushka usually played with her.... He used to pull her from under the bench by her hind legs, and play such tricks with her, that she saw green before her eyes, and ached in every joint. He would make her walk on her hind legs, use her as a bell, that is, shake her violently by the tail so that she squealed and barked, and give her tobacco to sniff.... The following trick was particularly agonizing: Fedyushka would tie a piece of meat to a thread and give it to Kashtanka, and then, when she had swallowed it he would, with a loud laugh, pull it back again from her stomach, and the more lurid were her memories the more loudly and miserably Kashtanka whined.

But soon exhaustion and warmth prevailed over melancholy. She began to fall asleep. Dogs ran by in her imagination: among them a shaggy old poodle, whom she had seen that day in the street with a white patch on his eye and tufts of wool by his nose. Fedyushka ran after the poodle with a chisel in his hand, then all at once he too was covered with shaggy wool, and began merrily barking beside Kashtanka. Kashtanka and he goodnaturedly sniffed each other's noses and merrily ran down the street....

III

New and Very Agreeable Acquaintances

When Kashtanka woke up it was already light, and a sound rose from the street, such as only comes in the day-time. There was not a soul in the room. Kashtanka stretched, yawned and, cross and ill-humoured, walked about the room. She sniffed the corners and the furniture, looked into the passage and found nothing of interest there. Besides the door that led into the passage there was another door. After thinking a little Kashtanka scratched on it with both paws, opened it, and went into the adjoining room. Here on the bed, covered with a rug, a customer, in whom she recognized the stranger of yesterday, lay asleep.

'Rrrrr...' she growled, but recollecting yesterday's dinner, wagged her tail, and began sniffing.

She sniffed the stranger's clothes and boots and thought they smelt of horses. In the bedroom was another door, also closed. Kashtanka scratched at the door, leaned her chest against it, opened it, and was instantly aware of a strange and very suspicious smell. Foreseeing an unpleasant encounter, growling and looking about her, Kashtanka walked into a little room with a dirty wall-paper and drew back in alarm. She saw something surprising and terrible. A grey gander came straight towards her, hissing, with its neck bowed down to the floor and its wings outspread. Not far from him, on a little mattress, lay a white tom-cat; seeing Kashtanka, he jumped up, arched his back, wagged his tail with his hair standing on end and he, too, hissed at her. The dog was frightened in earnest, but not caring to betray her alarm, began barking loudly and dashed at the cat.... The cat arched his back more than ever, mewed and gave Kashtanka a smack on the head with his paw. Kashtanka jumped back, squatted on all four paws, and craning her nose towards the cat, went off into loud, shrill barks; meanwhile the gander came up behind and gave her a painful peck in the back. Kashtanka leapt up and dashed at the gander.

'What's this?' They heard a loud angry voice, and the stranger came into the room in his dressing-gown, with a cigar between his teeth. 'What's the meaning of this? To your places!'

He went up to the cat, flicked him on his arched back, and said:

'Fyodor Timofeyitch, what's the meaning of this? Have you got up a fight? Ah, you old rascal! Lie down!'

And turning to the gander he shouted: 'Ivan Ivanitch, go home!'

The cat obediently lay down on his mattress and closed his eyes. Judging from the expression of his face and whiskers, he was displeased with himself for having lost his temper and got into a fight.

Kashtanka began whining resentfully, while the gander craned his neck and began saying something rapidly, excitedly, distinctly, but quite unintelligibly.

'All right, all right,' said his master, yawning. 'You must

live in peace and friendship.' He stroked Kashtanka and went on: 'And you, redhair, don't be frightened.... They are capital company, they won't annoy you. Stay, what are we to call you? You can't go on without a name, my dear.'

The stranger thought a moment and said: 'I tell you what... you shall be Auntie.... Do you understand? Auntie!'

And repeating the word 'Auntie' several times he went out. Kashtanka sat down and began watching. The cat sat motionless on his little mattress, and pretended to be asleep. The gander, craning his neck and stamping, went on talking rapidly and excitedly about something. Apparently it was a very clever gander; after every long tirade, he always stepped back with an air of wonder and made a show of being highly delighted with his own speech.... Listening to him and answering 'R-r-r-r,' Kashtanka fell to sniffing the corners. In one of the corners she found a little trough in which she saw some soaked peas and a sop of rye crusts. She tried the peas; they were not nice; she tried the sopped bread and began eating it. The gander was not at all offended that the strange dog was eating his food, but, on the contrary, talked even more excitedly, and to show his confidence went to the trough and ate a few peas himself.

IV
Marvels on a Hurdle

A little while afterwards the stranger came in again, and brought a strange thing with him like a hurdle, or like the figure II. On the crosspiece on the top of this roughly made wooden frame hung a bell, and a pistol was also tied to it; there were strings from the tongue of the bell, and the trigger of the pistol. The stranger put the frame in the middle of the room, spent a long time tying and untying something, then looked at the gander and said: 'Ivan Ivanitch, if you please!'

The gander went up to him and stood in an expectant attitude.

'Now then,' said the stranger, 'let us begin at the very beginning. First of all, bow and make a curtsey! Look sharp!'

Ivan Ivanitch craned his neck, nodded in all directions, and scraped with his foot.

'Right. Bravo.... Now die!'

The gander lay on his back and stuck his legs in the air. After performing a few more similar, unimportant tricks, the stranger suddenly clutched at his head, and assuming an expression of horror, shouted: 'Help! Fire! We are burning!'

Ivan Ivanitch ran to the frame, took the string in his beak, and set the bell ringing.

The stranger was very much pleased. He stroked the gander's neck and said:

'Bravo, Ivan Ivanitch! Now pretend that you are a jeweller selling gold and diamonds. Imagine now that you go to your shop and find thieves there. What would you do in that case?'

The gander took the other string in his beak and pulled it, and at once a deafening report was heard. Kashtanka was highly delighted with the bell ringing, and the shot threw her into so much ecstasy that she ran round the frame barking.

'Auntie, lie down!' cried the stranger; 'be quiet!'

Ivan Ivanitch's task was not ended with the shooting. For a whole hour afterwards the stranger drove the gander round him on a cord, cracking a whip, and the gander had to jump over barriers and through hoops; he had to rear, that is, sit on his tail and wave his legs in the air. Kashtanka could not take her eyes off Ivan Ivanitch, wriggled with delight, and several times fell to running after him with shrill barks. After exhausting the gander and himself, the stranger wiped the sweat from his brow and cried:

'Marya, fetch Havronya Ivanovna here!'

A minute later there was the sound of grunting. Kashtanka growled, assumed a very valiant air, and to be on the safe side, went nearer to the stranger. The door opened, an old woman looked in, and, saying something, led in a black and very ugly sow. Paying no attention to Kashtanka's growls, the sow lifted up her little hoof and grunted good-humouredly. Apparently it was very agreeable to her to see her master, the cat and Ivan Ivanitch. When she went up to the cat and gave him a light tap on the stomach with her hoof, and then made some remark to the gander, a great deal of good-nature was expressed in her movements, and the quivering of her tail. Kashtanka realized at once that to growl and bark at such a character was useless.

The master took away the frame and cried. 'Fyodor Timofeyitch, if you please!'

The cat stretched lazily, and reluctantly, as though performing a duty, went up to the sow.

'Come, let us begin with the Egyptian pyramid,' began the master.

He spent a long time explaining something, then gave the word of command, 'One...two...three!' At the word 'three' Ivan Ivanitch flapped his wings and jumped on to the sow's back.... When, balancing himself with his wings and his neck, he got a firm foothold on the bristly back, Fyodor Timofeyitch listlessly and lazily, with manifest disdain, and with an air of scorning his art and not caring a pin for it, climbed on to the sow's back, then reluctantly mounted on to the gander, and stood on his hind legs. The result was what the stranger called the Egyptian pyramid. Kashtanka yapped with delight, but at that moment the old cat yawned and, losing his balance, rolled off the gander. Ivan Ivanitch lurched and fell off too. The stranger shouted, waved his hands, and began explaining something again. After spending an hour over the pyramid their indefatigable master proceeded to teach Ivan Ivanitch to ride on the cat, then began to teach the cat to smoke, and so on.

The lesson ended in the stranger's wiping the sweat off his brow and going away. Fyodor Timofeyitch gave a disdainful sniff, lay down on his mattress, and closed his eyes; Ivan Ivanitch went to the trough, and the pig was taken away by the old woman. Thanks to the number of her new impressions, Kashranka hardly noticed how the day passed, and in the evening she was installed with her mattress in the room with the dirty wall-paper, and spent the night in the society of Fyodor Timofeyitch and the gander.

V
Talent! Talent!

A month passed.

Kashtanka had grown used to having a nice dinner every evening, and being called Auntie. She had grown used to the stranger too, and to her new companions. Life was comfortable and easy.

Every day began in the same way. As a rule, Ivan Ivanitch was the first to wake up, and at once went up to Auntie or to the cat, twisting his neck, and beginning to talk excitedly and persuasively, but, as before, unintelligibly. Sometimes he would crane up his head in the air and utter a long monologue. At first Kashtanka thought he talked so much because he was very clever, but after a little time had passed, she lost all her respect for him; when he went up to her with his long speeches she no longer wagged her tail, but treated him as a tiresome chatterbox, who would not let anyone sleep and, without the slightest ceremony, answered him with 'R-r-r-r!'

Fyodor Timofeyitch was a gentleman of a very different sort. When he woke he did not utter a sound, did not stir, and did not even open his eyes. He would have been glad not to wake, for, as was evident, he was not greatly in love with life. Nothing interested him, he showed an apathetic and nonchalant attitude to everything, he disdained everything and, even while eating his delicious dinner, sniffed contemptuously.

When she woke Kashtanka began walking about the room and sniffing the corners. She and the cat were the only ones allowed to go all over the flat; the gander had not the right to cross the threshold of the room with the dirty wall-paper, and Hayronya Ivanovna lived somewhere in a little outhouse in the yard and made her appearance only during the lessons. Their master got up late, and immediately after drinking his tea began teaching them their tricks. Every day the frame, the whip, and the hoop were brought in, and every day almost the same performance took place. The lesson lasted three or four hours, so that sometimes Fyodor Timofeyitch was so tired that he staggered about like a drunken man, and Ivan Ivanitch opened his beak and breathed heavily, while their master became red in the face and could not mop the sweat from his brow fast enough.

The lesson and the dinner made the day very interesting, but the evenings were tedious. As a rule, their master went off somewhere in the evening and took the cat and the gander with him. Left alone, Auntie lay down on her little mattress and began to feel sad.

Melancholy crept on her imperceptibly and took possession of her by degrees, as darkness does of a room. It began with the dog's losing every inclination to bark, to eat, to run about the rooms, and even to look at things; then vague figures, half dogs, half human beings, with countenances attractive, pleasant, but incomprehensible, would appear in her imagination; when they came Auntie wagged her tail, and it seemed to her that she had somewhere, at some time, seen them and loved them. And as she dropped asleep, she always felt that those figures smelt of glue, shavings, and varnish.

When she had grown quite used to her new life, and from a thin, long mongrel, had changed into a sleek, well-groomed dog, her master looked at her one day before the lesson and said:

'It's high time, Auntie, to get to business. You have kicked up your heels in idleness long enough. I want to make an artiste of you…. Do you want to be an artiste?'

And he began teaching her various accomplishments. At the first lesson he taught her to stand and walk on her hind legs, which she liked extremely. At the second lesson she had to jump on her hind legs and catch some sugar, which her teacher held high above her head. After that, in the following lessons she danced, ran tied to a cord, howled to music, rang the bell, and fired the pistol, and in a month could successfully replace Fyodor Timofeyitch in the 'Egyptian Pyramid'. She learned very eagerly and was pleased with her own success; running with her tongue out on the cord, leaping through the hoop, and riding on old Fyodor Timofeyitch, gave her the greatest enjoyment. She accompanied every successful trick with a shrill, delighted bark, while her teacher wondered, was also delighted, and rubbed his hands.

'It's talent! It's talent!' he said. 'Unquestionable talent! You will certainly be successful!'

And Auntie grew so used to the word talent, that every time her master pronounced it, she jumped up as if it had been her name.

VI
An Uneasy Night

Auntie had a doggy dream that a porter ran after her with a broom, and she woke up in a fright.

It was quite dark and very stuffy in the room. The fleas were biting. Auntie had never been afraid of darkness before, but now, for some reason, she felt frightened and inclined to bark.

Her master heaved a loud sigh in the next room, then soon afterwards the sow grunted in her sty, and then all was still again. When one thinks about eating one's heart grows lighter, and Auntie began thinking how that day she had stolen the leg of a chicken from Fyodor Timofeyitch, and had hidden it in the drawing-room, between the cupboard and the wall, where there were a great many spiders' webs and a great deal of dust. Would it not be as well to go now and look whether the chicken leg were still there or not? It was very possible that her master had found it and eaten it. But she must not go out of the room before morning, that was the rule. Auntie shut her eyes to go to sleep as quickly as possible, for she knew by experience that the sooner you go to sleep the sooner the morning comes. But all at once there was a strange scream not far from her which made her start and jump up on all four legs. It was Ivan Ivanitch, and his cry was not babbling and persuasive as usual, but a wild, shrill, unnatural scream like the squeak of a door opening. Unable to distinguish anything in the darkness, and not understanding what was wrong, Auntie felt still more frightened and growled: 'R-r-r-r....'

Some time passed, as long as it takes to eat a good bone; the scream was not repeated. Little by little Auntie's uneasiness passed off and she began to doze. She dreamed of two big black dogs with tufts of last year's coat left on their haunches and sides; they were eating out of a big basin some swill, from which there came a white steam and a most appetizing smell; from time to time they looked round at Auntie, showed their teeth and growled: 'We are not going to give you any!' But a peasant in a fur-coat ran out of the house and drove them away with a whip; then Auntie went up to the basin and began eating, but as soon as the peasant went out of the gate, the two black dogs rushed at her growling, and all at once there was again a shrill scream.

'K-gee! K-gee-gee!' cried Ivan Ivanitch.

Auntie woke, jumped up and, without leaving her mattress, went off into a yelping bark. It seemed to her that it was not Ivan Ivanitch that was screaming but someone else, and for some reason the sow again grunted in her sty.

Then there was the sound of shuffling slippers, and the master came into the room in his dressing-gown with a candle in his hand. The flickering light danced over the dirty wallpaper and the ceiling, and chased away the darkness. Auntie saw that there was no stranger in the room. Ivan Ivanitch was sitting on the floor and was not asleep. His wings were spread out and his beak was open, and altogether he looked as though he were very tired and thirsty. Old Fyodor Timofeyitch was not asleep either. He, too, must have been awakened by the scream.

'Ivan Ivanitch, what's the matter with you?' the master asked the gander. 'Why are you screaming? Are you ill?'

The gander did not answer. The master touched him on the neck, stroked his back, and said: 'You are a queer chap. You don't sleep yourself, and you don't let other people....'

When the master went out, carrying the candle with him, there was darkness again. Auntie felt frightened. The gander did not scream, but again she fancied that there was some stranger in the room. What was most dreadful was that this stranger could not be bitten, as he was unseen and had no shape. And for some reason she thought that something very bad would certainly happen that night. Fyodor Timofeyitch was uneasy too.

Auntie could hear him shifting on his mattress, yawning and shaking his head.

Somewhere in the street there was a knocking at a gate and the sow grunted in her sty. Auntie began to whine, stretched out her front-paws and laid her head down upon them. She fancied that in the knocking at the gate, in the grunting of the sow, who was for some reason awake, in the darkness and the stillness, there was something as miserable and dreadful as in Ivan Ivanitch's scream. Everything was in agitation and anxiety, but why? Who was the stranger who could not be seen? Then two dim flashes of green gleamed for a minute near Auntie.

It was Fyodor Timofeyitch, for the first time of their whole acquaintance coming up to her. What did he want? Auntie licked his paw, and not asking why he had come, howled softly and on various notes.

'K-gee!' cried Ivan Ivanitch, 'K-g-ee!'

The door opened again and the master came in with a candle. The gander was sitting in the same attitude as before, with his beak open, and his wings spread out, his eyes were closed.

'Ivan Ivanitch!' his master called him.

The gander did not stir. His master sat down before him on the floor, looked at him in silence for a minute, and said:

'Ivan Ivanitch, what is it? Are you dying? Oh, I remember now, I remember!' he cried out, and clutched at his head. 'I know why it is! It's because the horse stepped on you to-day! My God! My God!'

Auntie did not understand what her master was saying, but she saw from his face that he, too, was expecting something dreadful. She stretched out her head towards the dark window, where it seemed to her some stranger was looking in, and howled.

'He is dying, Auntie!' said her master, and wrung his hands. 'Yes, yes, he is dying! Death has come into your room. What are we to do?'

Pale and agitated, the master went back into his room, sighing and shaking his head. Auntie was afraid to remain in the darkness, and followed her master into his bedroom. He sat down on the bed and repeated several times: 'My God, what's to be done?'

Auntie walked about round his feet, and not understanding why she was wretched and why they were all so uneasy, and trying to understand, watched every movement he made. Fyodor

Timofeyitch, who rarely left his little mattress, came into the master's bedroom too, and began rubbing himself against his feet. He shook his head as though he wanted to shake painful thoughts out of it, and kept peeping suspiciously under the bed.

The master took a saucer, poured some water from his wash-stand into it, and went to the gander again.

'Drink, Ivan Ivanitch!' he said tenderly, setting the saucer before him; 'drink, darling.'

But Ivan Ivanitch did not stir and did not open his eyes. His master bent his head down to the saucer and dipped his beak into the water, but the gander did not drink, he spread his wings wider than ever, and his head remained lying in the saucer.

'No, there's nothing to be done now,' sighed his master. 'It's all over. Ivan Ivanitch is gone!'

And shining drops, such as one sees on the window-pane when it rains, trickled down his cheeks. Not understanding what was the matter, Auntie and Fyodor Timofeyitch snuggled up to him and looked with horror at the gander.

'Poor Ivan Ivanitch!' said the master, sighing mournfully. 'And I was dreaming I would take you in the spring into the country, and would walk with you on the green grass. Dear creature, my good comrade, you are no more! How shall I do without you now?'

It seemed to Auntie that the same thing would happen to her, that is, that she too, there was no knowing why, would close her eyes, stretch out her paws, open her mouth, and everyone would look at her with horror. Apparently the same reflections were passing through the brain of Fyodor Timofeyitch. Never before had the old cat been so morose and gloomy.

It began to get light, and the unseen stranger who had so

frightened Auntie was no longer in the room. When it was quite daylight, the porter came in, took the gander, and carried him away. And soon afterwards the old woman came in and took away the trough.

Auntie went into the drawing-room and looked behind the cupboard: her master had not eaten the chicken bone, it was lying in its place among the dust and spiders' webs. But Auntie felt sad and dreary and wanted to cry. She did not even sniff at the bone, but went under the sofa, sat down there, and began softly whining in a thin voice.

VII
An Unsuccessful Début

One fine evening the master came into the room with the dirty wall-paper, and, rubbing his hands, said:

'Well....'

He meant to say something more, but went away without saying it. Auntie, who during her lessons had thoroughly studied his face and intonations, divined that he was agitated, anxious and, she fancied, angry. Soon afterwards he came back and said:

'To-day I shall take with me Auntie and F'yodor Timofeyitch. To-day, Auntie, you will take the place of poor Ivan Ivanitch in the "Egyptian Pyramid". Goodness knows how it will be! Nothing is ready, nothing has been thoroughly studied, there have been few rehearsals! We shall be disgraced, we shall come to grief!'

Then he went out again, and a minute later, came back in his fur-coat and top hat. Going up to the cat he took him by the fore-paws and put him inside the front of his coat, while

Fyodor Timofeyitch appeared completely unconcerned, and did not even trouble to open his eyes. To him it was apparently a matter of absolute indifference whether he remained lying down, or were lifted up by his paws, whether he rested on his mattress or under his master's fur-coat.

'Come along, Auntie,' said her master.

Wagging her tail, and understanding nothing, Auntie followed him. A minute later she was sitting in a sledge by her master's feet and heard him, shrinking with cold and anxiety, mutter to himself:

'We shall be disgraced! We shall come to grief!'

The sledge stopped at a big strange-looking house, like a soup-ladle turned upside down. The long entrance to this house, with its three glass doors, was lighted up with a dozen brilliant lamps. The doors opened with a resounding noise and, like jaws, swallowed up the people who were moving to and fro at the entrance. There were a great many people, horses, too, often ran up to the entrance, but no dogs were to be seen.

The master took Auntie in his arms and thrust her in his coat, where Fyodor Timofeyirch already was. It was dark and stuffy there, but warm. For an instant two green sparks flashed at her; it was the cat, who opened his eyes on being disturbed by his neighbour's cold rough paws. Auntie licked his ear, and, trying to settle herself as comfortably as possible, moved uneasily, crushed him under her cold paws, and casually poked her head out from under the coat, but at once growled angrily, and tucked it in again. It seemed to her that she had seen a huge, badly lighted room, full of monsters; from behind screens and gratings, which stretched on both sides of the room, horrible faces looked out: faces of horses with horns, with long ears, and one fat, huge countenance with a tail instead of a nose, and two long gnawed bones sticking out of his mouth.

The cat mewed huskily under Auntie's paws, but at that moment the coat was flung open, the master said, 'Hop!' and Fyodor Timofeyitch and Auntie jumped to the floor. They were now in a little room with grey plank walls; there was no other furniture in it but a little table with a looking-glass on it, a stool, and some rags hung about the corners, and instead of a lamp or candles, there was a bright fan-shaped light attached to a little pipe fixed in the wall. Fyodor Timofeyitch licked his coat which had been ruffled by Auntie, went under the stool, and lay down. Their master, still agitated and rubbing his hands, began undressing....He undressed as he usually did at home when he was preparing to get under the rug, that is, took off everything but his underlinen, then he sat down on the stool, and, looking in the looking-glass, began playing the most surprising tricks with himself.... First of all he put on his head a wig, with a parting and with two tufts of hair standing up like horns, then he smeared his face thickly with something white, and over the white colour painted his eyebrows, his moustaches, and red on his cheeks. His antics did not end with that. After smearing his face and neck, he began putting himself into an extraordinary and incongruous costume, such as Auntie had never seen before, either in houses or in the street. Imagine very full trousers, made of chintz covered with big flowers, such as is used in working-class houses for curtains and covering furniture, trousers which buttoned up just under his armpits. One trouser leg was made of brown chintz, the other of bright yellow. Almost lost in these, he then put on a short chintz jacket, with a big scalloped collar, and a gold star on the back, stockings of different colours, and green slippers.

Everything seemed going round before Auntie's eyes and in her soul. The white-faced, sack-like figure smelt like her master, its voice, too, was the familiar master's voice, but there were moments when Auntie was tortured by doubts, and then she was ready to run away from the parti-coloured figure and to bark. The new place, the fan-shaped light, the smell, the transformation that had taken place in her master—all this aroused in her a vague dread and a foreboding that she would certainly meet with some horror such as the big face with the tail instead of a nose. And then, somewhere through the wall, some hateful band was playing, and from time to time she heard an incomprehensible roar. Only one thing reassured her—that was the imperturbability of Fyodor Timofeyitch. He dozed with the utmost tranquillity under the stool, and did not open his eyes even when it was moved.

A man in a dress coat and a white waistcoat peeped into the little room and said:

'Miss Arabella has just gone on. After her—you.'

Their master made no answer. He drew a small box from under the table, sat down, and waited. From his lips and his hands it could be seen that he was agitated, and Auntie could hear how his breathing came in gasps.

'Monsieur George, come on!' someone shouted behind the door. Their master got up and crossed himself three times, then took the cat from under the stool and put him in the box.

'Come, Auntie,' he said softly.

Auntie, who could make nothing out of it, went up to his hands, he kissed her on the head, and put her beside Fyodor Timofeyitch. Then followed darkness.... Auntie trampled on the cat, scratched at the walls of the box, and was so frightened that she could not utter a sound, while the box swayed and quivered, as though it were on the waves....

'Here we are again!' her master shouted aloud: 'here we are again!'

Auntie felt that after that shout the box struck against something hard and left off swaying. There was a loud deep roar, someone was being slapped, and that someone, probably the monster with the tail instead of a nose, roared and laughed so loud that the locks of the box trembled. In response to the roar, there came a shrill, squeaky laugh from her master, such as he never laughed at home.

'Ha!' he shouted, trying to shout above the roar. 'Honoured friends! I have only just come from the station! My granny's kicked the bucket and left me a fortune! There is something very heavy in the box, it must be gold, ha! ha! I bet there's a million here! We'll open it and look....'

The lock of the box clicked. The bright light dazzled Auntie's eyes, she jumped out of the box, and, deafened by the roar, ran quickly round her master, and broke into a shrill bark.

'Ha!' exclaimed her master. 'Uncle Fyodor Timofeyitch! Beloved Aunt, dear relations! The devil take you!'

He fell on his stomach on the sand, seized the cat and Auntie, and fell to embracing them. While he held Auntie tight in his arms, she glanced round into the world into which fate had brought her and, impressed by its immensity, was for a minute dumbfounded with amazement and delight, then jumped out of her master's arms, and to express the intensity of her emotions, whirled round and round on one spot like a top. This new world was big and full of bright light; wherever she looked, on all sides, from floor to ceiling there were faces, faces, faces, and nothing else.

'Auntie, I beg you to sit down!' shouted her master. Remembering what that meant, Auntie jumped on to a chair, and sat down. She looked at her master. His eyes looked at her gravely and kindly as always, but his face, especially his mouth and teeth, were made grotesque by a broad immovable grin. He laughed, skipped about, twitched his shoulders, and made a show of being very merry in the presence of the thousands of faces. Auntie believed in his merriment, all at once felt all over her that those thousands of faces were looking at her, lifted up her fox-like head, and howled joyously.

'You sit there, Auntie,' her master said to her, 'while Uncle and I will dance the Kamarinsky.'

Fyodor Timofeyitch stood looking about him indifferently, waiting to be made to do something silly. He danced listlessly, carelessly, sullenly, and one could see from his movements, his tail and his ears, that he had a profound contempt for the crowd, the bright light, his master and himself. When he had performed his allotted task, he gave a yawn and sat down.

'Now, Auntie!' said her master, 'we'll have first a song, and then a dance, shall we?'

He took a pipe out of his pocket, and began playing. Auntie, who could not endure music, began moving uneasily in her chair and howled. A roar of applause rose from all sides. Her master bowed, and when all was still again, went on playing…. Just as he took one very high note, someone high up among the audience uttered a loud exclamation:

'Auntie!' cried a child's voice, 'why it's Kashtanka!'

'Kashtanka it is!' declared a cracked drunken tenor.

'Kashtanka! Strike me dead, Fedyushka, it is Kashtanka. Kashtanka! Here!'

Someone in the gallery gave a whistle, and two voices, one a boy's and one a man's, called loudly: 'Kashtanka! Kashtanka!'

Auntie started, and looked where the shouting came from. Two faces, one hairy, drunken and grinning, the other chubby, rosy-cheeked and frightened-looking, dazed her eyes as the bright light had dazed them before.... She remembered, fell off the chair, struggled on the sand, then jumped up, and with a delighted yap dashed towards those faces. There was a deafening roar, interspersed with whistles and a shrill childish shout: 'Kashtanka! Kashtanka!'

Auntie leaped over the barrier, then across someone's shoulders. She found herself in a box: to get into the next tier she had to leap over a high wall. Auntie jumped, but did not jump high enough, and slipped back down the wall. Then she was passed from hand to hand, licked hands and faces, kept mounting higher and higher, and at last got into the gallery....

∞

Half an hour afterwards, Kashtanka was in the street, following the people who smelt of glue and varnish. Luka Alexandritch staggered and instinctively, taught by experience, tried to keep as far from the gutter as possible.

'In sin my mother bore me,' he muttered. 'And you, Kashtanka, are a thing of little understanding. Beside a man, you are like a joiner beside a cabinetmaker.'

Fedyushka walked beside him, wearing his father's cap. Kashtanka looked at their backs, and it seemed to her that she had been following them for ages, and was glad that there had not been a break for a minute in her life.

She remembered the little room with dirty wall-paper, the gander, Fyodor Timofeyitch, the delicious dinners, the lessons, the circus, but all that seemed to her now like a long, tangled, oppressive dream.

10

SLEEPY

Night. Varka, the little nurse, a girl of thirteen, is rocking the cradle in which the baby is lying, and humming hardly audibly:

> 'Hush-a-bye, my baby wee,
> While I sing a song for thee.'

A little green lamp is burning before the ikon; there is a string stretched from one end of the room to the other, on which baby-clothes and a pair of big black trousers are hanging. There is a big patch of green on the ceiling from the ikon lamp, and the baby-clothes and the trousers throw long shadows on the stove, on the cradle, and on Varka.... When the lamp begins to flicker, the green patch and the shadows come to life, and are set in motion, as though by the wind. It is stuffy. There is a smell of cabbage soup, and of the inside of a boot-shop.

The baby's crying. For a long while he has been hoarse and exhausted with crying; but he still goes on screaming, and there is no knowing when he will stop. And Varka is sleepy. Her eyes are glued together, her head droops, her neck aches. She cannot move her eyelids or her lips, and she feels as though her face is dried and wooden, as though her head has become as small as the head of a pin.

'Hush-a-bye, my baby wee,' she hums, 'while I cook the groats for thee....'

A cricket is churring in the stove. Through the door in the next room the master and the apprentice Afanasy are snoring.... The cradle creaks plaintively, Varka murmurs—and it all blends into that soothing music of the night to which it is so sweet to listen, when one is lying in bed. Now that music is merely irritating and oppressive, because it goads her to sleep, and she must not sleep; if Varka—God forbid!—should fall asleep, her master and mistress would beat her.

The lamp flickers. The patch of green and the shadows are set in motion, forcing themselves on Varka's fixed, half-open eyes, and in her half slumbering brain are fashioned into misty visions. She sees dark clouds chasing one another over the sky, and screaming like the baby. But then the wind blows, the clouds are gone, and Varka sees a broad high road covered with liquid mud; along the high road stretch files of wagons, while people with wallets on their backs are trudging along and shadows flit backwards and forwards; on both sides she can see forests through the cold harsh mist. All at once the people with their wallets and their shadows fall on the ground in the liquid mud. 'What is that for?' Varka asks. 'To sleep, to sleep!' they answer her. And they fall sound asleep, and sleep sweetly, while crows and magpies sit on the telegraph wires, scream like the baby, and try to wake them.

'Hush-a-bye, my baby wee, and I will sing a song to thee,' murmurs Varka, and now she sees herself in a dark stuffy hut.

Her dead father, Yefim Stepanov, is tossing from side to side on the floor. She does not see him, but she hears him moaning and rolling on the floor from pain. 'His guts have burst,' as he says; the pain is so violent that he cannot utter a single word, and can only draw in his breath and clack his teeth like the rattling of a drum:

'Boo—boo—boo—boo....'

Her mother, Pelageya, has run to the master's house to say that Yefim is dying. She has been gone a long time, and ought to be back. Varka lies awake on the stove, and hears her father's 'boo—boo—boo.' And then she hears someone has driven up to the hut. It is a young doctor from the town, who has been sent from the big house where he is staying on a visit. The doctor comes into the hut; he cannot be seen in the darkness, but he can be heard coughing and rattling the door.

'Light a candle,' he says.

'Boo—boo—boo,' answers Yefim.

Pelageya rushes to the stove and begins looking for the broken pot with the matches. A minute passes in silence. The doctor, feeling in his pocket, lights a match.

'In a minute, sir, in a minute,' says Pelageya. She rushes out of the hut, and soon afterwards comes back with a bit of candle.

Yefim's cheeks are rosy and his eyes are shining, and there is a peculiar keenness in his glance, as though he were seeing right through the hut and the doctor.

'Come, what is it? What are you thinking about?' says the doctor, bending down to him. 'Aha! Have you had this long?'

'What? Dying, your honour, my hour has come.... I am not to stay among the living.'

'Don't talk nonsense! We will cure you!'

'That's as you please, your honour, we humbly thank you, only we understand.... Since death has come, there it is.'

The doctor spends a quarter of an hour over Yefim, then he gets up and says:

'I can do nothing. You must go into the hospital, there they will operate on you. Go at once... You must go! It's rather late, they will all be asleep in the hospital, but that doesn't matter, I will give you a note. Do you hear?'

'Kind sir, but what can he go in?' says Pelageya. 'We have no horse.'

'Never mind. I'll ask your master, he'll let you have a horse.'

The doctor goes away, the candle goes out, and again there is the sound of 'boo—boo—boo.' Half an hour later someone drives up to the hut. A cart has been sent to take Yefim to the hospital. He gets ready and goes....

But now it is a clear bright morning. Pelageya is not at home; she has gone to the hospital to find what is being done to Yefim. Somewhere there is a baby crying, and Varka hears someone singing with her own voice:

'Hush-a-bye, my baby wee, I will sing a song to thee.'

Pelageya comes back; she crosses herself and whispers:

'They put him to rights in the night, but towards morning he gave up his soul to God.... The Kingdom of Heaven be his and peace everlasting.... They say he was taken too late.... He ought to have gone sooner....'

Varka goes out into the road and cries there, but all at once someone hits her on the back of her head so hard that her forehead knocks against a birch tree. She raises her eyes, and sees facing her, her master, the shoemaker.

'What are you about, you scabby slut?' he says. 'The child is crying, and you are asleep!'

He gives her a sharp slap behind the ear, and she shakes her head, rocks the cradle, and murmurs her song. The green patch and the shadows from the trousers and the baby-clothes move up and down, nod to her, and soon take possession of her brain again. Again she sees the high road covered with liquid mud. The people with wallets on their backs and the shadows have lain down and are fast asleep. Looking at them, Varka has a passionate longing for sleep; she would lie down with enjoyment, but her mother Pelageya is walking beside her, hurrying her on. They are hastening together to the town to find situations.

'Give alms, for Christ's sake!' her mother begs of the people they meet. 'Show us the Divine Mercy, kind-hearted gentlefolk!'

'Give the baby here!' a familiar voice answers. 'Give the baby here!' the same voice repeats, this time harshly and angrily. 'Are you asleep, you wretched girl?'

Varka jumps up, and looking round grasps what is the matter: there is no high road, no Pelageya, no people meeting them, there is only her mistress, who has come to feed the baby, and is standing in the middle of the room. While the stout, broad-shouldered woman nurses the child and soothes it, Varka stands looking at her and waiting till she has done. And outside the windows the air is already turning blue, the shadows and the green patch on the ceiling are visibly growing pale, it will soon be morning.

'Take him,' says her mistress, buttoning up her chemise over her bosom; 'he is crying. He must be bewitched.'

Varka takes the baby, puts him in the cradle and begins rocking it again. The green patch and the shadows gradually disappear, and now there is nothing to force itself on her eyes and cloud her brain. But she is as sleepy as before, fearfully sleepy! Varka lays her head on the edge of the cradle, and rocks her whole body to overcome her sleepiness, but yet her eyes are glued together, and her head is heavy.

'Varka, heat the stove!' she hears the master's voice through the door.

So it is time to get up and set to work. Varka leaves the cradle, and runs to the shed for firewood. She is glad. When one moves and runs about, one is not so sleepy as when one is sitting down. She brings the wood, heats the stove, and feels that her wooden face is getting supple again, and that her thoughts are growing clearer.

'Varka, set the samovar!' shouts her mistress.

Varka splits a piece of wood, but has scarcely time to light the splinters and put them in the samovar, when she hears a fresh order:

'Varka, clean the master's goloshes!'

She sits down on the floor, cleans the goloshes, and thinks how nice it would be to put her head into a big deep golosh, and have a little nap in it.... And all at once the golosh grows, swells, fills up the whole room. Varka drops the brush, but at once shakes her head, opens her eyes wide, and tries to look at things so that they may not grow big and move before her eyes.

'Varka, wash the steps outside; I am ashamed for the customers to see them!'

Varka washes the steps, sweeps and dusts the rooms, then heats another stove and runs to the shop. There is a great deal of work: she hasn't one minute free.

But nothing is so hard as standing in the same place at the kitchen table peeling potatoes. Her head droops over the table, the potatoes dance before her eyes, the knife tumbles out of her hand while her fat, angry mistress is moving about near her with her sleeves tucked up, talking so loud that it makes a ringing in Varka's ears. It is agonizing, too, to wait at dinner, to wash, to sew, there are minutes when she longs to flop on to the floor regardless of everything, and to sleep.

The day passes. Seeing the windows getting dark, Varka presses her temples that feel as though they were made of wood, and smiles, though she does not know why. The dusk of evening caresses her eyes that will hardly keep open, and promises her sound sleep soon. In the evening visitors come.

'Varka, set the samovar!' shouts her mistress. The samovar is a little one, and before the visitors have drunk all the tea they want, she has to heat it five times. After tea Varka stands for a whole hour on the same spot, looking at the visitors, and waiting for orders.

'Varka, run and buy three bottles of beer!'

She starts off, and tries to run as quickly as she can, to drive away sleep.

'Varka, fetch some vodka! Varka, where's the corkscrew? Varka, clean a herring!'

But now, at last, the visitors have gone; the lights are put out, the master and mistress go to bed.

'Varka, rock the baby!' she hears the last order.

The cricket churrs in the stove; the green patch on the ceiling and the shadows from the trousers and the baby-clothes force themselves on Varka's half-opened eyes again, wink at her and cloud her mind.

'Hush-a-bye, my baby wee,' she murmurs, 'and I will sing a song to thee.'

And the baby screams, and is worn out with screaming. Again Varka sees the muddy high road, the people with wallets, her mother Pelageya, her father Yefim. She understands everything, she recognizes everyone, but through her half sleep she cannot understand the force which binds her, hand and foot, weighs upon her, and prevents her from living. She looks round, searches for that force that she may escape from it, but she cannot find it. At last, tired to death, she does her very utmost, strains her eyes, looks up at the flickering green patch, and listening to the screaming, finds the foe who will not let her live.

That foe is the baby.

She laughs. It seems strange to her that she has failed to grasp such a simple thing before. The green patch, the shadows, and the cricket seem to laugh and wonder too.

The hallucination takes possession of Varka. She gets up from her stool, and with a broad smile on her face and wide unblinking eyes, she walks up and down the room. She feels pleased and tickled at the thought that she will be rid directly of the baby that binds her hand and foot.... Kill the baby and then sleep, sleep, sleep....

Laughing and winking and shaking her fingers at the green patch, Varka steals up to the cradle and bends over the baby. When she has strangled him, she quickly lies down on the floor, laughs with delight that she can sleep, and in a minute is sleeping as sound as the dead.

11

BOYS

'Volodya's come!' someone shouted in the yard.

'Master Volodya's here!' bawled Natalya the cook, running into the dining-room. 'Oh, my goodness!'

The whole Korolyov family, who had been expecting their Volodya from hour to hour, rushed to the windows. At the front door stood a wide sledge, with three white horses in a cloud of steam. The sledge was empty, for Volodya was already in the hall, untying his hood with red and chilly fingers. His school overcoat, his cap, his snowboots, and the hair on his temples were all white with frost, and his whole figure from head to foot diffused such a pleasant, fresh smell of the snow that the very sight of him made one want to shiver and say 'brrr!'

His mother and aunt ran to kiss and hug him. Natalya plumped down at his feet and began pulling off his snowboots, his sisters shrieked with delight, the doors creaked and banged, and Volodya's father, in his waistcoat and shirt-sleeves, ran out into the hall with scissors in his hand, and cried out in alarm:

'We were expecting you all yesterday? Did you come all right? Had a good journey? Mercy on us! you might let him say "how do you do" to his father! I am his father after all!'

'Bow-wow!' barked the huge black dog, Milord, in a deep bass, tapping with his tail on the walls and furniture.

For two minutes there was nothing but a general hubbub of joy. After the first outburst of delight was over the Korolyovs noticed that there was, besides their Volodya, another small person in the hall, wrapped up in scarves and shawls and white with frost. He was standing perfectly still in a corner, in the shadow of a big fox-lined overcoat.

'Volodya darling, who is it?' asked his mother, in a whisper.

'Oh!' cried Volodya. 'This is—let me introduce my friend Lentilov, a schoolfellow in the second class…. I have brought him to stay with us.'

'Delighted to hear it! You are very welcome,' the father said cordially. 'Excuse me, I've been at work without my coat…. Please come in! Natalya, help Mr Lentilov off with his things. Mercy on us, do turn that dog out! He is unendurable!'

A few minutes later, Volodya and his friend Lentilov, somewhat dazed by their noisy welcome, and still red from the outside cold, were sitting down to tea. The winter sun, making its way through the snow and the frozen tracery on the window-panes, gleamed on the samovar, and plunged its pure rays in the tea-basin. The room was warm, and the boys felt as though the warmth and the frost were struggling together with a tingling sensation in their bodies.

'Well, Christmas will soon be here,' the father said in a pleasant sing-song voice, rolling a cigarette of dark reddish tobacco. 'It doesn't seem long since the summer, when mamma was crying at your going…and here you are back again…. Time flies, my boy. Before you have time to cry out, old age is upon you. Mr Lentilov, take some more, please help yourself! We don't stand on ceremony!'

Volodya's three sisters, Katya, Sonya, and Masha (the eldest was eleven), sat at the table and never took their eyes off the newcomer.

Lentilov was of the same height and age as Volodya, but not as round-faced and fair-skinned. He was thin, dark, and freckled; his hair stood up like a brush, his eyes were small, and his lips were thick. He was, in fact, distinctly ugly, and if he had not been wearing the school uniform, he might have been taken for the son of a cook. He seemed morose, did not speak, and never once smiled. The little girls, staring at him, immediately came to the conclusion that he must be a very clever and learned person. He seemed to be thinking about something all the time, and was so absorbed in his own thoughts, that, whenever he was spoken to, he started, threw his head back, and asked to have the question repeated.

The little girls noticed that Volodya, who had always been so merry and talkative, also said very little, did not smile at all, and hardly seemed to be glad to be home. All the time they were at tea he only once addressed his sisters, and then he said something so strange. He pointed to the samovar and said:

'In California they don't drink tea, but gin.'

He, too, seemed absorbed in his own thoughts, and, to judge by the looks that passed between him and his friend Lentilov, their thoughts were the same.

After tea, they all went into the nursery. The girls and their father took up the work that had been interrupted by the arrival of the boys. They were making flowers and frills for the Christmas tree out of paper of different colours. It was an attractive and noisy occupation. Every fresh flower was greeted by the little girls with shrieks of delight, even of awe, as though the flower had dropped straight from heaven; their father was in ecstasies too, and every now and then he threw the scissors on the floor, in vexation at their bluntness. Their mother kept running into the nursery with an anxious face, asking:

'Who has taken my scissors? Ivan Nikolaitch, have you taken my scissors again?'

'Mercy on us! I'm not even allowed a pair of scissors!' their father would respond in a lachrymose voice, and, flinging himself back in his chair, he would pretend to be a deeply injured man; but a minute later, he would be in ecstasies again.

On his former holidays Volodya, too, had taken part in the preparations for the Christmas tree, or had been running in the yard to look at the snow mountain that the watchman and the shepherd were building. But this time Volodya and Lentilov took no notice whatever of the coloured paper, and did not once go into the stable. They sat in the window and began whispering to one another; then they opened an atlas and looked carefully at a map.

'First to Perm ...' Lentilov said, in an undertone, 'from there to Tiumen, then Tomsk... then...then...Kamchatka. There the Samoyedes take one over Behring's Straits in boats.... And then we are in America.... There are lots of furry animals there....'

'And California?' asked Volodya.

'California is lower down.... We've only to get to America and California is not far off.... And one can get a living by hunting and plunder.'

All day long Lentilov avoided the little girls, and seemed to look at them with suspicion. In the evening he happened to be left alone with them for five minutes or so. It was awkward to be silent.

He cleared his throat morosely, rubbed his left hand against his right, looked sullenly at Katya and asked:

'Have you read Mayne Reid?'

'No, I haven't…. I say, can you skate?'

Absorbed in his own reflections, Lentilov made no reply to this question; he simply puffed out his cheeks, and gave a long sigh as though he were very hot. He looked up at Katya once more and said:

'When a herd of bisons stampedes across the prairie the earth trembles, and the frightened mustangs kick and neigh.'

He smiled impressively and added:

'And the Indians attack the trains, too. But worst of all are the mosquitoes and the termites.'

'Why, what's that?'

'They're something like ants, but with wings. They bite fearfully. Do you know who I am?'

'Mr Lentilov.'

'No, I am Montehomo, the Hawk's Claw, Chief of the Ever Victorious.'

Masha, the youngest, looked at him, then into the darkness out of window and said, wondering:

'And we had lentils for supper yesterday.'

Lentilov's incomprehensible utterances, and the way he was always whispering with Volodya, and the way Volodya seemed now to be always thinking about something instead of playing… all this was strange and mysterious. And the two elder girls, Katya and Sonya, began to keep a sharp look-out on the boys. At night, when the boys had gone to bed, the girls crept to their bedroom door, and listened to what they were saying. Ah, what they discovered! The boys were planning to run away to America to dig for gold: they had everything ready for the journey, a pistol, two knives, biscuits, a burning glass to serve instead of matches, a compass, and four roubles in cash. They learned that the boys would have to walk some thousands of miles, and would have to fight tigers and savages on the road: then they would get gold and ivory, slay their enemies, become pirates, drink gin, and finally marry beautiful maidens, and make a plantation.

The boys interrupted each other in their excitement. Throughout the conversation, Lentilov called himself 'Montehomo, the Hawk's Claw', and Volodya was 'my paleface brother!'

'Mind you don't tell mamma,' said Katya, as they went back to bed. 'Volodya will bring us gold and ivory from America, but if you tell mamma he won't be allowed to go.'

The day before Christmas Eve, Lentilov spent the whole day poring over the map of Asia and making notes, while Volodya, with a languid and swollen face that looked as though it had been stung by a bee, walked about the rooms and ate nothing. And once he stood still before the holy image in the nursery, crossed himself, and said:

'Lord, forgive me a sinner; Lord, have pity on my poor unhappy mamma!'

In the evening he burst out crying. On saying good-night he gave his father a long hug, and then hugged his mother and sisters. Katya and Sonya knew what was the matter, but little Masha was puzzled, completely puzzled. Every time she looked at Lentilov she grew thoughtful and said with a sigh:

'When Lent comes, nurse says we shall have to eat peas and lentils.'

Early in the morning of Christmas Eve, Katya and Sonya

slipped quietly out of bed, and went to find out how the boys meant to run away to America. They crept to their door.

'Then you don't mean to go?' Lentilov was saying angrily. 'Speak out: aren't you going?'

'Oh dear,' Volodya wept softly. 'How can I go? I feel so unhappy about mamma.'

'My pale-face brother, I pray you, let us set off. You declared you were going, you egged me on, and now the time comes, you funk it!'

'I...I...I'm not funking it, but I...I...I'm sorry for mamma.'

'Say once and for all, are you going or are you not?'

'I am going, only...wait a little...I want to be at home a little.'

'In that case I will go by myself,' Lentilov declared. 'I can get on without you. And you wanted to hunt tigers and fight! Since that's how it is, give me back my cartridges!'

At this Volodya cried so bitterly that his sisters could not help crying too. Silence followed.

'So you are not coming?' Lentilov began again.

'I...I...I am coming!'

'Well, put on your things, then.'

And Lentilov tried to cheer Volodya up by singing the praises of America, growling like a tiger, pretending to be a steamer, scolding him, and promising to give him all the ivory and lions' and tigers' skins.

And this thin, dark boy, with his freckles and his bristling shock of hair, impressed the little girls as an extraordinary remarkable person. He was a hero, a determined character, who knew no fear, and he growled so ferociously, that, standing at the door, they really might imagine there was a tiger or lion inside. When the little girls went back to their room and dressed, Katya's eyes were full of tears, and she said:

'Oh, I feel so frightened!'

Everything was as usual till two o'clock, when they sat down to dinner. Then it appeared that the boys were not in the house. They sent to the servants' quarters, to the stables, to the bailiff's cottage. They were not to be found. They sent into the village—they were not there.

At tea, too, the boys were still absent, and by supper-time Volodya's mother was dreadfully uneasy, and even shed tears.

Late in the evening they sent again to the village, they searched everywhere, and walked along the river bank with lanterns. Heavens! what a fuss there was!

Next day the police officer came, and a paper of some sort was written out in the dining-room. Their mother cried....

All of a sudden a sledge stopped at the door, with three white horses in a cloud of steam.

'Volodya's come,' someone shouted in the yard.

'Master Volodya's here!' bawled Natalya, running into the dining-room. And Milord barked his deep bass, 'bow-wow.'

It seemed that the boys had been stopped in the Arcade, where they had gone from shop to shop asking where they could get gunpowder.

Volodya burst into sobs as soon as he came into the hall, and flung himself on his mother's neck. The little girls, trembling, wondered with terror what would happen next. They saw their father take Volodya and Lentilov into his study, and there he talked to them a long while.

'Is this a proper thing to do?' their father said to them. 'I only pray they won't hear of it at school, you would both be expelled. You ought to be ashamed, Mr Lentilov, really. It's not at all the thing to do! You began it, and I hope you will be punished by your parents. How could you? Where did you spend the night?'

'At the station,' Lentilov answered proudly.

Then Volodya went to bed, and had a compress, steeped in vinegar, on his forehead.

A telegram was sent off, and next day a lady, Lentilov's mother, made her appearance and bore off her son.

Lentilov looked morose and haughty to the end, and he did not utter a single word at taking leave of the little girls. But he took Katya's book and wrote in it as a souvenir: 'Montehomo, the Hawk's Claw, Chief of the Ever Victorious'.

12

THE LOTTERY TICKET

Ivan Dmitritch, a middle-class man who lived with his family on an income of twelve hundred a year and was very well satisfied with his lot, sat down on the sofa after supper and began reading the newspaper.

'I forgot to look at the newspaper today,' his wife said to him as she cleared the table. 'Look and see whether the list of drawings is there.'

'Yes, it is,' said Ivan Dmitritch; 'but hasn't your ticket lapsed?'

'No; I took the interest on Tuesday.'

'What is the number?'

'Series 9,499, number 26.'

'All right... we will look... 9,499 and 26.'

Ivan Dmitritch had no faith in lottery luck, and would not, as a rule, have consented to look at the lists of winning numbers, but now, as he had nothing else to do and as the newspaper was before his eyes, he passed his finger downwards along the column of numbers. And immediately, as though in mockery of his scepticism, no further than the second line from the top, his eye was caught by the figure 9,499! Unable to believe his eyes, he hurriedly dropped the paper on his knees without looking to see the number of the ticket, and, just as though some one had given him a douche of cold water, he felt an agreeable chill in the pit of the stomach; tingling and terrible and sweet!

'Masha, 9,499 is there!' he said in a hollow voice.

His wife looked at his astonished and panic-stricken face, and realized that he was not joking.

'9,499?' she asked, turning pale and dropping the folded tablecloth on the table.

'Yes, yes… It really is there!'

'And the number of the ticket?'

'Oh, yes! There's the number of the ticket too. But stay… wait! No, I say! Anyway, the number of our series is there! Anyway, you understand….'

Looking at his wife, Ivan Dmitritch gave a broad, senseless smile, like a baby when a bright object is shown it. His wife smiled too; it was as pleasant to her as to him that he only mentioned the series, and did not try to find out the number of the winning ticket. To torment and tantalize oneself with hopes of possible fortune is so sweet, so thrilling!

'It is our series,' said Ivan Dmitritch, after a long silence. 'So there is a probability that we have won. It's only a probability, but there it is!'

'Well, now look!'

'Wait a little. We have plenty of time to be disappointed. It's on the second line from the top, so the prize is seventy-five thousand. That's not money, but power, capital! And in a minute I shall look at the list, and there—26! Eh? I say, what if we really have won?'

The husband and wife began laughing and staring at one another in silence. The possibility of winning bewildered them; they could not have said, could not have dreamed, what they both needed that seventy-five thousand for, what they would buy, where they would go. They thought only of the figures 9,499 and 75,000 and pictured them in their imagination, while somehow they could not think of the happiness itself which was so possible.

Ivan Dmitritch, holding the paper in his hand, walked several times from corner to corner, and only when he had recovered from the first impression began dreaming a little.

'And if we have won,' he said—'why, it will be a new life, it will be a transformation! The ticket is yours, but if it were mine I should, first of all, of course, spend twenty-five thousand on real property in the shape of an estate; ten thousand on immediate expenses, new furnishing... travelling... paying debts, and so on…. The other forty thousand I would put in the bank and get interest on it.'

'Yes, an estate, that would be nice,' said his wife, sitting down and dropping her hands in her lap.

'Somewhere in the Tula or Oryol provinces…. In the first place we shouldn't need a summer villa, and besides, it would always bring in an income.'

And pictures came crowding on his imagination, each more gracious and poetical than the last. And in all these pictures he saw himself well-fed, serene, healthy, felt warm, even hot! Here, after eating a summer soup, cold as ice, he lay on his back on the burning sand close to a stream or in the garden under a lime-tree…. It is hot…. His little boy and girl are crawling about near him, digging in the sand or catching ladybirds in the grass. He dozes sweetly, thinking of nothing, and feeling all over that he need not go to the office today, tomorrow, or the day after. Or, tired of lying still, he goes to the hayfield, or to the forest for mushrooms, or watches the peasants catching fish with a net. When the sun sets he takes a towel and soap and saunters to the bathing-shed, where he undresses at his leisure, slowly rubs his bare chest with his hands, and goes into the water. And in the water, near the opaque soapy circles, little fish flit to and fro and green water-weeds nod their heads. After bathing there is tea with cream and milk rolls.... In the evening a walk or vint with the neighbours.

'Yes, it would be nice to buy an estate,' said his wife, also dreaming, and from her face it was evident that she was enchanted by her thoughts.

Ivan Dmitritch pictured to himself autumn with its rains, its cold evenings, and its St. Martin's summer. At that season he would have to take longer walks about the garden and beside the river, so as to get thoroughly chilled, and then drink a big glass of vodka and eat a salted mushroom or a soused cucumber, and then—drink another.... The children would come running from the kitchen-garden, bringing a carrot and a radish smelling of fresh earth.... And then, he would lie stretched full length on the sofa, and in leisurely fashion turn over the pages of some illustrated magazine, or, covering his face with it and unbuttoning his waistcoat, give himself up to slumber.

The St. Martin's summer is followed by cloudy, gloomy weather. It rains day and night, the bare trees weep, the wind is damp and cold. The dogs, the horses, the fowls—all are wet, depressed, downcast. There is nowhere to walk; one can't go out for days together; one has to pace up and down the room, looking despondently at the grey window. It is dreary!

Ivan Dmitritch stopped and looked at his wife.

'I should go abroad, you know, Masha,' he said.

And he began thinking how nice it would be in late autumn to go abroad somewhere to the South of France... to Italy.... to India!

'I should certainly go abroad too,' his wife said. 'But look at the number of the ticket!'

'Wait, wait!...'

He walked about the room and went on thinking. It occurred to him: what if his wife really did go abroad? It is pleasant to travel alone, or in the society of light, careless women who live in the present, and not such as think and talk all the journey about nothing but their children, sigh, and tremble with dismay over every farthing. Ivan Dmitritch imagined his wife in the train with a multitude of parcels, baskets, and bags; she would be sighing over something, complaining that the train made her head ache, that she had spent so much money.... At the stations he would continually be having to run for boiling water, bread and butter.... She wouldn't have dinner because of its being too dear....

'She would begrudge me every farthing,' he thought, with a glance at his wife. 'The lottery ticket is hers, not mine! Besides, what is the use of her going abroad? What does she want there? She would shut herself up in the hotel, and not let me out of her sight.... I know!'

And for the first time in his life his mind dwelt on the fact that his wife had grown elderly and plain, and that she was saturated through and through with the smell of cooking, while he was still young, fresh, and healthy, and might well have got married again.

'Of course, all that is silly nonsense,' he thought; 'but... why should she go abroad? What would she make of it? And yet she would go, of course.... I can fancy... In reality it is all one to her, whether it is Naples or Klin. She would only be in my way. I should be dependent upon her. I can fancy how, like a regular woman, she will lock the money up as soon as she gets it.... She will hide it from me.... She will look after her relations and grudge me every farthing.'

Ivan Dmitritch thought of her relations. All those wretched brothers and sisters and aunts and uncles would come crawling about as soon as they heard of the winning ticket, would begin whining like beggars, and fawning upon them with oily, hypocritical smiles. Wretched, detestable people! If they were given anything, they would ask for more; while if they were refused, they would swear at them, slander them, and wish them every kind of misfortune.

Ivan Dmitritch remembered his own relations, and their faces, at which he had looked impartially in the past, struck him now as repulsive and hateful.

'They are such reptiles!' he thought.

And his wife's face, too, struck him as repulsive and hateful. Anger surged up in his heart against her, and he thought malignantly:

'She knows nothing about money, and so she is stingy. If she won it she would give me a hundred roubles, and put the rest away under lock and key.'

And he looked at his wife, not with a smile now, but with hatred. She glanced at him too, and also with hatred and anger. She had her own daydreams, her own plans, her own reflections; she understood perfectly well what her husband's dreams were. She knew who would be the first to try and grab her winnings.

'It's very nice making daydreams at other people's expense!'

is what her eyes expressed. 'No, don't you dare!'

Her husband understood her look; hatred began stirring again in his breast, and in order to annoy his wife he glanced quickly, to spite her at the fourth page on the newspaper and read out triumphantly:

'Series 9,499, number 46! Not 26!'

Hatred and hope both disappeared at once, and it began immediately to seem to Ivan Dmitritch and his wife that their rooms were dark and small and low-pitched, that the supper they had been eating was not doing them good, but lying heavy on their stomachs, that the evenings were long and wearisome....

'What the devil's the meaning of it?' said Ivan Dmitritch, beginning to be ill-humoured. 'Wherever one steps there are bits of paper under one's feet, crumbs, husks. The rooms are never swept! One is simply forced to go out. Damnation take my soul entirely! I shall go and hang myself on the first aspen-tree!'